They were noble, proud, and fierce.
This collection captures the courage of
the Indians who fought for the honor of
their tribes.

THE BEST OF THE WEST

Anthologies of new and old stories
written with gusto and realism by your
favorite Western authors.

Other Best of the West anthologies
edited by Bill Pronzini and Martin H. Greenberg:

THE LAWMEN
THE OUTLAWS
THE COWBOYS

THE WARRIORS

Edited by Bill Pronzini & Martin H. Greenberg

FAWCETT GOLD MEDAL • NEW YORK

Contents

Acknowledgments

"Lapwai Winter" by Will Henry. Copyright © 1959 by Will Henry. From *From Where the Sun Now Stands*. Reprinted by permission of the author.

"The Young Warrior" by Oliver La Farge. Copyright 1938 by Consuelo Baca de La Farge. Copyright renewed © 1966 by Consuelo La Farge. First published in *Esquire*. Reprinted by permission of the Marie Rodell-Frances Collin Literary Agency.

"A Man Called Horse" by Dorothy M. Johnson. Copyright 1949 by Dorothy M. Johnson. Copyright renewed © 1977 by Dorothy M. Johnson. First published in *Collier's*. Reprinted by permission of McIntosh and Otis, Inc.

"A Kind of Courage" by T. V. Olsen. Copyright © 1970 by The Western Writers of America. First published in *With Guidons Flying*. Reprinted by permission of the author and the Lenniger Literary Agency, Inc.

"Arrows Fly Westward" by Tom W. Blackburn. Copyright 1945 by Popular Publications, Inc. New York. First published in *15 Western Tales*, October 1945. Reprinted by permission of the author.

"Potlatch" by Edward Wellen. Copyright © 1970 by Zane Grey Western Magazine, Inc. First published in *Zane Grey Western Magazine*. Reprinted by permission of the author.

"Great Medicine" by Steve Frazee. Copyright 1953 by Flying Eagle Publications, Inc. First published in *Gun-*

Introduction

The Warriors is the fourth in a series of Best of the West anthologies dedicated to making available the finest in short Western fiction to contemporary readers. In the first three books in the series, *The Lawmen, The Outlaws,* and *The Cowboys*, we brought you stories of the famous, the near-famous, and the unsung among Old West peace officers, lawbreakers, and working cowboys. In *The Warriors* you will find some of the finest tales penned over the past seventy-five years about the American Indian—warriors, braves, Indian women, and many more.

We have tried to find stories about American Indians as they really were—the good and the bad—and about the problems they caused others and the problems others caused them. Few groups in American history have received worst treatment than our "native Americans," but they were and are courageous people. This book is dedicated to them. Here, in fictional form, you will meet members of some of the greatest Indian tribes and nations—Cheyennes, Apaches, Sacs, Kwakiutls, Crows, Comanches, and Arapahoes.

Future Best of the West anthologies will contain stories about the men who built and rode and, in some cases, stole from the railroads and the great steamboats—stories by such important writers in the field as Will Henry, Brian Garfield, John Jakes, and many more.

May *The Warriors*, and all the other anthologies in the series, give you many hours of reading enjoyment.

—Bill Pronzini and
Martin H. Greenberg

Henry Herbert Knibbs was a leading novelist and poet of the Old West, whose career began in the early years of the twentieth century and spanned several decades. His novels include Overland Red, Lost Farm Camp, and Sundown Slim; his best-known book of verse is Songs of the Outlands (1914). "Apuni Oyis," which tells the tale of an Indian Lodge in the mountains of Arizona, ranks high among his Western rhymes.

Apuni Oyis
(Butterfly Lodge)

Henry Herbert Knibbs

There's a lodge in Arizona where the rugged pines are marching
Straight and stalwart up the hillside till they gather on the crest,
And around their feet the grasses and the purple flowers are arching
In the dim and golden glamour of the sunlight in the West.

In the lodge—Apuni Oyis—dwells the Chief who writes the stories
Of the Blackfeet—mighty hunters in the pleasant days of old—
Tales of love and war and friendship, tales of mysteries and glories,
When the prairie moon was silver and the sun was faëry gold.

3

*And the trails along the mountains, o'er the mesa and the
    river,*
  *Lead to far and hidden cañons where the sleeping red men
    lie,*
*Wrapped in silence as above them myriad aspen leaves
    aquiver*
  *Whisper secrets to the west wind as the pack-train ambles
    by;*

*Where the swart Apache hunts and dreams of warriors now
    a-dreaming;*
  *Where the mountain stream runs swiftly, talking loudly to
    the day,*
*To the rock-rimmed pool and onward as an unexpected
    gleaming*
  *Marks the trout that leaps to vanish in a burst of silver
    spray:*

*Trails that climb the rocky fortress of the ridge and have
    their ending*
  In forlorn and ravaged temples of a people all unknown;
*Trails we make, and did we know it—on and on forever blend-
    ing*
  *With the red man's, toward the sunset—are no clearer
    than his own.*

Oh, the hills of Arizona in the pleasant autumn weather!
  Oh, the lodge—Apuni Oyis—where is happiness and rest!
*May the dreams we share come true, and may we live them
    all together,*
  *We who love the ancient magic of the mountains of the
    West.*

Warpath

Stanley Vestal

*L*ong Orphan was tired. Intolerably, incredibly tired. So tired that it seemed impossible to stick on the bare back of his loping pony for even one more jump. His back ached, his head ached, every bone in his long brown body ached from the long, hour-after-hour, day-and-night pounding upon his horse's hard spine. On top of that, his empty belly ached. But far worse than any of these discomforts was the terrible pain in his eyes—the stinging, insistent, cruel pain of eyes which have stared too long into the glare of the sun on the snow-patched plains. But Long Orphan was a Cheyenne. He did not complain. He rode.

He was so tired, so bounded by his own physical misery, that only at long intervals was he aware of other sensations, sensations which had been beating upon his nerves for a day and night. Only when his pony swerved or broke its loping gait did he force his red-rimmed eyes open. Then he would glimpse the plains, and catch sight of his comrades, with buffalo robes belted around them, plunging along at his side. He would see the backs and heads and manes of the stolen ponies just ahead, rising and falling and tossing like the waves of a wind-swept prairie lake.

The rest of the time Long Orphan rode in darkness, where the only sensations were the thud of unshod hoofs, the labored breathing of the ponies, the creak of No Heart's saddle, the smell of sweaty horses, sweaty men, smoke-tanned buckskins, and his own bleeding flesh. This was Long Orphan's first warpath, and it was not what he had expected.

As his name indicated, he was an orphan, and used to hardship and privation. That helped, but his pride helped more. For in spite of his poverty and insignificance, Long Orphan was desperately proud of his ancestry. His grandfather had been a famous warrior. And so he rode. Nobody was going to have the laugh on him. He would not complain or ask for favors. He was no woman!

Besides, Long Orphan knew there was no pity to be expected from his comrades. They were all picked men, seasoned veterans, who resented his presence among them. Long Orphan had no rating as a warrior, no friends of any importance, no relatives to ask him to join a war party. Nobody wanted him along. And so, when he heard that No Heart was going on the warpath against the Crows, Long Orphan had had to volunteer, had had to sneak along behind the party until it was three days' march from camp—too far for the warriors to turn back and take him home again.

When Long Orphan turned up and joined them at last, No Heart was so enraged that he lashed the youngster with his heavy quirt. No Heart wanted only the cream of the warriors on such a dangerous raid. But nothing could turn Long Orphan back. And so No Heart set to work to make the young man's life a burden.

It was the custom to haze a youngster on his first warpath; such treatment was said to make his heart strong. Long Orphan was prepared for that. But he had not expected malice. And No Heart was merciless.

It was the custom to douse a lazy man with water if he failed to turn out at the second call: No Heart doused Long Orphan while he slept, without any warning whatever. It was the custom to send a green warrior after water for the others: No Heart sent Long Orphan after water when there was none within miles of the line of march. It was usual to have him cook the food of the leader, to make up his bed: No Heart made Long Orphan do these things over and over. It was customary for him to carry the leader's pack: No Heart slipped rocks into his pack to make it heavy for Long Orphan.

During the long hike up the Yellowstone and over the divide to the enemy's country, the young man was continually being sent to some distant hilltop to look for game, or ordered back for miles to recover some article deliberately dropped along the way. When the party stopped to sleep, every man who happened to wake up found some excuse to waken Long Orphan also. And when finally, that last night, the party neared the Crow camp on the Musselshell, No Heart made Long Orphan stay with the packs, while he and the others sneaked into the camp just before dawn and captured horses.

Long Orphan was given no chance to steal a pony, no chance to make a name for himself. He was cheated of the reward of all his labors. Yet all he craved was a warrior's name—the rating of a man.

Ever since that dawn Long Orphan had been riding, riding, riding—one bare-backed, raw-boned bronc after another. For as fast as one horse was winded, the warriors would rope and mount another. Even if he had wished to stop and rest, he dared not; No Heart had seen to that.

No Heart had put his arrow through a sleeping Crow woman, had scalped her, stripped her, and tied her bloody dress to his saddle as a trophy. After that, so he told Long Orphan, the Crows were sure to follow. Long Orphan was not to be allowed to quit. No Heart intended to ride him to death.

But Big Tree and the other warriors called a halt. The sun

was up, and the whole country behind them was brightly lighted with its rays. Not an enemy was in sight. They had ridden more than a day and a night. Besides, they had not all been as lucky as No Heart, who had captured a pony with a saddle on its back; they were tired.

They stopped in the scanty brush along a small stream which flowed into the Yellowstone River from the north. It was an easy day's ride eastward to their home camp on Powder River.

When Long Orphan slipped from his pony's back, he fell down. His legs were like sticks. It was some time before he could stand. But No Heart gave him no chance to rest.

Long Orphan was sent to gather wood, told to make a fire, to cook breakfast. He was sent after water, and had to fill the skin only a little at a time from the low water hole. Yet the paunch in which he brought it was emptied before his eyes: No Heart said the water was dirty.

Long Orphan had to gather brush to spread under No Heart's buffalo robe, had to rub down his pony with dry grass while the others sat by the fire, eating, resting and smoking. Last of all he was told to pull sagebrush and throw it on the fire to make a smoke. That smoke was visible for a day's ride in the light of the morning sun. No Heart wanted to signal the folks at home that he was on his way back, victorious. No Heart always made the most of his achievements.

While Long Orphan was busy at these chores, No Heart divided the loot. He himself took the lion's share—ten horses. Other warriors got one, two, three head each. Long Orphan got nothing.

"Why should I give you anything?" No Heart demanded. "You behaved like a woman. You hid in the brush while the rest of us went into the enemy's camp and stole the ponies. Your bones would be lying on the prairie if I had not saved your life by letting you ride some of my horses away from that camp. It is about time you made yourself useful. Now we warriors are going to sleep. You go up on that butte and keep watch until sundown."

Long Orphan had had no breakfast; he was staggering with fatigue. No Heart's command was like a blow on the head. The tall young man stood silent, swaying, squinting through red eyes at the leader, at his comrades who watched him without a word. For the first time he thought he sensed a little sympathy in those hard brown faces.

Now Long Orphan, according to Cheyenne standards, had been well brought up. His mother had been the daughter of a famous man, and the boy had been taught to respect his elders. It was hard for him to argue with an older man. But now he doubted that he could carry out that order. His strength and patience seemed gone. Dully he heard his own voice, like that of another, mumbling his protest.

"My eyes are sore, Grandfather. I cannot keep good watch. If you think the Crows are coming after us, why did you make that smoke?"

No Heart was caught. He had to think fast for an excuse then. He glared at the young man and began to scold him in a loud voice.

"I am the leader here, boy. You will do as I say. You are only a boy, no better than a woman. What do you know about war? Do you know why I made that smoke signal? To call the Crows! I want them to come, so that we can have a good fight. Maybe they will kill you, and then I shall be rid of you. Now go up on that butte and keep watch. Go quickly, before I lay my quirt on your lazy back!"

No Heart raised the heavy, notched handle of his quirt, and whirled the double lash around his head. He was furious.

Long Orphan was too tired to resist. Slowly he turned, and, dragging his buffalo robe by one corner, walked up the long slope to the rocky hilltop. The men stood silent, watching him go. One or two of them stirred uneasily. Big Tree ventured to protest. He appealed to No Heart.

"My friend, you are too hard on this young man. You know it was never our custom to keep watch. When one sleeps, all sleep. My uncle, who was a leader of warriors, told me that it is the duty of the leader himself to keep watch and protect his men, if necessary. The leader is responsible for the lives of the warriors. Listen to me, my friend. If I were leader and feared surprise, I would not rely on the watchfulness of a worn-out growing boy with sore eyes. That is a duty for a scout.''

No Heart laughed. ''I do not think the Crows will come so far. How can they? We have all their best ponies. If you are afraid, go and keep watch with Long Orphan. I am going to sleep.''

Big Tree replied, ''My friend, that was a small village we raided. Maybe there was another Crow camp not far off where they have plenty of ponies.''

No Heart did not listen. He rolled up in his robe and closed his eyes. Big Tree said no more. Within three minutes all the Cheyennes were sound asleep. All but Long Orphan.

Long Orphan sat on the butte, hidden among the rocks there, facing the west, his back to the morning sun. Even with the light at his back, it was impossible to look out over the dry, whitened prairie for more than a few seconds at a time, snatching glimpses of the back trail. But he stuck to his duty, though there was nothing to see.

While the sun was low behind him, it was hard enough. But when it was high in the heavens, the young man was in agony. His vigil was torture. He could only squint at the dazzling landscape for a split second, quickly sweeping the country with smarting, red-rimmed eyes, then shutting them tight for long minutes of rest. And whenever his eyes were closed, he had to fight off sleep.

Cold, hungry, tired, sick with pain, time after time he caught himself reeling. There could be only one end to that kind of thing. Shortly after noon, Long Orphan was snoring.

He dreamed that No Heart was lashing him, flogging him with that heavy quirt. Again and again the heavy double lash fell on the robe wrapped around his body. Long Orphan groaned and stirred, covering his face with his arms to shield himself. Then he felt the stinging lash again—this time on his bare wrist. His eyes flew open. It was no dream. No

Heart stood over him, flailing him with his heavy quirt. All around stood the other men, panting from their run up the butte, their faces fierce with anger.

Long Orphan jumped up, jumped back out of reach of the lash. "What is the matter?" he demanded. The whole war party was there, hostile, ready to go for him.

"Plenty," Big Tree growled, his voice hoarse with fury. "While you slept, the Crows came. They have run off our horses. We are all afoot. Look."

Long Orphan squinted after the man's pointing finger. A mile to the westward the prairie was blotched by a dark mass of moving horseflesh. The Crows—a heap of Crows—were riding behind the captured herd. Long Orphan's mouth dropped open in surprise and shame. But No Heart gave him no chance to speak.

"You dog," he barked. "They might have killed us . . . Strip him, men. I'll show him what a Dog Soldier whipping is like."

At his command, the whole party rushed the youngster. One man grabbed him by his long braids, others by his arms. A scalping knife slit his buckskin shirt up the back from tail to neckhole; two others cut away his leggings. They snatched off his quiver, emptied it and broke the arrows. Big Tree cracked the bow over his knee, then snatched the young man's knife from its sheath and hurled it, spinning away, into the snow.

Before Long Orphan's eyes they slit his buffalo robe into ribbons. And almost before he realized that all this had happened, he found himself suddenly released. Then the air seemed full of flying thongs, as the Dog Soldiers plied the lashes of their notched quirts upon his naked body.

"Run him down the butte," No Heart commanded. "Run him back to our camp so that he can pick up my pack again."

It was death to resist the Dog Soldiers. Long Orphan did not resist. He knew without thinking that he did not want to die—not yet. Not until he had wiped out the disgrace of his offense, not until he had won a name worthy of his grandfather, not until he had got even with No Heart.

Long Orphan covered his face with his arms to save his eyes, and stumbled down the slope to camp. His bare back was laced with blood when he reached it. But even then the malice of No Heart was unsatisfied.

"Put the woman's dress on him, friends," he ordered. "He behaved like a woman, let him dress like one. And I want him to carry my pack."

At that, Long Orphan's eyes flashed, and he clenched his fists. But he controlled himself. He did not want to die —yet. The warriors put the dress over his head, yanked it down upon him. Then they stood back and laughed at the result. The dress was too wide—and too short. It barely reached below the young man's knees. They laughed and No Heart laughed loudest of all.

"Now, Sister," he commanded, "make up my pack, and let's go. If you stand around barelegged like that, you'll get chilblains."

Long Orphan did not budge. His face was defiant. "I am not going with you. Carry it yourself."

No Heart laughed. That struck him as a good joke.

"Friends, did you hear? She is not going with us. She is going to stay here. Well, Sister, if you stay here, I am afraid you will not live long. There are many Crows in that war party. They have not forgotten that I killed one of their women. When they have hidden their ponies in some safe place, they will all come riding back to fight us. And the first man they will try to kill is the man who has on their woman's dress."

"Then I will wear it," said Long Orphan. "Is that why you gave it to me? You want to get rid of it before the enemy gets too close. You are a brave man. You can kill a woman sleeping, but when you see her men coming, you are afraid."

No Heart sneered at that. "Friends, our sister is very brave. She has never seen a battle. She cannot understand that we are few and afoot, and that the Crows are many and on horseback. They will ride us down unless we can find a safe place to defend ourselves.''

Then No Heart advanced, raising his quirt. ''But nobody is going to call me coward,'' he said, beginning to strike at Long Orphan.

Big Tree interfered. He grabbed the quirt, wrenched it from No Heart's hands. ''My friend,'' he protested, ''if you want to fight, the Crows are coming. Unless you lead us to a place where we can defend ourselves, you will soon have more fighting than you can eat. Are you our leader or only a crazy fool? Leave the boy alone.''

Other warriors grunted agreement; they were in haste to be on their way. No Heart saw that his rating as a war chief would suffer if he delayed longer; and his rating was his dearest possession. Where that was concerned he was stubborn as a mule. Grumbling to himself, he stooped to make up his pack. He threw out the stones first.

At that, Long Orphan laughed. That long-legged youth, unarmed, and in that shameful woman's dress, laughed aloud.

''Yes, hurry,'' he taunted No Heart. ''You are their leader. You are always out in front—when the enemy is after you. Then you can run faster than anybody. Hurry up now, the Crows will dance over your hair!''

Standing there, easy and empty-handed, Long Orphan laughed again.

One of the warriors echoed the laugh. Perhaps that warrior was jealous of the fame of No Heart. Perhaps the mere novelty of that boy in his silly costume laughing at a war chief amused him. But that warrior's laugh was too much for No Heart. It stung him into action. He stood up, threw down his pack and turned on Long Orphan.

''Let the Crows come,'' he growled, his dark face set and stubborn. ''I am not afraid. I stay here. This is a good place to die.''

The warriors, taken by surprise, stood speechless. In that silence, Long Orphan's laugh sounded louder than a rifle shot.

"Show-off," he taunted. "They call you No Heart, but you have a heart—a woman's heart. You talk fire, but your words are only smoke. You have weapons. If you really wished to die, you would not hide here in the brush. You would go to meet the enemy!"

Long Orphan had found his tongue at last. He had thrown away his body—all that mattered to him now was his self-respect.

No Heart had never been so insulted in his life. His dark face worked with a fury which made it almost impossible for him to speak. But at last he got out the words: "Like you?"

"*Hau*—yes," Long Orphan assented, his young face stern and resolved. "I will not die hiding in the brush like a scared woman." He turned and started off after the Crows.

The warriors stood silent, amazed at the young man's courage. They knew, of course, that boys green to war were sometimes bolder than more seasoned warriors. But they had never seen anything to match this. Long Orphan, a boy, and unarmed, was starting off to meet an enemy they feared to face. For a time they neither stirred nor spoke.

Then Big Tree took his knife from his sheath and ran after the young man. When he had caught up with him, he handed him the knife and said, "When you meet the enemy, you will need a weapon. We are both Cheyennes." Big Tree's tone was one of respect.

"*Ah-ho*—thanks," said Long Orphan. Big Tree's friendly offer, his respectful tone, heartened the young man. He took the knife, and with it new courage. He was so ashamed of his disgrace, so determined to outdo No Heart, that even without the knife he would not have faltered. But now, he hoped, he could kill one Crow, take one scalp, before the enemy killed him. Big Tree's friendship warmed his heart. Long Orphan trudged away, a strange figure in his woman's dress. But only No Heart jeered.

"He is a foolish boy—just a foolish boy. He cannot fight. He will hide from the Crows as soon as he is out of our sight."

But Long Orphan did not head for the brush along the

creek. Instead, he started up the bare slopes of the butte where he had been stationed to keep watch. He intended to fight and die in full view of his comrades, so that his fame would outshine No Heart's forever after. Straight to the flat top of the butte he climbed, scrambled over the low broken rimrock, and took his stand, facing westward, toward the country of the Crows.

The Cheyennes behind him, down below, almost forgot their own danger in watching him.

Suddenly Long Orphan began to signal to his enemies. They were coming back, and he wanted them to come straight to him. He stooped, scooped up a double handful of sand. He tossed it high into the air, as a buffalo bull paws up the dust before he charges. The wind caught the sand and spread it into a broad tawny banner, visible for miles. It was the Indian call to battle.

The Crows were coming for him now. Long Orphan began to dance and sing on his level hilltop, thus advertising his readiness to fight them. When the Cheyennes down below saw him making gestures in the sign language, they knew that the Crows must be coming close.

"Come on—kill me!" he signaled. "I have only this knife!"

The Crows needed no further invitation. As fast as their tired ponies could go up that steep slope, they came yelling and shooting, their leader well out in front. Long Orphan kept right on dancing as they advanced, and for that reason none of their bullets took effect. It was not easy to shoot accurately from the bare back of a pony heaving itself up the slope, when the target was never still for a moment.

Long Orphan watched them come. Far in the lead rode a man in a war bonnet, its long feather mane flying out behind him in the wind. His spotted pony plunged up the long slope, and the sun flashed from the barrel of his rifle. Long Orphan hoped that Crow was brave enough to come to close quarters to fight—where he could use his knife. He did not want to be shot down from a distance like a rabbit.

But the Crow had no intention of risking a stab from the

knife of that lone Cheyenne who had already shown such
strong courage. Ten paces from the rimrock the Crow reined
up his horse. The pony stood quiet. The Crow raised his rifle and took aim.

Long Orphan grasped his knife and ran toward that edge
of the level top of the butte. As he ran, he threw his body
from side to side, trying to avoid the bullet. But the Crow
pulled the trigger before the Cheyenne could reach him.

TCHOW!

White powder smoke hid the Crow from sight. Long Orphan saw that smoke—and nothing more. But the Cheyennes watching below saw Long Orphan's head jerk, saw
him stop suddenly, spin half round and stumble down upon
the rimrock.

No Heart laughed. "They killed him easy," he sneered.
"I told you he could not fight."

The other Cheyennes said nothing. They could hear the
Crows yelling in triumph on the other side of the butte as
they dashed up the hill. On top they could see the victorious
Crow in the war bonnet jump off his horse, lay down his rifle and rush scrambling over the broken rocks toward Long
Orphan. The Crow was in haste to reach the fallen man first,
to count the coup and capture the knife before anyone else
could get there. But his haste was his undoing.

The lariat tied around the spotted pony's neck was fastened at the other end to the Crow's belt. It was coiled and
tucked under his belt, and paid out as he ran forward. But
when the Crow dismounted, his pony turned down the
slope, and the rope was not long enough.

The Crow found himself brought up short before he
reached Long Orphan, and had to stop and haul the pony
forward again. This delay allowed Long Orphan to regain
consciousness. And when the Crow, dragging on the pony's
rope, raised his head above the level of the rimrock, the
wind caught the long tail of his war bonnet and whipped it
about his face, blinding him. By the time the Crow had
clawed the tail of his bonnet from his eyes he found himself

confronted by the man he had just shot and thought was dead.

Still dizzy, his face covered with blood from the scalp wound which had downed him, Long Orphan towered above the Crow. Before the astonished Crow could draw his own knife and clamber to the level of his enemy, Long Orphan grabbed the man's knife hand and stabbed him twice in the side of the neck. The Crow went down in a flutter of eagle feathers.

Leaving him wriggling on the rocks, Long Orphan stumbled down and picked up the rifle. He grinned under the mask of blood.

It was a repeating rifle, and there were still some cartridges in the magazine. He dropped behind a rock and began shooting at the Crows coming up the slope. One of them swayed and caught at the horn of his saddle; the pony of another Crow began to buck. Long Orphan sighted, grinning, along the shining barrel. It was a good rifle—a better gun than he had ever hoped to own.

Evidently the Crows knew it was a good rifle. Startled as they were by the sudden and unexpected death of their chief, they had not the courage to rush the man on the hilltop now that he was armed and shooting. They halted, turned and raced down the hill.

Long Orphan kept on shooting at them until the hammer clicked and the magazine was empty. Long Orphan was out of the fight. He went back to the Crow he had killed, took his knife and scalped him. Then he stood up, facing the Cheyennes in the valley, waved the trophy over his head and yelled, in mockery of No Heart.

That yell was more than No Heart could stand. He and his men were well hidden in the brush, in no immediate danger. But now he jumped out of his concealment, fired off his rifle and shouted defiance to the enemy.

At that, the Crows, glad enough to leave Long Orphan alone, turned to attack this new challenger. They swept round the butte and scouted up the creek toward No Heart's party. But this time they were in no mood to rush recklessly in against a hidden foe. They dismounted, tied up their ponies in a clump of cottonwood trees and advanced on foot, trying to drive the Cheyennes into the open. They made use of every bit of cover, and though No Heart's men fought bravely, the Crows kept the Cheyennes on the move.

From the top of the butte Long Orphan watched all this in disgust. Both Cheyennes and Crows had forgotten him. For a while everybody had been watching him, but now No Heart was playing the hero's part. Long Orphan was the spectator. He did not like that. He made up his mind to do something.

Taking his useless rifle, Long Orphan got on the spotted horse and rode down the butte. The only way down—for a horse—was that up which the Crows had charged. The butte was between him and the fight along the creek. He had to circle it.

Passing around it, he had to go near the cottonwood trees where the Crows had left their horses. As he approached, one of the animals nickered to his own horse. The spotted pony answered, but nothing followed. Evidently the Crows had left nobody to guard their mounts. Long Orphan was not much surprised. They outnumbered the Cheyennes, and had them afoot and fighting for their lives. Besides, now that the Crows had lost their chief, there was no one with the authority to post a guard. Long Orphan rode in among the cottonwoods.

There was nobody there—only the horses. Long Orphan licked his lips. These were all war horses—far better animals than the ones No Heart had taken from the Crow camp. If he could bring home such a herd as that, Long Orphan knew his name would be high among his people. No Heart would be put to shame. It was worth any risk.

Quickly, Long Orphan rounded up the animals, drew them out through the trees. He circled back around the butte and brought the ponies safely down the creek in the rear of the fighting Cheyennes. He found them much farther up the creek then they had been before. The Crows had been driving them back.

There was a chance that, when they saw the ponies coming, some Cheyenne might take a shot at Long Orphan. And so he sang an old war song, a favorite of his grandfather's: "Friends, I bring you their horses . . ."

The first man Long Orphan saw was Big Tree, who sat leaning back against a tree trunk, nursing his wounded knee. Big Tree saw the young man coming with the horses and covered his mouth with his hands in sheer astonishment. Then Big Tree laughed and said, "*Ah-ho*, thanks. Today you have saved my life." Big Tree called to his comrades, and they all came dodging back through the brush, eager to mount the horses Long Orphan had brought.

No Heart was sick with chagrin when he saw what the young man had done. He mounted a horse and then said: "Good. Now we can charge them on horseback." He wanted to do something brave then, to outdo the boy who had taunted him.

But Big Tree was loud in objection. "No," he said, "let's go home. We have taken these horses and a scalp. We are lucky to get away alive. That is enough for one day. Three good men have been wounded already. Besides, these horses all belong to our friend Long Orphan. If we ride them, we must do as he says. Of course, if anyone wants to stay here and fight on foot, let him do it. What do you say, friend?"

They all looked at Long Orphan, waiting for him to speak. He had become their leader. He glanced at No Heart—the man's face was fixed with a look of furious envy. Long Orphan said, "Let's do as Big Tree says. Let's go home."

When the Cheyennes rode away across the prairie, the Crows ran out of the brush and stood staring after them, amazed, afoot and two days' ride from home. The Cheyennes laughed and made gestures at the foolish Crows. All but No Heart. There was no laughter in him.

That night in camp the Cheyennes held council. It was agreed that they would all ride home together the next day, timing their arrival about noon so that the whole camp would see them come in victorious. All the people would be awake and about then, and they would make a good showing. They planned this in advance, for if one or two men slipped away and reached home before the others, the news of their victory would be stale when they got in, and half the fun of the celebration would be lost to them.

Long Orphan was well pleased with this plan, for he was the hero of the expedition. But No Heart left the camp and sat alone on the hillside, smoking and thinking until after the others had gone to bed.

Next morning, before it was light, Long Orphan was up and went out looking for his horses. He expected to find them near the water at that hour, but failed to do so. All the animals seemed to have vanished. He hurried back to tell his comrades. But they pointed to the place where No Heart had slept and to a broad trail of horses moving toward the home camp. No Heart had taken the horses and the scalp, and had gone on ahead. He wanted to steal some of the glory of Long Orphan and make everybody look first at himself.

There was one horse left in the camp of the war party—Big Tree's. For Big Tree had been wounded. He could not walk, and he was taking no chances on being left afoot a second time. He had tied his pony's lariat around his own body before he went to sleep, and No Heart had been afraid that he might waken Big Tree if he tried to take that horse along. So Big Tree told Long Orphan to take the horse and go after No Heart. Long Orphan lost no time. He went on the run.

About the middle of the morning, he saw No Heart driving the herd along ahead of him. Quirting his pony on both flanks, Long Orphan quickly came up to the man. He rode up on the right side, like a man about to shoot a buffalo. But Long Orphan did not shoot; he did not say a word. He pushed his horse between No Heart and the horses he had stolen.

No Heart would not give way. He was angry. He turned in his saddle, raised his quirt and lashed Long Orphan across the face.

Then Long Orphan lost his temper. He was too angry to

speak. Instead he lifted the barrel of his rifle suddenly and brought it down across No Heart's head. No Heart dropped from his saddle and lay on the ground without stirring.

"Lie there, dog!" said Long Orphan. "You beat me for disobeying orders. Now it is my turn."

Long Orphan took the horses back to his waiting comrades. When they all passed that way again, later in the day, No Heart still lay where he had fallen. They flung him across a saddle, like a dead man, and packed him into camp. He was still out when they finished the scalp dance the next morning.

But nobody seemed to miss No Heart at the scalp dance. Everyone was too busy celebrating the victory of a new warrior with a new name—that long-legged orphan boy whom everyone had thought was of no account. The chiefs had thrown his old name away and given him a new title in honor of his brave exploit.

That name was Woman's Dress.

"The West" is a relative term that not only depends on where you live, but when you were writing. Hamlin Garland's West in most of his stories was such states as Kansas and Nebraska, because he was writing from the perspective of his native Boston. However, he was fully capable (at least once in a while) of setting his tales further west, as in "Lone Wolf's Old Guard," which appeared in his The Book of the American Indian *in 1923.*

Lone Wolf's Old Guard

Hamlin Garland

Now it happened that Lone Wolf's camp was on the line between the land of the Cheyennes and the home of his own people, the Kiowas, but he did not know this. He had lived there long, and the white man's maps were as unimportant to him as they had been to the Cheyennes. When he moved there he considered it to be his—a gift direct from the Creator—with no prior rights to be overstepped.

But the Consolidated Cattle Company, having secured the right to enclose a vast pasture, cared nothing for any red man's claim, provided they stood in with the government. A surveying party was sent out to run lines for fences.

Lone Wolf heard of these invaders while they were at work north of him, and learned in some mysterious way that they were to come down the Elk and cut through his camp. To his friend John, the interpreter, he sent these words:

"The white man must not try to build a fence across my land. I will fight if he does. Washington is not behind this thing. He would not build a fence through my lines without talking with me. I have sent to the agent of the Kiowas, he knows nothing about it—it is all a plan of the cattlemen to steal my lands. Tell them that we have smoked over this news—we have decided. This fence will not be built."

When "Johnny Smoker" brought this stern message to the camp of the surveyors, some of them promptly threw up their hands. Jim Bellows, scout and interpreter, was among these, and his opinion had weight, for he wore his hair long and posed as an Indian fighter of large experience.

"Boys," he began, impressively, "we got to get out o' here as soon as darkness covers us. We're sixty miles from the fort, and only fifteen all told, and not half-armed. Old Lone Wolf holds over us, and we might as well quit and get help."

This verdict carried the camp, and the party precipitately returned to Darlington to confer with the managers of the company.

Pierce, the chief man, had reasons for not calling on the military authorities. His lease was as yet merely a semiprivate arrangement between the Secretary of the Interior and himself, and he feared the consequences of a fight with Lone Wolf—publicity, friction, might cause the withdrawal of his lease; therefore he called in John Seger, and said:

"Jack, can you put that line through?"

"I could, but I don't want to. Lone Wolf is a good friend of mine, and I don't want to be mixed up in a mean job."

"Oh, come now—you mustn't show the white flag. I need you. I want you to pick out five or six men of grit and go along and see that this line is run. I can't be fooling around here all summer. Here's my lease, signed by the Secretary, as you see. It's all straight, and this old fool of an Indian must move."

Jack reluctantly consented, and set to work to hire a half-dozen men of whose courage he had personal knowledge. Among these was a man by the name of Tom Speed, a borderman of great hardihood and experience. To him he said:

"Tom, I don't like to go into this thing; but I'm hard up, and Pierce has given me the contract to build the fence if we run the line, and it looks like we got to do it. Now I wish you'd saddle up and help me stave off trouble. How does it strike you?"

"It's nasty business, Jack; but I reckon we might better do it than let some tenderfoot go in and start a killin'. I'm busted flat, and if the pay is good, I jest about feel obliged to take it."

So it happened that two avowed friends of the red man led this second expedition against Lone Wolf's camp. Pierce sent his brother as boss, and with him went the son of one of the principal owners, a Boston man, by the name of Ross. Speed always called him "the Dude," though he dressed quite simply, as dress goes in Roxbury. He wore a light suit of gray wool, "low-quartered shoes," and a "grape box hat." He was armed with a pistol, which wouldn't kill a turtledove at fifteen feet. Henry Pierce, on the contrary, was a reckless and determined man.

Moving swiftly across the Divide, they took up the line on Elk Creek, and started directly towards Lone Wolf's camp. As they were nearing the bend in the river where Lone Wolf was camped, a couple of young warriors came riding leisurely up from the south. They were very cordial in their greeting, and, after shaking hands all around, pleasantly inquired:

"What are you doing here?"

"Running a line to mark out the land which the cattlemen have leased of the Cheyennes."

"We will go along and see where you are going," they replied.

A couple of hours later, while they were still with the camp, two others came riding quietly in from the east. They said, "We are looking for horses," and after shaking hands and asking Seger what the white men were doing, rode forward to join their companions, who seemed deeply interested in the surveyors and their instruments. Turning to Pierce, Jack said:

"You noticed that these four men were armed, I reckon?"

"Oh, yes, but they are all right. Didn't you see how they shook hands all round? They're just out hunting up ponies."

"Yes, I saw that; but I noticed they had plenty of ammunition and that their guns were bright. Indians don't hunt horses in squads, Mr. Pierce."

Pierce smiled, giving Seger a sidewise glance. "Are you getting nervous? If you are, you can drop to the rear."

Now Seger had lived for the larger part of his life among the red people, and knew their ways. He answered, quietly:

"There are only four of them now; you'll see more of them soon," and he pointed away to the north, where the heads of three mounted men were rising into sight over a ridge. These also proved to be young Kiowas, thoroughly armed, who asked the same question of the manager, and in conclusion pleasantly said:

"We'll just go along and see how you do it."

As they rode forward, Seger uttered a more pointed warning.

"Mr. Pierce, I reckon you'd better make some better disposition of your men. They are all strung out here, with their guns on their backs, in no kind of shape to make a defense."

Pierce was a little impressed by the scout's earnestness, and took trouble to point out the discrepancy between "a bunch of seven cowardly Indians" and his own band of twenty brave and experienced men.

"That's all right," replied Seger, "but these seven men are only spies, sent out to see what we are going to do. We'll have to buckle up with Lone Wolf's whole band very soon."

A few minutes later, the seven young men rode quietly by and took a stand on a ridge a little in front of the surveyors. As he approached them, Seger perceived a very great change in their demeanor. They no longer smiled; they seemed grim, resolute, and much older. From a careless, laughing group of young men they had become soldiers—determined, disciplined, and dignified. Their leader, riding forth, held up his hand, and said:

"Stop; you must wait here till Lone Wolf comes."

Meanwhile, in the little city of tents, a brave drama was being enacted. Lone Wolf, a powerful man of middle age, was sitting in council with his people. The long-expected had happened—the cattlemen had begun to mark off the red man's land as their own, and the time had come either to submit or to repel the invaders. To submit was hard, to fight hopeless. Their world was still narrow, but they had a benumbing conception of the power and the remorseless greed of the white man.

"We can kill those who come," said Lone Wolf. "They are few, but behind them are the soldiers and men who plough."

At last old White Buffalo rose—he had been a great leader in his day, and was still much respected, though he had laid aside his chieftainship. He was bent and gray and wrinkled, but his voice was still strong, and his eyes keen.

"My friends, listen to me! During seventy years of my life, I lived without touching the hand of a white man. I have always opposed warfare, except when it was necessary; but now the time has come to fight. Let me tell you what to do. I see here some thirty old men, who, like me, are nearing the grave. This thing we will do—we old men—we will go out to war against these cattlemen. We will go forth and die in defense of our lands. Big Wolf, come—and you, my brother, Standing Bear."

As he called the roll of the gray old defenders, the old women broke into heart-piercing wailing, intermingled with exultant cries as some brave wife or sister caught the force of the heroic responses, which leaped from the lips of their fathers and husbands. A feeling of awe fell over the young men as they watched the fires flame once more in the dim eyes of their grandsires, and when all had spoken, Lone Wolf rose and stepped forth, and said:

"Very well; then I will lead you."

"Whosoever leads us goes to certain death," said White Buffalo. "It is the custom of the white men to kill the leader. You will fall at the first fire. I will lead."

Lone Wolf's face grew stern. "Am I not your war chief? Whose place is it to lead? If I die, I fall in combat for my land, and you, my children, will preserve my name in song. We do not know how this will end, but it is better to end in battle than to have our lands cut in half beneath our feet."

The bustle and preparation began at once. When all was ready, the thirty gray and withered old men, beginning a low humming song, swept through the camp and started on their desperate charge, Lone Wolf leading them. "Some of those who go will return, but if the white men fight, I will not return," he sang, as they began to climb the hill on whose top the white men could be seen awaiting their coming.

Halfway up the hill, they met some of the young warriors. "Go bring all the white men to the council," said Lone Wolf.

As the white men watched the band leaving the village and beginning to ascend the hill, Speed turned and said: "Well, Jack, what do you think of it? Here comes a war party—painted and armed."

"I think it's about an even chance whether we ever cross the Washita again or not. Now, you are a married man with children, and I wouldn't blame you if you pulled out right this minute."

"I feel meaner about this than anything I ever did," replied Speed, "but I am going to stay with the expedition."

As Lone Wolf and his heroic old guard drew near, Seger thrilled with the significance of this strange and solemn company of old men in full war-paint, armed with all kinds of old-fashioned guns, and bows and arrows. As he looked into their wrinkled faces, the scout perceived that these grandsires had come resolved to die. He divined what had taken place in camp. Their exalted heroism was written in the somber droop of their lips. "We can die, but we will not retreat!" In such wise our grandsires fought.

Lone Wolf led his Spartan host steadily on till it was near enough to be heard without effort. He then halted, took off his war-bonnet, and hung it on the pommel of his saddle. Lifting both palms to the sky, he spoke, and his voice had a solemn boom in it: "The Great Father is looking down on us. He sees us. He knows I speak the truth. He gave us this land. We are the first to inhabit it. No one else has any claim to it. It is ours, and I will go under the sod before any cattlemen shall divide it and take it away from us. I have said it."

When this was interpreted for him, Pierce, with a look of inquiry, turned to Speed. "Tell the old fool this line is going to be run, and no old scarecrows like these can stop us."

Seger, lifting his hand, signed: "Lone Wolf, you know me. I am your friend. I do not come to do you harm. I come to tell you you are wrong. All the land on my left hand the Great Father says is Cheyenne land. All on my right hand is Kiowa land. The Cheyennes have sold the right to their land to the white man, and we are here to mark out the line. We take only Cheyenne land."

"I do not believe it," replied the chief. "My agent knows nothing of it. Washington has not written anything to me about it. This is the work of robbers. Cattlemen will do anything for money. They are wolves. They shall not go on."

"What does he say?" asked Pierce.

"He says we must not go on."

"You tell him he can't run any such bluff on me with his old scarecrow warriors. This line goes through."

Lone Wolf, tense and eager, asked, "What says the white chief?"

"He says we must run the line."

Lone Wolf turned to his guard. "You may as well get ready," he said, quietly.

The old men drew closer together with a mutter of low words, and each pair of dim eyes selected their man. The clicking of their guns was ominous, and Pierce turned white.

Speed drew his revolver-holster round to the front. "They're going to fight," he said. "Every man get ready!"

But Seger, eager to avoid the appalling contest, cried out to Pierce:

"Don't do that! It's suicide to go on. These old men have come out to fight till death." To Lone Wolf he signed: "Don't shoot, my friend!—let us consider this matter. Put up your guns."

Into the hot mist of Pierce's wrath came a realization that these old men were in mighty earnest. He hesitated.

Lone Wolf saw his hesitation, and said: "If you are here by right, why do you not get the soldier chief to come and tell me? If the Great Father has ordered this—then I am like a man with his hands tied. The soldiers do not lie. Bring them!"

Seger grasped eagerly at this declaration. "There is your chance, Pierce. The chief says he will submit if the soldiers come to make the survey. Let me tell him that you will bring an officer from the fort to prove that the government is behind you."

Pierce, now fully aware of the desperate bravery of the old men, was looking for a knothole of escape. "All right, fix it up with him," he said.

Seger turned to Lone Wolf. "The chief of the surveyors says: 'Let us be friends. I will not run the line.' "

"Ho, ho!" cried the old warriors, and their faces, grim and wrinkled, broke up into smiles. They laughed, they shook hands, while tears of joy filled their eyes. They were like men delivered from sentence of death. The desperate courage of their approach was now revealed even to Pierce. They were joyous as children over their sudden release from slaughter.

Lone Wolf, approaching Seger, dismounted, and laid his arm over his friend's shoulder. "My friend," he said, with grave tenderness, "I wondered why you were with these men, and my heart was heavy; but now I see that you were here to turn aside the guns of the cattlemen. My heart is big with friendship for you. Once more you have proved my good counselor." And tears dimmed the fierceness of his eyes.

A week later, a slim, smooth-cheeked second lieutenant, by virtue of his cap and the crossed arms which decorated his collar, ran the line, and Lone Wolf made no resistance. "I have no fight with the soldiers of the Great Father," he said, "they do not come to gain my land. I now see that Washington has decreed that this fence shall be built." Nevertheless, his heart was very heavy, and in his camp his heroic old guard sat waiting, waiting!

Lapwai Winter

Will Henry

I recall the day as though it were but one or two suns gone. It had been an early spring in the northeast Oregon country, the weather in mid-April being already clear and warm as late May. I was on the hillside above our village on the Wallowa River when Itsiyiyi, Coyote, the friend of my heart in those boyhood times, came racing up from the lodges below.

Poor Coyote. His eyes were wild. His nostrils were standing wide with breath. His ragged black hair was tossing like the mane of a bay pony. I pitied the little fellow. He was always so alarmed by the least affair. Now I wondered calmly what small thing brought him dashing up from the village, and I awaited his news, very superior in the advantage of my fourteen summers to his twelve.

But Coyote had the real news that morning.

Joseph, our chief, had decided to accept the invitation of White Bird and Toohoolhoolzote to go with them to Montana and hunt the buffalo. Since White Bird and Too-

31

hoolhoolzote were the chiefs of the fierce White Bird and Salmon River bands—what we called the "wild" or "fighting Indians" as against our own more peaceful Wallowa people—no news could possibly have been more exciting to a Nez Perce boy. With a cry as high-pitched as Coyote's, I dashed off down the hill to catch up my pony and get ready.

Within the hour, the entire village was packed and our horse herd strung out on the Imnaha Trail to Idaho and the Salmon River country, where the wild bands lived. There was no trouble crossing the Snake late that afternoon, and early the following sunrise we were off up the Salmon to see the famous warrior tribes.

The prospects sent my heart soaring higher than a hawk on hunting wing. Even though my mother, who was a Christian and had gone many years to the white man's missionary school at Lapwai, talked very strong against such "Indian nonsense" as going to the buffalo, and assured me with plenty of threats that I was going to spend that coming winter at Agent Monteith's reservation school whether Joseph and my father agreed to it or not, I still could not restrain my joy at the adventure which lay ahead. I knew this was a time of times for any Nez Perce boy to remember, and I certainly was not going to let my mother's stern beliefs in her Lord Jesus, nor any of her threats about the white man's school, spoil it for me. I was an Indian, and this was a time for Indians.

It was spring. A fine shower during the night had washed the sky clean as a river stone. The sun was warm and sweet. Above us on the steepening hillsides the pine jays scolded with a good will. Below us along the rushing green water of the river the redwing reed-birds whistled cheerily. Tea Kettle, my dear mouse-colored pony, tried to bite me in the leg and buck me off. Yellow Wolf, my young uncle who was as fierce as any fighting Indian, jogged by on his traveling mare and gave me a friendly sign. Even Joseph, that strange, sad-eyed man who almost never smiled, brightened to nod and wave at me as I passed him where he sat his horse by the trail watching and counting to be sure all of his people were safe across the Snake and settled right upon the trail up the Salmon.

I looked all about me at the lovely pine-scented country and at those handsome, good-natured Nez Perce people riding up the sparkling river carefree and noisy-throated as the mountain birds around them and, doing that, I thought to myself that I might well take this moment to offer up some word of thanks to Hunyewat, our own Indian god. There was, too, good and real reason for the gratitude. Due to President Grant's good treaty of the year before, the trouble between our people and the white man was over for all time. The Wallowa, our beautiful Valley of the Winding Water, had been given back to us and, surely, as of that moment there among the Idaho hills there was nothing but blue sky and bird-songs in the Nez Perce world.

Bobbing along on my little gray pony, I bowed my head to the morning sun and said my humble word to Hunyewat.

Indians are supposed to be very brave, even the little boys. I was not such a good Indian, I fear. When we got to White Bird Canyon where the first village of wild bands was located, I am afraid I did great shame to my fourteen years. I certainly did not act like a boy but three summers away from his manhood.

White Bird—it was his village nestled there on the canyon floor—was not at home. Neither were his warriors. There were only the old men, the women, and the children left in the silent village. Some of the old men rode out to tell us what had happened.

Word had come that the white settlers in Kamiah Valley had stopped our Nez Perce cattle herds at Kamiah Crossing of the Clearwater River. The white men had showed the Nez Perce herdsmen the rifle and told them they could not bring their cattle into the Kamiah any more from that time. It was white man's grass now. The Indian was going to have to stay off of it. White Bird had gone that same morning to gather up Toohoolhoolzote and the Salmon River warriors to ride to the crossing. Eeh-hahh! Bad, very bad. There was going to be real trouble now.

The moment I heard this I knew our trip to the buffalo country was ruined. It was then the tear came to my eye, the sniffle to my nose. Fortunately no one saw me. There were graver things to watch. Joseph's face had grown hard as the mountain rock above us.

It was a wrong thing, he told the old men, for the settlers to have closed the historic Indian Road to the Kamiah grass. The Nez Perce has used that trail and those pastures since the grayest chief could remember. But it would also be a wrong thing to let White Bird and Toohoolhoolzote come up to the river ready to fight. They were dangerous Indians.

"Ollikut, Elk Water, Horse Blanket, Yellow Wolf," said Joseph quickly, "you four come with me. Go get your best horses, pick your buffalo racers, we must go fast."

"Where are we going?" asked Ollikut, Joseph's tall, young brother.

"To Kamiah Crossing. We must stop these angry men or there will be shooting. We have given our word against that. Do you agree?"

"Yes," said Ollikut. "We will get our horses."

In bare minutes they had mounted up and gone hammering down the trail around Buzzard Mountain to the Clearwater River. I sat there, feeling my heart tear apart within me. Suddenly I saw Coyote motioning to me urgently. I guided Tea Kettle over toward him. He was on his scrubby brown colt and he had a pudgy White Bird boy with him. The boy had his own horse, a spavined paint with feet like snowshoes. I drew myself up, looking haughty.

"Well," I challenged Coyote, "what do you want?"

"This is Peopeo Hihhih," he replied, indicating his companion.

"Yes? What is so remarkable about that?"

"Not much. Only his father's name is Peopeo Hihhih, too."

"Coyote, what are you trying to say to me?"

"This much—this boy's father is Chief White Bird."

"No!"

I could not believe it. This small, ugly little animal the true son of White Bird? Impossible.

"Boy," I said, "is my friend's tongue straight? Are you the blood son of Chief White Bird?"

"No. Only the near-son. My mother was his sister. But he raised me in his tepee and gave me his name. Everybody calls me Little Bird. You look like a nice boy; what's your name?"

"Heyets."

"Very fine name. It means Mountain Sheep."

"That's very smart of you, boy. And you only seven or eight summers. Imagine!"

"Seven summers." The pudgy boy smiled. "Ten more and I will be a warrior like you."

I watched him closely, but he was not bright enough to be flattering me. He actually thought I had seventeen summers. Clearly, although not clever, neither was he as stupid as I had believed. I began to feel better about my lot.

"Well," I said cheerfully, "what shall we do? Ride down the river and stone the potholes for mallard hens? Go for a swim in the Salmon? Hunt rabbits? Have a pony race?"

Instantly the fat White Bird boy was frowning at Coyote.

"I thought you said he would want to go over to the Clearwater and creep up on the fight at Kamiah Crossing," he said accusingly.

"I did! I did!" protested Coyote. "But with Heyets you can't tell. He changes his mind like a woman. You can't trust his mind. Neither can he."

I did not care to stand there listening to a simpleton like Coyote explaining the workings of my thoughts to a seven-year-old White Bird Indian. I grew angry.

"Be quiet!" I ordered. "Of course I would like to go to the Clearwater and see the fight. But what is the use of such talk? It will be all over before we could get these poor crowbaits of ours halfway around the mountain." I paused, getting madder. "Coyote," I said, "from here where I now say good-by to you, I will speak no more to you in this life. I warned you, now we are through *Taz alago*—!''

"Well, all right, good-by." Coyote shrugged. "Have it your way, Heyets. But I just thought you would like to beat Joseph and the men to Kamiah Crossing. That's why I wanted you to see Little Bird. He knows a way."

I spun Tea Kettle around.

"He knows what way?" I demanded.

"The secret way of his people over the mountain, instead of around it. It's a way he says we can get our poor horses to the crossing before any of them. Before Elk Water, your father. Before Horse Blanket, Yellow Wolf's father. Before Ollikut, Joseph's brother. Before—''

"Enough! Enough!" I cried. "Is this true, Little Bird?"

Little Bird lifted his three small chins. "I am the son of a war chief," he said. "Would I lie to a Wallowa?"

I made as though I did not understand the insult, and said, "Eeh-hahh, there has been too much talk. Let's go."

"Yes, that's right," spoke up Little Bird. "We have a tall mountain to get over. Follow me. And when we get up high, let your ponies have their heads. There are some places up there you will not want to look over. Eeh-hahh!"

Coyote and I understood that kind of instruction. We gave a happy laugh, hit our ponies with our buffalo-hide quirts, went charging off after Little Bird's splayfooted paint. We were gone as quickly as the men before us.

That was a wild track up over that mountain but it was a good one. We got to the Clearwater before Joseph and before even the White Bird and Salmon River warriors.

Little Bird led us off the mountain down a creek bed which had a cover of timber all the way to its joining with the river. This was below the crossing, up near which we could plainly see the white men sitting around their campfire making loud talk and boasting of the easy way they had run off the Indian herders that morning.

The day was well gone now. Whippoorwills were crying

on the mountain. Dusk hawks were about their bug hunting. The sun was dropped from sight beyond the western hills. Only its last shafts were striking the face of the cliffs above us. North and east, heavy clouds were coming on to rain. The river was starting to drift a chilly mist.

I shivered and suggested to my companions that we circle the white camp and go on up the river to the village of Looking Glass, the Asotin Nez Perce chief. Up there we could get a warm sleep in a dry tepee, also some good hot beef to eat for our supper.

But Little Bird had not come over the mountain to visit the Asotin, who were even more settled than the Wallowa.

"No," said the fat rascal, "I won't go up there. My father says Looking Glass is strong, but his people are weak. They take the white man's way. *Kapsis itu*, that's a bad thing."

"Well," I countered, "it's going to rain. We'll get soaked and lie here on the ground shaking all night. That's a bad thing, too."

"Eeh!" was all he would say to me. "I am a Nez Perce; you Wallowas are all women."

"Not this Wallowa!" cried Coyote. "I fear no rain. I fear no white man. I fear no fat White Bird boy. Ki-yi-yi-yi-yi!"

He threw back his head and burst into his yipping personal call before I could move to stop him. My stomach closed up within me like a bunching hand. Only one thing saved us from instant discovery. Coyote made such an excellent imitation of the little brush wolf for which he was named that the white men were fooled. One of them picked up his rifle and shied a shot our way. The bullet slapped through our cover at the same time my hand took Coyote across his yammering mouth. He gave a startled yelp and shut up. The white man laughed and put down his gun and said, "By damn, I must have clipped the leetle varmint. How's thet fer luck?"

We didn't answer him, letting him think what he wanted.

It got pretty quiet.

Presently Little Bird said respectfully to me, "What I

suggest, Heyets, is that we creep up the river bed and listen to the white man's talk. Coyote said your mother has been to the school at Lapwai and has taught you their language. You can tell us what they are saying up there, eh?''

I started to give him some good reason why we should not attempt this riskful thing but was fortunately spared the need. Happening to glance up the river as he spoke, my eyes grew wide.

"Eeh!'' I whispered excitedly. "It is too late. Look up there on the cliff!''

I flung out my arm, and my friends, following the point of my rigid finger to the mountainside above the white man's fire, became very still. Everything all around became very still. That was the kind of a sight it was.

On the crest of the last rise past the settler campfire, sitting their horses quiet as so many statues carved from the mountain granite, were too craggy-faced war chiefs and half a hundred unfriendly-looking, eagle-feathered fighting Indians.

"Nanitsch!'' hissed Little Bird, filling the silence with the fierce pride of his words. "Look, you Wallowas! See who it is yonder on the hillside. It is my father, White Bird, and his friend Toohoolhoolzote, come to kill the Kamiah white man!''

The fighting Indians came down the hill. They came very slow, giving us time to slip up through the river brush to be close to it all when it happened. As they rode forward, the white men left their fire and took up their rifles. They walked out on foot to meet the mounted Indians in the way such things were done. Both parties stopped about an arrow shot apart. For the Indians White Bird and Toohoolhoolzote rode out. For the white men it was a lanky fellow with no whiskers and a foxy eye, and a square-built man with blunt whiskers and a glinting eye like a rooting pig. We knew them both. They were Narrow Eye Chapman and Agent Monteith.

The talk began but did not go far.

Neither White Bird nor Toohoolhoolzote spoke a word of

English. Monteith knew our tongue a little, yet had to wait for Chapman to explain many things for him. Chapman was a squaw man, living with an Umatilla woman up in White Bird Canyon. The Indians knew him from a long time and took him as their friend. Still the talk kept stopping because of Agent Monteith. Toohoolhoolzote, famous for his harsh temper, began to grow angry. He glared at the Lapwai agent and growled the one English saying he knew at Narrow Eye Chapman.

"Damn-to-hell," he said, "I will not stay here and listen to any more of this delaying. We know why we are here. You know why we are here. Why do we argue? I am going to ride back a ways and return with my gun cocked for shooting."

"No, no," the squaw man pleaded. "Wait now, old friend, don't do that. You haven't heard the whole story yet."

Toohoolhoolzote looked at him.

"Do you deny these men stopped our cattle?" he asked.

"No, I can't deny that. But—"

"Never mind, I only want to know if you stopped the cattle. Now I will ask it of you one more time. Can the cattle go over the river into the Kamiah grass?"

Chapman looked around like a rabbit caught by dogs in an open meadow. Then he spoke rapidly to Agent Monteith, telling him what Toolhoolhoolzote had said. The agent got very dark in the face.

"You tell that Indian," he ordered, "to bring his cattle and come to live upon the reservation as the other Nez Perce have done. Tell him there is plenty of grass at Lapwai, and be done with him. Tell him I will send for the soldiers if he does not do as I say."

But Narrow Eye knew better than that. He shook his head.

"No," he said quickly, "we can't do that. I will ask him to wait until morning with his decision. That will give us time to send back for more men. We will need every gun in the Kamiah if we stay here. We wouldn't last five minutes if they started shooting now, and they're mortal close to doing it. Those Indians are mad.''

Agent Monteith peered at the angry faces of the fighting Indians, and of a sudden his own stubborn face changed. Even from as far away as our river bushes we could see him get pale above his whiskers. At once he agreed to the squaw man's plan, and Chapman turned and told the big lie to the Indians.

Toohoolhoolzote was for war right then. But White Bird looked up at the sky and said "no." The light was already too far gone for good shooting. The morning would be time enough. There were only a dozen white men and by good daybreak light they could be more sure they got every one of them. For a moment I let out my listening breath, thinking everything was going to rest quiet at that agreement, giving Joseph time to get up and perhaps prevent the fight. I finished translating what had been said for my two friends, not thinking how they might take the white man's treachery. I had still much to learn about fighting Indians, even very small fat ones.

Little Bird, the moment he heard of Chapman's deceitful words to Monteith, burst from our cover like a stepped-on cottontail. Bounding through the twilight toward the Nez Perce, he kept shouting in our tongue for them to beware, to fight right then, that Narrow Eye Chapman was sending for more guns, maybe even for the horse soldiers, that all of them would be killed if they waited for the morning.

When Little Bird did that—jumped and ran—I didn't know what to do, but crazy Coyote, he knew what to do. He jumped and ran after him, yelling, "Wait for me! Wait for me! Wait for me—!"

One of the white men, a heavy one with yellow-stained red whiskers, cursed, using his God's name, and called out to the others, "Come on, boys, we had better beat through them willows. Might be a whole litter of them red whelps in thar!"

With the words, he leaped on his horse and plunged him into the brush where I was running around in senseless circles trying to decide which way to go. He reached down and seized me by the back of my hunting shirt, rode back with me dangling in one great hand.

"Here, by cripes!" he bellowed. "Lookit here what I found. Damn me if it ain't a leetle red swamp rat!"

Well, it was no little red swamp rat, but the fourteen-year-old son of Elk Water, the Wallowa Nez Perce. Still it was no time for false pride. Nor anything else for that matter. Before the red-whiskered man could bring me back to the campfire and before the startled Indians could form their line to charge upon the treacherous whites, a single shot rang out upon the mountainside.

The lone bullet splashed a whining mark of lead on a big rock which stood midway in the meadow between the settlers and our angry people, and a deep voice rolled down from above saying, "Do not fight. The first man on either side to ride beyond the rock will be shot."

We all fell still, looking upward toward the cliff down which winded the Clearwater trail.

There, fiery red in the reflected light of the disappeared sun, tall as giants on their beautiful buffalo horses, were Joseph and Ollikut, with my father and Yellow Wolf's father and Yellow Wolf himself. All save Joseph had their rifles pointed toward the midway rock, and there was still smoke curling from Ollikut's gun, showing it was he who had fired the lone shot. For himself, Joseph did not even have a gun. He was commanding the stillness with his upheld hand alone. It was a strange thing. All the Indians and all the white men likewise did his bidding. Not one man made to move himself, or his horse, or his loaded rifle in all the time it took our Wallowa chief to ride down from the cliff.

It was the first time I had seen the power of Joseph's hand. It was the first time I knew that he possessed this *wyakin*, this personal magic to command other men. I think that many of the Nez Perce had not seen it or felt it before this time either. It was as if they did not know this Joseph, like he was a stranger among them.

The stillness hurt the ears as he made his way across the meadow toward the white men from Kamiah.

Joseph talked straight with the white men. The other Indians came into the settler fire and stood at the edge of its outer light and listened without moving. But they did not talk, only Joseph talked.

In his patient way, he went back to the beginning of the agreements on paper between our two peoples. He reminded Agent Monteith of the Walla Walla Peace Council of 1855 of which only the Nez Perce had stood faithful to the white man, and in which all the other tribes, the Yakimas, the Umatillas, the Palouse, Spokanes, Couer d'Alenes—all of them save the Nez Perce—spoke against the paper and would not sign it.

Always, Joseph said, the Nez Perce had abided by that treaty. Only when the Thieves Treaty took away their lands in 1863, after gold was discovered at Oro Fino, had the Nez Perce faltered in their friendship. Even then they had made no war, only stayed apart from the white man, asking nothing but to be let alone. Now there was President Grant's good paper that returned the Wallowa country to the Nez Perce. Now all should be as it was in the old friendly days. But here was the white man trying to steal the Indian's grass again. The Kamiah was Indian country. There was no treaty keeping Nez Perce cattle away from it, yet here was the white man standing at Kamiah Crossing flourishing the rifle and saying hard things to Joseph, who was trying to keep the peace.

Was it not enough, cried Joseph, throwing wide his arms, that the white man had torn the gold from the Indian earth? That he had taken the best farmlands for himself? That he had built his whiskey stores along the Indian trails? That he had lured the Indian children away from their parents into his Christian school? Had taught them to pray to Jesus Christ and to sneer at the old Indian gods? Had made them forget the ways of their own fathers and mothers, and led them to think their own people were lower than dogs and the white man the lord of all on earth? That he had lied to, stolen from, cheated on the poor, trusting Nez Perce for seventy snows and more? Were not all these things enough? Did he now also have to starve the Indian as well? To stomp in his water and stale in it, too? Must he not only take what grass he needs, alone, but also that small amount necessary to the Indian's poor few cattle?

What did such a situation leave Joseph to say to White Bird and Toohoolhoolzote? What could he tell his angry brothers to keep them from fighting in the morning? If any of the white men had the answer to that question, he had better give it to Joseph now.

There was a long silence then while Chapman translated and the white men talked it over. Then Agent Monteith showed his stumpy teeth and stood forth to talk unfriendly.

It was time, he said, for the Nez Perce to realize they could no longer move themselves and their cattle about the land as they pleased. They were going to have to keep themselves and their herds in one place from now on, even as the white man did. There was no choice. If they would not do it, the soldiers would come and make them do it. Was that perfectly clear to Joseph?

Joseph was a wise man. He did not say "yes" just to make a good feeling. He shook his head and said "no," he did not think he understood what Agent Monteith was saying. It seemed there was possibly more intended than was stated. Would the agent try again, Joseph asked Chapman, this time with his tongue uncurled?

Chapman winced and said to Joseph, "I hope you understand that my heart is with you. I think much of my wife's people. But I am white, what can I do?"

"Do nothing," answered Joseph, "that you do not think I would do."

"Thank you, my brother," said Chapman, and went back to Monteith. The latter proved quite ready to repeat his exact meaning. He did not like Joseph, because he could not fool him, so he took refuge in hard talk.

"All right," he scowled, "here is precisely what I mean: you and your people are not going to the buffalo anymore;

you are not leaving your lands to do anything. Such moving around makes the young men restless and wild. When you put your cattle out to grass and go to the buffalo, you are away six months. The children are kept out of school, they have no chance to learn the ways of the new life that will let them live side by side with the white man. This is a wrong thing, Joseph. We must start with the children. They must be put in school and kept there. It is the only way to real peace between our people. We must have a common God and common ways. Only through the children may this be done.''

When Joseph heard this, he asked only what putting the children in school had to do with showing the rifle at Kamiah Crossing. Monteith answered him at once. Peaceful Indians, he said, were Indians who stayed in one place. Moving Indians were fighting Indians. And the day of the moving Indian was all done. From this time forward, the Nez Perce must do as Indian Agent John Monteith said, not as White Bird said, not as Toohoolhoolzote said, not as any other fighting chief said. And what Agent Monteith said was that the Wallowas must now stay in their level valley, the White Birds in their deep canyon, the Salmon Rivers behind their big mountain. To guarantee this obedience there was but one sure way: put the children in the reservation school and raise them as white boys and girls. It was up to Joseph to make this clear to the other Nez Perce. Did Joseph understand?

Our chief nodded slowly. The hurt in his face would have made a stone weep. Yes, he said, for the very first time he did understand. Now it was revealed to him what the white man really wanted of the Indian. It was not to live in peace with him, as brother with brother. When the agent said that about not going to the buffalo, about the cattle not going into Kamiah, that was nothing. It was only an excuse. The white man knew that to shut up the Indian in a small place was to destroy his spirit, to break his heart, to kill him.

If that was what Agent Monteith now wanted Joseph to tell the other chiefs, he would do it. He would tell them that either they went home and stayed there or the horse soldiers would come and drive them upon the reservation. He would tell them that in any case their children must soon be sent into Lapwai School and made to live there. But he must warn the agent that he was asking a very dangerous thing.

With this low-voiced agreement, Joseph turned away from Monteith and told the fighting Indians what he had said.

I had a very good look at this last part of it. I was being held in the camp tent. The red-whiskered man was in there with me holding his bad-smelling hand across my mouth the whole time. But I could see between his fat fingers and through the slight parting of the tent flap. Of course none of the Nez Perce knew I was in there. They all thought I had gotten away down the river and would come into their camp when I had the chance.

When Joseph told the others about not going to the buffalo anymore, about the horse soldiers putting them on the reservation if they moved around, about Agent Monteith demanding the surrender of the children as the earnest of their good faith, the Indians did a strange thing. Their faces grew not angry but very sad, and when Joseph had finished the last word, they turned and went back upon the mountainside without a sound. Only old Toohoolhoolzote stayed behind with Joseph, and with our Wallowa chief he now went toward the white men.

Coming up to Monteith, Joseph said, "I have told my people what you said. Now Toohoolhoolzote will tell you what my people say in return." He stood back, giving over his place to the older man. Toohoolhoolzote stared at all the white men for a moment, then nodded.

"I will be brief," he said in Nez Perce to Chapman, but fixing his gaze upon the Lapwai agent. "Tomorrow, if you are still here, there will be shooting. We are going to the buffalo. We will graze our cattle where we wish. We will not bring our children into Lapwai. Joseph is a good man and he is your friend. Toohoolhoolzote is a bad man and he is not your friend. When the sun comes up, remember that. *Taz alago*, Agent Monteith. Sleep light.''

For a time the old man stood there, the firelight making a black spiderweb of the seams and dry canyons in his face skin. His mouth was set in a line wide and ugly as a war-ax cut. His eyes burned like a wolf's eyes. His expression was unmoving. Suddenly I was as afraid of him as the white men. The sight of him braced there, lean and dark and strong as a pine tree for all his sixty-eight winters, staring down all that bitter talk and all those menacing white rifles with nothing save his Nez Perce *simiakia*, his terrible Indian pride, put a chill along my spine from tail to neckbone. When he finally turned away to follow his warriors up onto the mountain, it was even more quiet than when Joseph came down the cliff trail.

Now there was only my own chief left.

He told Chapman in Nez Perce that he was sad that Agent Monteith had done this dangerous thing to the spirit of the wild bands. He promised he would yet do what he could to prevent the shooting in the morning but begged Chapman to try and get the white settlers to leave the crossing when it was full dark, to be far, far from it when the sun came over Buzzard Mountain next day. Then he, too, turned to go. In the last breath, however, Agent Monteith requested him to wait a moment. Wearily Joseph did so, and Monteith wheeled toward the camp tent and said, ''Bates, bring that boy up here.''

Redbeard Bates grinned and spat and shoved me stumbling out of the tent. Outside, he pushed me forward into the fire's light to face my chief.

Joseph's tired face softened as he saw me.

But Agent Monteith's face grew hard.

''Joseph,'' he said, ''tell your people over on the mountain that I don't trust them. I will hold the boy with us until we see there is no shooting and no following us away from here. The boy will be perfectly all right. After a time you come into Lapwai and we will talk about him. I know this boy is of your own blood, and I have an idea for him you would do well to listen to. It may be that we can use him to lead in the others. Do you understand that?''

Joseph understood it.

But to Agent Monteith he merely nodded without words, while to me he spoke ever so gently in his deep voice.

"No harm will come to you, little Heyets," he said. "Go with the agent and do not fear. I shall come for you. As you wait, think well upon what you have seen here. Do you think you can remember it?''

I drew myself up.

"Yes, my chief, I will always remember it.''

"Good. It is a lesson about the white man that you will never learn in his school at Lapwai.'' He smiled, touching me softly on the shoulder. "*Taz alago*, Heyets,'' he said, and turned for the last time away from that dark fire by the Clearwater.

"*Taz alago*, my chief,'' I called into the twilight after him, and was glad he did not look back to see the tears that stood in my eyes no matter that I was fourteen summers and would be a warrior soon.

I had never been to Lapwai longer than one day. Say, as on a Sunday to watch the tame Indians pray, or on a Saturday when they drew their agency beef and might favor a visiting "wild" relative with a bit of fat meat to take home at the white man's expense. Accordingly, as I now rode toward the mission school with the agent and the Kamiah settlers, I began to recover from my fright and to wonder how it might be to live on the reservation over here in Idaho for a longer while, like perhaps two or three days, or even a whole week.

But I did not get to find out.

We had been riding most of the night, having slipped away from the crossing as Joseph advised. Now, as the sun came up, we stopped to boil water and make coffee. Before the water started to roll in the old black pot, five Nez Perce came out of a brushy draw nearby and rode up to our fire. We knew them all. They were Joseph, Ollikut, Horse Blanket, Yellow Wolf, and Elk Water, my own father.

"Well, Joseph," demanded Agent Monteith at once, "what is this? Have you tricked me? What do you want here?"

Joseph looked at him steadily.

"It is not my way to play tricks," he said. "Last night I gave you the boy so there would be no trouble with those White Birds and Salmon Rivers. There was no trouble. Now I want the boy back, that is all."

"Give them the kid!" I heard Narrow Eye Chapman whisper to Monteith, but the agent set his stubborn jaw and said no, he wouldn't do it.

Ollikut, great, handsome Ollikut, pushed his roan buffalo racer forward. He cocked his gun. "Agent," he said, "we want the boy."

"For God's sake," said Chapman out of the side of his mouth to Monteith, "give them the kid and get shut of them. What are you trying to do, get us all killed? That damned Ollikut will tackle a buzzsaw barehanded. Smarten up, you hear? These ain't agency Indians you're fooling with."

Agent Monteith stuck out his stubby beard still farther and bared his many small teeth like a cornered cave bat, but he gave in.

"Joseph," he said, "I am charging you with this matter. I want this boy in school this winter. You know why. It is the only way he can learn the white man's way."

"Yes, but he should have his say what he will do."

"No, he should not. That is the trouble with you Indians. You let the children run over you. You never say 'no' to them and you never punish them for doing wrong. Children must be taught to do as they are told."

"We teach them. But what has that to do with striking them and saying no to everything they want? There are other ways to show them wisdom."

"Joseph, I won't argue with you. I leave it to your own mind. Whether this boy is going to grow up Indian or white is up to you. You and I are grown men, we will not change our ways. I have one God, you have another. My father taught from the Holy Book, your father tore up the Holy

Book. We are as we are, you and I, but the boy can be anything which you say he can be. You are the head chief of the Wallowas, the most powerful band of the Nez Perce. If you send this boy of your own band and blood to go to school at Lapwai this winter, you will have said to all the other wild bands that you intend to take the white man's way, to obey your agent, to learn to live the new life. It will be a powerful thing for peace, an important thing for your people. What do you say? The decision is your own. You alone can make it.''

It was a hard talk. I could see that Joseph was thinking much on it. I held my breath for I was frightened again now. Of a sudden I lost all my bravery about going to Lapwai for a few days. This was serious. They were talking about the whole winter, perhaps about several winters. This could be a sad thing. I had heard many stories of boys dying at the school of broken hearts and bad food and lonesomeness for tepee smoke and boiled cowish and dried salmon and roast elk and of horse sweat and saddle leather and gun oil and powder smell and all of the other grand things a wild Nez Perce lad grew up with around him in his parents' lodge, his home village, and his native hunting lands. Joseph, too, knew of these poor boys. The thought of them weighed heavy on him and made him take such a long time that Ollikut threw him a sharp glance and said, ''Come on, brother, make up your mind. I feel foolish standing here with this gun cocked.''

Joseph nodded to him and sighed very deep.

''All right,'' he said to Agent Monteith, ''give us the boy now. When the grass grows brown and the smell of the first snow is like a knife in the wind, I shall bring him to you at Lapwai.''

In May, in the land of the Nez Perce, the spring sun comes first to the southern slopes of the tumbling hills which guard the wide valleys and shadowed canyons. Here in the warm sandy soil the cowish plant breaks through the mountain loam even before the snows are all gone from the rock hollows and catch basins which hold it there to water this sturdy rootling of the upper hills. To these cowish patches in that month of May would come my people hungry and eager for the taste of fresh vegetables after the long winter of dried camass and smoked salmon.

The juicy roots of the cowish baked in the Nez Perce way had a breadlike, biscuity flavor, giving the plant its white man's name of biscuitroot. We called it kouse, and from that the settlers sometimes called us the Kouse Eaters. My people loved this fine food, which was the gift of Hunyewat, and the time of its gathering was a festival time for us. All we children looked forward through the winter to the May travel to the cowish fields. Yet in that May of the year we did not go to the buffalo, I sang no gathering songs, danced no thankful dances, ate no kouse at the great feast held at that traditional Time of the First Eating. I sat apart and thought only of September and of that first smell of snow in the sharpening wind.

June was the time of going to the camass meadows. In that month my people took up the tepees and journeyed happily to the upland plateaus where, in the poorly drained places, large flats of snow-melt water would collect and stand. Up out of these meadow shallows, springing like green spears from the black soil beneath the water, would come the fabled blue camass plant—the lovely water hyacinth or Indian lily of the Northwest.

Even within a few days the surfaces of the water flats would be bright-grown as new meadow grass with its spreading leaves. Then, short weeks later, the brilliant bells of its blue blossoms would stalk out for their brief flowering. As the swift blooming passed, all the nourishment of Hunyewat's warm sky and cool snow water would go from the faded flower down into its underground bulb to store up strength and hardy life for its fortunate harvesters.

All this glad time of waiting for the camass root to come ripe and dry up for the digging, my band was camped with the other Nez Perce bands in the shady pines above the meadow. There was much gay chanting and dancing the whole while, but I did not take part in any of it. Instead, I stayed out on the mountain by myself thinking of September and the snow wind.

Under the mellow sun of July, the shallow waters of the camass fields evaporated, the rich muck dried, the great Indian harvest began. Now while the men sat at their gambling games or raced their famous Appaloosa horses, and while the children played at stick-and-hoop, or fished and hunted the summer away, the women took out the digging tools with their stubby wooden handles and pronged elkhorn tips, and pried up the ripened bulbs of the blue lily.

After that came the cooking.

As many as thirty bushels of the bulbs were covered with wet meadow grass and steamed over heated stones. Then the bulbs were mashed, shaped into loaves, sunbaked into a nourishing Indian bread. This bread would keep easily six to eight moons. It was a good and valuable food, having a flavor much like a sweet yam. With the flesh of the salmon, the meat of the elk, the deer, and the antelope, it fed us through the severest winter. Thus, the July camass harvest was a time of tribal joy and gratitude for the Nez Perce. But I did not join in the Thankful Sing. I only wandered afar with Tea Kettle, my small gray pony, and looked with aching loneliness out across the blue peaks, hazy canyons, lapping waters, and lofty pines of the homeland I would see no more after the grass was brown beneath the autumn wind.

In late summer, in August, after the high spring floodwater had fallen and all the rivers were running low and clear, it was the Time of Silver Waters, of the great Columbia salmon run from the sea to the headwater creeks of Nez Perce country. This was the end of the Indian year, the very highest time of thanks for my people, and the very hardest time of work for them.

When the flashing salmon came at last, the men would strain from dawn to dusk with spear and net at every leaping falls from the mighty Celilo upward to the least spawning creeklets which fed the main forks of the Salmon, the Snake, the Clearwater, Grande Ronde, Wallowa, and Imnaha rivers. The sandy beaches would soon be heaped to a small child's waist with the great hump-backed fish. Then the women would work like packhorses to split, clean, rack, and smoke the bright-red slabs of that blessed flesh which provided nine of every ten Nez Perce meals around the year and which made my people immune to the famine which periodically visited the other Northwestern tribes.

Yes, August and the Time of Silver Waters was the real time to offer final thanks to Hunyewat. Yet even then I could think of no gratitude, no contentment, no happiness, but only of Joseph and Agent Monteith. And after them only of the brown grass and snow smell of September and of the log-walled prison waiting for me in the school at Lapwai.

At last the Moon of Smoky Sunshine, September, was but three suns away. In that brief space it would be Sapalwit, Sunday, and Joseph would ride up to the tepee of my father and call out in his soft deep voice, "Elk Water, where is the boy? Where is Heyets, our little Mountain Sheep? The grass is grown brown again, the skies have turned the color of gun steel. I smell snow in the wind. It is the time to keep our word to Agent Monteith."

I let two of those last three suns torture me. Then on the final night, late and when the chilling winds had blown out all the cook-fire embers and no one stirred in all that peaceful camp, I crept beneath the raised rear skins of my father's tepee.

Moving like a shadow, I found my faithful friend Tea Kettle where I had tethered him in a dark spruce grove that same afternoon. He whickered and rubbed me with his soft nose and I cried a little and loved him with my arms about his bony neck. It was a bad time, but I did not think of turning back. I only climbed on his back and guided him on into the deepening timber away from the camp of my father's people there beside the salmon falls of the Kahmuenem, the Snake River, nine miles below the entrance of the Imnaha.

I was bound for the land of our mortal foes, the Shoshoni. My reasoning was that if I could take an enemy scalp I would no longer be considered a boy. I would be a man, a warrior, fourteen summers or no, and they would no more think of sending me to school with Agent Monteith than they would my fierce uncle Yellow Wolf.

As for equipment I had Tea Kettle, who could barely come up to a lame buffalo at his best speed. I had a *kopluts*, or war club, which was no war club at all but a rabbit-throwing stick cut off short to make it look like a *kopluts*. Also I had a rusted camp ax with the haft split and most of the blade broken off, a bow-and-arrow set given me by Joseph on my tenth birthday, a much-mended horse soldier blanket marked "U.S." in one corner and stolen for me by my father from the big fort at Walla Walla, three loaves of camass bread, a side of dried salmon, and my *wyakin*, my personal war charm, a smoked baby bear's foot, cured with the claws and hair left on. And, oh, yes, I had my knife. Naturally. No Nez Perce would think of leaving his tepee without putting on his knife. He might not put on his pants, but he would always put on his knife.

So there I was, on my way to kill a Shoshoni, a Snake warrior far over across the Bitterroot Mountains in the Wind River country. I might, in addition, while I was over there and for good measure, steal a few horses. About that I had not entirely decided. It would depend on circumstances. Meanwhile, more immediate problems were developing.

I had left home in good spirit if weak flesh. Now, however, after a long time of riding through the dark forest, the balance was beginning to come even. It occurred to me, thinking about it, that I had ridden many miles. It might well be that I needed food to return my strength. Perhaps I had better stop, make a fire, roast some salmon, warm a slice of bread. When I had eaten, I would feel my old power once more. Then, although I had already ridden a great distance that night, I would go on yet farther before lying down to sleep.

I got off Tea Kettle and gathered some moss and small sticks which I laid properly in the shelter of a windfallen old pine giant. With my flint, I struck a tiny flame and fed it into a good little Nez Perce fire, say the size of a man's two hands spread together, and clear and clean in the manner of its burning as a pool of trout water in late autumn. I cut a green spitting stick and propped a piece of salmon and one of camass over the flames. Then I put the soldier blanket around my shoulders and leaned back against the big log to consider my journey plans. The next thing I knew a shaft of sunlight was prying at my eyes and two very familiar Indians were crouched at my fire eating my salmon and camass bread.

"Good morning." Chief Joseph nodded. "This is fine food, Heyets. You had better come and have some of it with us."

"Yes," said Elk Water, my father. "It is a long ride to Lapwai."

"What is the matter?" I mumbled, my mind bewildered, my eyes still spiderwebbed with sleep. "What day is this? What has happened to bring you here?"

"This is Sunday," answered Joseph in his easy way. "And what has happened to bring us here is that we have come to ride with you to Agent Monteith's school. You must have left very early, Heyets. That showed a good spirit. Probably you did not wish to bother us to rise so soon. Probably it was in your heart to let us have a good morning's sleep."

"Yes," agreed my father. "Surely that was it. Heyets is a fine boy. He wanted to let us sleep. He wanted also to ride into the white man's school alone so that we would be certain his heart was strong and he was not afraid. Is that not so, Heyets?"

My eyes had grown clearer, and it was in my mind to lie to them, to say, yes, that they were right about my thoughtful actions. Yet I could not bring myself to do it. To my father I might have lied, for he was a simple man and would not have guessed the difference, no, and would not have cared a great deal for it. But Joseph, ah, Joseph was completely another matter and another man. His great quiet face, soft deep voice, and sad brown eyes touched me with a faith and a feeling which would not let my tongue wander.

"No," I replied, low-worded. "That is not the way it was at all. I was running away. I was going to the Snake country to take a Shoshoni scalp so that you would think I was a man and would not send me to Agent Monteith's school. My heart was like a girl's. I was weak and sore afraid. I wanted only to stay with my people, with my father, and with my chief."

There was a silence then, and my father looked hard at Joseph. He turned his head away from both Joseph and me, but I could see the large swallowing bone in his throat moving up and down. Still, he did not say anything. He waited for Joseph to speak.

At last my chief raised his eyes to me and said gently:

"I beg your pardon, Heyets. The wind was making such a stir in the pine trees just now that I do not believe I heard what you said. Did you hear him, Elk Water?"

"No," answered my father, "I don't think I did. What was it you said, boy?"

I looked at Elk Water, my father, and at Joseph, my chief. Then I looked beyond them up into the pine boughs above us. There was no wind moving up there, no wind at all. I shook my head and got to my feet.

"Nothing," I said, untying Tea Kettle and kicking dirt upon my little fire. "Let us go to Lapwai and keep the word with Agent Monteith."

It will not take long, now, to tell of that Lapwai winter. It was not a good thing. The memory of it turns in me like a badly knitted bone. Yet, like a badly knitted bone, it will not let me forget.

I was sick much of the time, homesick all of the time. It was a hard winter, very cold, with a lot of wet-crust snow and heavy river ice the whole while. Some of my little Indian friends who sickened at the school did not grow well again. They were not watched over by Hunyewat as Heyets was. They lay down in the night and did not get up again in the morning. When we saw them the others of us wept, even we big boys. It hurt us very bad.

If they were Christian Indian children, they were buried

in the churchyard. Their mothers were there, their fathers were there. All their many friends of the reservation were there to stand and say good-by to them, and to sprinkle the handful of mother earth on them as was the old custom. Agent Monteith read from the Holy Book at the graveside, and the proper songs of Jesus were sung over them. They were treated like something.

But if they were wild Indian children, like myself, their little bodies were let to lie out overnight and freeze solid like dog salmon. Then they were stacked, like so many pieces of stovewood, in the open shed behind the schoolhouse. There they waited, all chill and white and alone, until such time as their parents could come in over the bad trails to claim them for the simple Nez Perce ceremony of The Putting to the Last Sleep.

It was not a happy or a kind place for a boy raised in the old free Indian way. It made my heart sad and lonely to stay there. In consequence, and although I knew I was being watched closely because of my kinship with Joseph, both by my own and the agency people, I grew all the while more determined against the Lapwai, or white man's, way.

Naturally I learned but little at the school.

I already knew how to speak the white tongue from my mother. But I did not let this help me. I would not learn to write, and in reading I was like a child of but six or seven. This blind pride was my father's blood, the old Nez Perce blood, the spirit, the *simikia* of my untamed ancestors, entering into me. I was not a wicked boy, but neither was I willing to work. I was like a young horse caught from out a wild herd. I knew nothing but the longing to escape. The only chance to teach me anything was to first gentle me down, and there was no chance at all to gentle me down. I thought, of course, and many times, about Joseph's faith in me. I wanted to do what was right for the sake of my chief's hope that I would serve as an example to the other wild bands that they might send their children in safety, and with profit, to the white man's school at Lapwai. But my own faith was no match for my chief's. Daily I grew more troublesome to Agent Monteith. Daily he grew less certain of my salvation.

When I had been with him five moons—through the time of Christmas and into that of the new year—it had at last become plain to Agent Monteith that I was not "settling down," as he put it, and Joseph was sent for. When my chief arrived, I was called in and stood by as interpreter while the talk was made about me. Joseph began it with his usual quiet direction, getting at once to the point.

"This boy's mother," he said, "reports to me that she has visited him here at the school and you have told her that her son is a bad boy, that he will not work, and that he is as bad for the other children as for himself." He paused, looking steadily at Agent Monteith. "Now I do not remember that Heyets is a bad boy. Perhaps my memory has failed me. Since I am also of his blood, you had better tell me what you told his mother."

Agent Monteith grew angry, his usual way.

"Now see here, Joseph," he blustered, "are you trying to intimidate me?"

"Excuse me. I do not understand what you mean."

"Are you trying to frighten me?"

"Never. What I want is the truth. Should that frighten you?"

"Of course not! This boy simply will not buckle down and study as he should. He will not work with the others. The class is told to draw a picture of our Lord Jesus humbly astride a lowly donkey and this boy draws a lurid picture of an armed warrior on an Appaloosa stallion. I ask him, 'What picture is that, Heyets?' and he says, 'Why, that is a picture of Yellow Wolf on Sun Eagle going to the buffalo.' Now I put it to you, Joseph, is that the right way for a boy to behave before the others? A boy upon whom we have all placed so much hope? A boy the other bands are watching to see how he fares at Lapwai? Answer me. Say what you think."

My chief frowned and pulled at his broad chin.

"I don't know," he said carefully. "Does he draw well?"

"He draws extremely well, easily the best in the class."

"He draws a good horse? A proper Indian?"

"Very good, very proper." Agent Monteith scowled. "Perfect likenesses, especially of the horse. He puts all the parts on the animal and when I reprimand him he offers to take me to the Wallowa and show me that Sun Eagle is, indeed, a horse among horses."

Agent Monteith blew out his fat cheeks, filling them like the gas-blown belly of a dead cow.

"Now you listen to me, Joseph! You promised to bring this boy here and to make him behave himself and work hard to learn the white man's way. This has since become a serious matter for the school. It can no longer be ignored. Heyets is creating a grave discipline problem for me. I mean among the other older boys. Some of them are beginning to draw pictures of spotted Nez Perce ponies in their study Bibles. I insist to you that this is no way for this boy of your blood to carry out our bargain."

Joseph shook his head in slow sympathy.

"You are right, Agent," he said, "if what you tell me is true. But before I make a decision I would like to have you tell me one special thing Heyets has done—show me some example of his evil ways that I may see with my own eyes—so that I shall know what it is you and I are talking about."

He hesitated a little, looking at the agent.

"Sometimes, you know," he said, "the white brother says one thing and really means several others. It becomes difficult for an Indian to be sure."

Agent Monteith's blunt beard jutted out, but he kept his voice reasonable.

"Joseph, you are the most intelligent Indian I know. You are a shrewd man by any standards, red or white. You have been to this very school yourself in the old days. You were the best pupil they ever had here before your father, Old Joseph, tore up the Bible and took you away. You understand exactly what I mean and you do not have to ask me for any examples.''

Joseph only nodded again and said, ''Nevertheless, show me one special bad thing the boy has done.''

The agent turned away quickly and picked up a study Bible from the desk of James Redwing, a Christian Wallowa boy of my own age and my best friend among the reservation Indians. He opened the book and handed it to Joseph.

''Very well,'' he snapped. ''Look at that!''

Joseph took the book and studied it thoughtfully.

''Let us see here,'' he said. ''Here is a picture of a young baby being carried in his mother's arms. She is riding a small mule led by her husband. They are leaving an old town of some sort in a strange land, and they are not going very fast with such a poor beast to take them. Nevertheless, they are in a great hurry. There is fear in their faces, and I believe the enemy must be pursuing them. Is there something else I have missed?''

Agent Monteith stamped his foot.

''You know very well that is the Christ Child fleeing Bethlehem with Mary and Joseph!''

''Oh yes, so it is. A fine picture of all of them, too. Better than in the book they had here before.''

''You know equally well,'' Agent Monteith continued, very cold-eyed, ''what else I am talking about, and what else it is you have missed. What is printed under the picture of the Christ Child?''

Joseph nodded and held the book up for me to tell him the words. I did so, and he turned back to Agent Monteith and said, ''The words there are 'Jesus Fleeing the Holy City.' ''

''Exactly. And what has some heathen pupil scrawled in by hand under that sacred title, with a Nez Perce arrow pointing to the donkey?''

My chief's face never changed. Again he held the book up to me, and again I whispered the words to him. Looking back at Agent Monteith, he shifted the Bible as though to get a better light on it and answered, ''Oh, yes, there is something else, sure enough. It says, 'If he had used an Appaloosa pony, his enemies never would have caught up to him.' Is that what you mean?"

"That is precisely what I mean, Joseph."

The agent took time to get a good breath and let some of it puff back out of his cheeks.

"That added writing was done by James Redwing, a Christian Indian of your own Wallowa band and a very fine boy who, until these past months, has been our star pupil. James is fifteen years old and I have worked with him a long time, Joseph. He had become a white boy in his thoughts and in his actions. I had saved him. He prayed on his knees every day and he had given over his life gladly to the service of his Saviour. Now he writes such things as you see there and the other boys all laugh."

"That is not right," said Joseph softly, "but they are only boys, all of them. Boys are full of tricks, Agent."

"Indeed they are!" cried Monteith, puffing up again. "And I will tell you about just one of those tricks!"

"Do that, my friend. My ears are uncovered."

"Well, this past Christmas we celebrated the birth of our Lord by making a little stable scene with the manger, and so forth, in Bethlehem. Of course there was the little packmule tied as the faithful ass beside the sleeping babe. And do you know what some monstrous boy had done to the innocent brute?"

Joseph shook his head wonderingly. "I could never imagine," he said. "Tell me."

"He had taken—he had stolen—some of the mission's whitewash and dappled the rear of that animal to imitate a Nez Perce Appaloosa horse, and had marked in red paint on the two halves of his rump the name 'Sun Eagle.' Now what do you think of that for your fine boy? He admitted it, you know. It was his work."

My chief put his chin down to his chest. He seemed to be having some trouble with his swallowing. It was as though he had caught a fishbone crosswise in his throat and were trying to be polite about choking on it. But after a bit he was able to raise his head and continue.

"I think it is very unfortunate," he answered the agent. "It is true my own father tore up the Bible and that I have followed his way, but I will not tolerate Wallowa boys making laughs about your God. What do you suggest we do?"

"Heyets must be punished severely."

"In what manner?"

"He should be flogged."

"Have you flogged him before, Agent?"

"No. Frankly, I've been afraid to try it. The rascal told me that if I touched him he would have his uncle Yellow Wolf come in and kill me."

"His uncle Yellow Wolf is but a boy himself, Agent."

"You do not need to tell me of Yellow Wolf. I know him very well. He has the eye of a mad dog. I wouldn't trust him ten feet away."

"I see. How else have you thought to punish Heyets?"

"He must be made to say the school prayers, on his knees, in front of the other boys."

"Alone?"

"Yes, alone."

"Has he prayed like this before, Agent?"

"Not once. He says he believes in Hunyewat. He says he did not come here to study Jesus Christ. He tells wild tales of the power of Hunyewat to the Christian boys and has them believing that anything Jesus of Nazareth did in 'ten moons' Hunyewat could do in 'two suns.' He asks them such sacrilegious questions as, 'Did you ever see a picture of Hunyewat riding a packmule?' and he has the entire class so disorganized they spend more time learning the Brave Songs, Scalp Chants, and Salmon Dances from him than they do the Sunday-school hymns from me. I will not tolerate it a day longer, Joseph. I simply cannot and will not do it. The matter is your entire responsibility and you must make the final decision on it right now."

Joseph moved his head in understanding and raised his hand for the agent to calm himself and wait while both of them thought a little while.

Presently he went on.

"Very well, Agent," he said. "Do you know what my father, Old Joseph, told me about this same school many snows ago when he came to take me away from it?"

"I can very well imagine what the old heathen might have said," agreed Agent Monteith. "But go ahead and tell it your way. You will anyway. That's the Indian of it."

"It is," replied Joseph, "and here is the way my father told it to me. He said, 'My son, always remember what I am about to say. A school is a good thing when it teaches school thoughts from schoolbooks. But the place for God and for His Book is in the church. Pray in the church if you wish, and choose which god pleases you. But in the school do not pray. In the school work hard all the time at the printed thoughts of reading and writing and of the white man's way of figuring with numbers. Do that six days and on the seventh day go to church and pray all you want.' "

"Your father was a very wise man," admitted Agent Monteith, "until he left the church."

"He was a wise man after he left the church, too," said Joseph. "And here is the rest of his wisdom which you did not allow me to finish. The old chief finally said to me, 'But, my son, when the time comes that they will not let you learn your lessons except at the price of kneeling to their God, when they demand of you to become of their faith before they will give you a schoolbook, or feed you your food, or allow you your decent shelter from the snow and cold, then that is the time to tell them that they do not follow the way of their own Lord Jesus, which He taught in the Holy Land two thousand snows before our little time here upon our mother earth. I once believed in Jesus Christ the Saviour,' said my father, 'and I know His words as well as any agent. It was not His way to ask for payment, neither before nor after He gave of Himself or of His goods!' "

"In heaven's name," fumed Agent Monteith, breaking in again, "what are you trying to say, Joseph?" And Joseph answered him very quietly, "I am only trying to say that it is not my way either," and after that both men stood a considerable time staring right at each other.

"Well," laughed Agent Monteith at last and somewhat nervously, "that is scarcely anything new. You have not been in church since your father tore up the Bible on this same spot eleven years ago."

"That is not what I mean, Agent."

"All right, all right, what is it that you do mean?"

"I mean about the boy."

"What about the boy?"

"I am doing with him as my father did with me when they would not teach me unless I prayed first."

"Joseph, I warn you!"

"It is too late for warning. All has been said. It is you and I who have failed, Agent, not this child. There is nothing he can do here. In his way he is wiser than either of us. He knows he is an Indian and cannot be a white man. I am taking him back to his own people, Agent. You will not see him in this place again. *Taz alago*."

I could not have been more stunned.

Since I knew the importance of my position at the school, I had been waiting to learn what kind of punishment would be agreed upon as the terms of my staying there. Yet, instead, here was my chief taking me proudly by the hand and leading me out of that log-walled schoolhouse there at Lapwai, Idaho, in the severe winter of 1875, without one more spoken word of parting, or rearward glance of consideration, for powerful Indian Agent John Monteith.

I will say that it was a strange and wonderful feeling.

Thrilling to it, I got up behind Joseph on his broad-backed old brown traveling horse, and we set out through the falling snow toward the snug tepees along the Imnaha River where, since the most ancient among them could remember, our Nez Perce people had spent their winters.

In all the long way home, Joseph and I said not a word to one another and that, too, was the Indian way. As he himself put it, all had been said back at Lapwai. Now was the time for riding in rich silence and, if a grateful Nez Perce boy remained of the old beliefs, for offering up a final humble word to Hunyewat.

So it was I bowed my small head behind Joseph's great shoulders and said my first prayer in five moons.

So it was I ended my Lapwai winter.

This unusual story is one of the few that reverses the standard Western formula of describing an Indian raid through the eyes of white men: it tells how the Indians (Apaches, in this case) felt during just such a raid, and gives us an insight into their lives and motivations. Oliver La Farge, who won a Pulitzer Prize for his Indian novel, Laughing Boy, *has written no better short story than "The Young Warrior"—and that is high praise, indeed.*

The Young Warrior

Oliver La Farge

"**W**e had good profit and good fun," he said. "Truly, we were much amused, and on the way home we laughed a lot. And I tell you that that Nantai, he is a great leader."

He was about eighteen years old, at the age when young men wish to prove themselves and to recite their exploits in the presence of young women. He sprawled beside the fire in the camp of his cousin's band, aware that he had an audience, men who had proved themselves on the warpath, old men, boys his age who had not yet gone fighting, and girls. The fire burnt generously in front of his cousin's wickeyup, he had an audience, and he had something to tell.

He wore the usual knee-high Apache moccasins, a breechclout, a white man's coat of very fine green material, much too large for him, and a heavy turban of shining, blue silk covered with a design of small, pink and yellow flowers. Across his lap he nursed one of the new, short rifles that load from the back.

Supper was over. He had been quiet, saying nothing

65

about himself, until at last one of the old men asked him about the war party. He lit a corn-husk cigarette. Seeing that they all waited, listening, he went on with his narrative. Now and again a man grunted approval, from time to time a woman would laugh.

We set out on foot for the Mexican settlement at Cottonwood River. There were five of us young men, and Nantai, who had agreed to come as our leader. The raid there was nothing. Most of the people had gone further east for a fiesta, so we simply took what horses we could find, a small amount of goods, and set the houses on fire. The few who were there ran away, and we did not bother hunting for them. There was really very little there, we each got a horse, that was about all. So Nantai took us to the north, to see what we could find.

The next day we came into sight of the road that runs from the far east to the big settlement at Muddy Flat. We rode to the westward, in sight of it. About noon we came up with a train of four wagons, heading west. Nantai took us around them in a circle, and showed us how to watch them.

These were Americans, and we young men were greatly interested in studying them. There were ten American men, several of their women, and two Mexicans. The wagons were drawn by oxen. We spent that day studying the party, while Nantai sent Comes Fighting to scout the back trail, and Crooked Nose ahead, to make sure that they were traveling alone, and no one would interfere with us. Sometimes we rode or walked just out of sight, watching them. Sometimes we hid in the sagebrush and let them travel by us.

They say that Americans are very great fighters. That may be so, but they are easy to scout. If one sits still and makes himself hard to see, the peaceful Indians may none-the-less see one, the Mexicans do sometimes, but the Americans almost never. It is the color of their eyes, I think. By nightfall we knew them pretty well, and after dark we came in close and enjoyed ourselves watching how they did.

Back when we were at peace with the Americans, before they tied up our chief and flogged him that time, Nantai used to go among them. Now he pointed things out to us. For instance, save for one man, they sat staring into the fire, blinding themselves. They built their fire large, here in enemy country, and they slept close to it. The one man who kept his back to the fire, there were things about his way of dressing that Nantai told us to notice. He said that that man was surely one of the Americans from Taos, the ones who go everywhere trapping beaver. Those men are dangerous, he said. It was because of the trapper that their night guard was well kept up, and it would not be easy to run off their stock. They had good saddle horses, and some mules.

When they had gone to sleep, and we had studied their way of placing their guards, we went back to a place where we could camp. There we talked over what we had seen. We were amused about a young man and woman we had watched. The woman seemed to be the daughter of an elderly man, rather fat, who rode mostly in one of the wagons. We thought he was a chief of some kind. The young man wished to court her, but her father did not like it. During the day they dropped back, behind the Mexicans who were herding the spare horses, but then the father mounted a horse, and they separated. In camp at night, they looked towards each other, and yet stayed apart. We joked about the young man's chances, and wondered what the father's objection was. The young man was well dressed, and he rode a good horse.

The next day, some of us wanted to make a quick rush for the spare horses, to see if we could drive some off. Nantai told us to be patient. We were no longer children, he said. It would be many days yet before the train came near to Muddy Flat, let us see what turned up. So we followed them again all that day, amusing ourselves with the courtship and other such matters.

The next night Crooked Nose and I were lying in wait where the young lover stood on guard, when the girl came out to see him. They whispered, hugged each other, and put their mouths together. They pushed their mouths against each other as a form of lovemaking. It seemed to us that here was a chance to take two prisoners. What sort of warrior was this who dealt with a woman while he was on war duty? His power would be destroyed, his eyes dimmed, his medicine would not protect him. It would have been easy to capture them both at those times when their faces were touching. I went off to find Nantai. He called the others, and we all crept back.

Crooked Nose came to meet us. The girl had gone back to the wagons, he said, and the young man was watchful once more. He had been so close to them that he could have touched them with his spear. They had had a long talk, and he thought that they had decided something, he said. We watched awhile longer, then went to our camp. There Crooked Nose and I described what we had seen, and we laughed about the lovemaking.

The next morning the train came to where a road branched off northwards, to the American settlement at the Silver Mine. The settlement was only a few hours' ride away, beyond a range of hills, and we knew that there were soldiers there. We were afraid that the wagons might turn that way, but they went on by.

Very shortly after that I was sitting in a clump of oaks watching the wagons pass. I saw the young man riding a chestnut horse, even better than the one he had had the day before. He dropped back, behind the spare horses, then worked over to the right, the north side of the valley, near the cliffs. He had his gun across his saddle, and acted as if he were hunting.

Pretty soon the girl rode out to the right. She, too, was well mounted, on a buckskin. She idled, looking over the country, and by and by drifted behind the oak clump in which I was hiding. As soon as she was hidden from the wagons, she whipped up her horse and rode fast to the cliffs, meeting the man in the mouth of a little canyon. I signaled to the others, then I went ahead to where I could see these two.

They spoke together for a moment, then they went north, up the canyon, riding hard.

We assembled on top of the cliffs, looking down into the canyon. Nantai was pleased.

"They are running away," he said. "This afternoon, they can reach the Silver Mine; there they will marry each other. This is fine. They are bait."

He told Crooked Nose to follow well in the rear. Then he made us ride along the high ground, where the going was difficult. He had us take great care so that if anybody followed the couple, he could see no sign of an enemy on the trail.

We came to the head of the canyon, and climbed up to the flat country on top. Pretty soon we saw them. They were traveling at a steady trot now, well ahead of us. We made a wide circle around them. Then we reached a long valley, leading up to a sort of pass, a notch, where the piñon and oak brush were thick. We went into that notch, and lay in wait there. Nantai gave us our instructions.

We could watch that couple coming towards us. It made one want to laugh. They were looking at each other much of the time while they rode; they were thinking only of each other and getting married. Then we saw Crooked Nose, slipping along behind them.

Nantai gave the mourning dove call, so Crooked Nose came up on a high place and signaled that no one was following. Then he hid himself. We lay there, thinking of the surprise we were about to cause.

They came along blindly, so close to where we lay that you could see their strange, colorless, American eyes. Then Nantai whooped and we opened fire. We put four arrows and a spear into the man, one arrow into the woman. The man came down dead. We pulled the woman off her horse. First she fought and screamed, then she stood still, then she tried to break away to get to the man, whom Nantai was scalping. Comes Fighting and Short Bow held her, the rest of us stood watching her.

We wanted to keep her until later, but Nantai said there

was no time for that. He asked us, "Do you want fun or horses?" Then he put his spear through her, and Walks Slowly took the scalp. Just then Crooked Nose called like a hawk, so we knew others were coming. Nantai had us drive the two horses we had taken, and our own, on to the north through the notch, making a clear trail. Then we hid the animals, and came back to hide near the bodies.

Two men came along riding fast. One was the plump, chief man I mentioned, the woman's father. The other was the trapper. The plump man just watched the tracks and sometimes looked ahead, the trapper kept looking all about him, watching everything. We could see that he was a scout, and that we should have to lie very still when he drew near. It was he who saw the bodies first, when he was about a hundred paces away. They were partly hidden by the brush. He exclaimed, and reined in his horse.

The other man cried out. He did not stop, although the trapper called to him. He galloped right up to them, jumped off his horse, and knelt down by his daughter. We could have killed him easily then, but the trapper had dismounted, too, and was standing with his rifle ready. So we stayed quiet. How well Nantai had foreseen this, how wise he had been to make us ride in the hard going, away to one side, so that there was no sign of us, how wise to kill that girl so that we were not burdened.

When nothing had happened for a long time, the trapper came up slowly. The plump man was still kneeling, saying things in a low voice. The trapper still looked around, until he saw the tracks heading north. Then he said something to the father, and bent over, touching his shoulder.

That way, they both faced to the right, the side on which I was. We on the right lay still. Nantai, Short Bow, and Horse Frightener rose up on the other side and loosed their arrows. That was all there was to it, it was so simple.

Then we went over them for goods of value. While we were doing that, Crooked Nose came up. We were all much interested by the way the woman was dressed. Her skirt was really two skirts, one for each leg, and under it were many layers of clothing, mostly white. We examined them, wondering why anyone should make herself so uncomfortable, and joking about how hard she would be to undress. Then Nantai told us to stop fooling. We took our plunder and the captured horses, and swung back in a wide circle to the road.

We found the wagon train late in the afternoon. It had gone a few miles, and then stopped, to wait for its leader, we supposed. Now its leader and two more of its men were dead. We stayed quiet till after dark. They had fewer men to stand watch, and no one with real experience. A little before dawn two of us started shooting from one side, with the new rifles we had captured. The rest of us came along on the other side and ran off sixteen of their horses.

We met together on the south side of the valley, and rode all that day, making camp in comfort at sunset. Then we divided what we had taken.

On the back of her saddle, that woman had tied a bundle containing a dress of beautiful, smooth material. This new headband of mine—look—is a part of it. She also had more of those clothes for wearing underneath, of fine materials. Horse Frightener put on some of them, and we joked with him. I received that headband, this coat—it belonged to the father—this new rifle that loads from the back, and four horses. Then we came home at our leisure, talking over all that we had seen, and finding much to laugh at.

Dorothy M. Johnson is frequently referred to as "The First Lady of Western Fiction," a title she richly deserves. Although her work is well known to hundreds of thousands of Western readers, the films based on her stories "The Man Who Shot Liberty Valance," "The Hanging Tree" (the title of a fine short-story collection), and "A Man Called Horse" have been viewed by millions of moviegoers. The present selection is one of the most powerful stories of courage and endurance that you will ever read.

A Man Called Horse

Dorothy M. Johnson

*H*e was a young man of good family, as the phrase went in the New England of a hundred-odd years ago, and the reasons for his bitter discontent were unclear, even to himself. He grew up in the gracious old Boston home under his grandmother's care, for his mother had died in giving him birth; and all his life he had known every comfort and privilege his father's wealth could provide.

But still there was the discontent, which puzzled him because he could not even define it. He wanted to live among his equals—people who were no better than he and no worse either. That was as close as he could come to describing the source of his unhappiness in Boston and his restless desire to go somewhere else.

In the year 1845, he left home and went out West, far beyond the country's creeping frontier, where he hoped to find his equals. He had the idea that in Indian country, where there was danger, all white men were kings, and he wanted

72

to be one of them. But he found, in the West as in Boston, that the men he respected were still his superiors, even if they could not read, and those he did not respect weren't worth talking to.

He did have money, however, and he could hire the men he respected. He hired four of them, to cook and hunt and guide and be his companions, but he found them not friendly.

They were apart from him and he was still alone. He still brooded about his status in the world, longing for his equals.

On a day in June, he learned what it was to have no status at all. He became a captive of a small raiding party of Crow Indians.

He heard gunfire and the brief shouts of his companions around the bend of the creek just before they died, but he never saw their bodies. He had no chance to fight, because he was naked and unarmed, bathing in the creek, when a Crow warrior seized and held him.

His captor let him go at last, let him run. Then the lot of them rode him down for sport, striking him with their coup sticks. They carried the dripping scalps of his companions, and one had skinned off Baptiste's black beard as well, for a trophy.

They took him along in a matter-of-fact way, as they took the captured horses. He was unshod and naked as the horses were, and like them he had a rawhide thong around his neck. So long as he didn't fall down, the Crows ignored him.

On the second day they gave him his breeches. His feet were too swollen for his boots, but one of the Indians threw him a pair of moccasins that had belonged to the halfbreed, Henri, who was dead back at the creek. The captive wore the moccasins gratefully. The third day they let him ride one of the spare horses so that the party could move faster, and on that day they came in sight of their camp.

He thought of trying to escape, hoping he might be killed in flight rather than by slow torture in the camp, but he never had a chance to try. They were more familiar with escape than he was and, knowing what to expect, they forestalled it. The only other time he had tired to escape from anyone, he had succeeded. When he had left his home in Boston, his father had raged and his grandmother had cried, but they could not talk him out of his intention.

The men of the Crow raiding party didn't bother with talk.

Before riding into camp they stopped and dressed in their regalia, and in parts of their victims' clothing; they painted their faces black. Then, leading the white man by the rawhide around his neck as though he were a horse, they rode down toward the tepee circle, shouting and singing, brandishing their weapons. He was unconscious when they got there; he fell and was dragged.

He lay dazed and battered near a tepee while the noisy, busy life of the camp swarmed around him and Indians came to stare. Thirst consumed him, and when it rained he lapped rain water from the ground like a dog. A scrawny, shrieking, eternally busy old woman with ragged graying hair threw a chunk of meat on the grass, and he fought the dogs for it.

When his head cleared, he was angry, although anger was an emotion he knew he could not afford.

It was better when I was a horse, he thought—when they led me by the rawhide around my neck. I won't be a dog, no matter what!

The hag gave him stinking, rancid grease and let him figure out what it was for. He applied it gingerly to his bruised and sun-seared body.

Now, he thought, I smell like the rest of them.

While he was healing, he considered coldly the advantages of being a horse. A man would be humiliated, and sooner or later he would strike back and that would be the end of him. But a horse had only to be docile. Very well, he would learn to do without pride.

He understood that he was the property of the screaming old woman, a fine gift from her son, one that she liked to show off. She did more yelling at him than at anyone else, probably to impress the neighbors so they would not forget what a great and generous man her son was. She was bossy and proud, a dreadful sag of skin and bones, and she was a devilish hard worker.

The white man, who now thought of himself as a horse, forgot sometimes to worry about his danger. He kept making mental notes of things to tell his own people in Boston about this hideous adventure. He would go back a hero, and he would say, "Grandmother, let me fetch your shawl. I've been accustomed to doing little errands for another lady about your age."

Two girls lived in the tepee with the old hag and her warrior son. One of them, the white man concluded, was his captor's wife and the other was his little sister. The daughter-in-law was smug and spoiled. Being beloved, she did not have to be useful. The younger girl had bright, wandering eyes. Often enough they wandered to the white man who was pretending to be a horse.

The two girls worked when the old woman put them at it, but they were always running off to do something they enjoyed more. There were games and noisy contests, and there was much laughter. But not for the white man. He was finding out what loneliness could be.

That was a rich summer on the plains, with plenty of buffalo for meat and clothing and the making of tepees. The Crows were wealthy in horses, prosperous and contented. If their men had not been so avid for glory, the white man thought, there would have been a lot more of them. But they went out of their way to court death, and when one of them met it, the whole camp mourned extravagantly and cried to their God for vengeance.

The captive was a horse all summer, a docile bearer of burdens, careful and patient. He kept reminding himself that he had to be better-natured than other horses, because he could not lash out with hoofs or teeth. Helping the old woman load up the horses for travel, he yanked at a pack and said, "Whoa, brother. It goes easier when you don't fight."

The horse gave him a big-eyed stare as if it understood his language—a comforting thought, because nobody else did, But even among the horses he felt unequal. They were able to look out for themselves if they escaped. He would simply starve. He was envious still, even among the horses.

Humbly he fetched and carried. Sometimes he even offered to help, but he had not the skill for the endless work of the women, and he was not trusted to hunt with the men, the providers.

When the camp moved, he carried a pack trudging with the women. Even the dogs worked then, pulling small burdens on travois of sticks.

The Indian who had captured him lived like a lord, as he had a right to do. He hunted with his peers, attended long ceremonial meetings with much chanting and dancing, and lounged in the shade with his smug bride. He had only two responsibilities: to kill buffalo and to gain glory. The white man was so far beneath him in status that the Indian did not even think of envy.

One day several things happened that made the captive think he might sometime become a man again. That was the day when he began to understand their language. For four months he had heard it, day and night, the joy and the mourning, the ritual chanting and sung prayers, the squabbles and the deliberations. None of it meant anything to him at all.

But on that important day in early fall the two young women set out for the river, and one of them called over her shoulder to the old woman. The white man was startled. She had said she was going to bathe. His understanding was so sudden that he felt as if his ears had come unstopped. Listening to the racket of the camp, he heard fragments of meaning instead of gabble.

On that same important day the old woman brought a pair of new moccasins out of the tepee and tossed them on the ground before him. He could not believe she would do anything for him because of kindness, but giving him moccasins was one way of looking after her property.

In thanking her, he dared greatly. He picked a little hand-ful of fading fall flowers and took them to her as she squatted in front of her tepee, scraping a buffalo hide with a tool made from a piece of iron tied to a bone. Her hands were hideous—most of the fingers had the first joint miss-ing. He bowed solemnly and offered the flowers.

She glared at him from beneath the short, ragged tangle of her hair. She stared at the flowers, knocked them out of his hand and went running to the next tepee, squalling the story. He heard her and the other women screaming with laughter.

The white man squared his shoulders and walked boldly over to watch three small boys shooting arrows at a target. He said in English, "Show me how to do that, will you?"

They frowned, but he held out his hand as if there could be no doubt. One of them gave him a bow and one arrow, and they snickered when he missed.

The people were easily amused, except when they were angry. They were amused, at him, playing with the little boys. A few days later he asked the hag, with gestures, for a bow that her son had just discarded, a man-size bow of horn. He scavenged for old arrows. The old woman cackled at his marksmanship and called her neighbors to enjoy the fun.

When he could understand words, he could identify his people by their names. The old woman was Greasy Hand, and her daughter was Pretty Calf. The other young woman's name was not clear to him, for the words were not in his vo-cabulary. The man who had captured him was Yellow Robe.

Once he could understand, he could begin to talk a little, and then he was less lonely. Nobody had been able to see any reason for talking to him, since he would not understand anyway. He asked the old woman, "What is my name?" Until he knew it, he was incomplete. She shrugged to let him know he had none.

He told her in the Crow language, "My name is Horse." He repeated it, and she nodded. After that they called him Horse when they called him anything. Nobody cared except the white man himself.

They trusted him enough to let him stray out of camp, so that he might have got away and, by unimaginable good luck, might have reached a trading post or a fort, but winter was too close. He did not dare leave without a horse; he needed clothing and a better hunting weapon than he had, and more certain skill in using it. He did not dare steal, for then they would surely have pursued him, and just as certainly they would have caught him. Remembering the warmth of the home that was waiting in Boston, he settled down for the winter.

On a cold night he crept into the tepee after the others had gone to bed. Even a horse might try to find shelter from the wind. The old woman grumbled, but without conviction. She did not put him out.

They tolerated him, back in the shadows, so long as he did not get in the way.

He began to understand how the family that owned him differed from the others. Fate had been cruel to them. In a short, sharp argument among the old women, one of them derided Greasy Hand by sneering, "You have no relatives!" and Greasy Hand raved for minutes of the deeds of her father and uncles and brothers. And she had had four sons, she reminded her detractor—who answered with scorn, "Where are they?"

Later the white man found her moaning and whimpering to herself, rocking back and forth on her haunches, staring at her mutilated hands. By that time he understood. A mourner often chopped off a finger joint. Old Greasy Hand had mourned often. For the first time he felt a twinge of pity, but he put it aside as another emotion, like anger, that he could not afford. He thought: What tales I will tell when I get home!

He wrinkled his nose in disdain. The camp stank of animals and meat and rancid grease. He looked down at his naked, shivering legs and was startled, remembering that he was still only a horse.

He could not trust the old woman. She fed him only because a starved slave would die and not be worth boasting about. Just how fitful her temper was he saw on the day when she got tired of stumbling over one of the hundred dogs that infested the camp. This was one of her own dogs, a large, strong one that pulled a baggage travois when the tribe moved camp.

Countless times he had seen her kick at the beast as it lay sleeping in front of the tepee, in her way. The dog always moved, with a yelp, but it always got in the way again. One day she gave the dog its usual kick and then stood scolding at it while the animal rolled its eyes sleepily. The old woman suddenly picked up her axe and cut the dog's head off with one blow. Looking well satisfied with herself, she beckoned her slave to remove the body.

It could have been me, he thought, if I were a dog. But I'm a horse.

His hope of life lay with the girl, Pretty Calf. He set about courting her, realizing how desperately poor he was both in property and honor. He owned no horse, no weapon but the old bow and the battered arrows. He had nothing to give away, and he needed gifts, because he did not dare seduce the girl.

One of the customs of courtship involved sending a gift of horses to a girl's older brother and bestowing much buffalo meat upon her mother. The white man could not wait for some far-off time when he might have either horses or meat to give away. And his courtship had to be secret. It was not for him to stroll past the groups of watchful girls, blowing a flute made of an eagle's wing bone, as the flirtatious young bucks did.

He could not ride past Pretty Calf's tepee, painted and bedizened; he had no horse, no finery.

Back home, he remembered, I could marry just about any girl I'd want to. But he wasted little time thinking about that. A future was something to be earned.

The most he dared do was wink at Pretty Calf now and then, or state his admiration while she giggled and hid her face. The least he dared do to win his bride was to elope with her, but he had to give her a horse to put the seal of tribal approval on that. And he had no horse until he killed a man to get one. . . .

His opportunity came in early spring. He was casually accepted by that time. He did not belong, but he was amusing to the Crows, like a strange pet, or they would not have fed him through the winter.

His chance came when he was hunting small game with three young boys who were his guards as well as his scornful companions. Rabbits and birds were of no account in a camp well fed on buffalo meat, but they made good targets.

His party walked far that day. All of them at once saw the two horses in a sheltered coulee. The boys and the man crawled forward on their bellies, and then they saw an Indian who lay on the ground, moaning, a lone traveler. From the way the boys inched eagerly forward, Horse knew the man was fair prey—a member of some enemy tribe.

This is the way the captive white man acquired wealth and honor to win a bride and save his life: He shot an arrow into the sick man, a split second ahead of one of his small companions, and dashed forward to strike the still-groaning man with his bow, to count first coup. Then he seized the hobbled horses.

By the time he had the horses secure, and with them his hope for freedom, the boys had followed, counting coup with gestures and shrieks they had practiced since boyhood, and one of them had the scalp. The white man was grimly amused to see the boy double up with sudden nausea when he had the thing in his hand. . . .

There was a hubbub in the camp when they rode in that evening, two of them on each horse. The captive was noticed. Indians who had ignored him as a slave stared at the brave man who had struck first coup and had stolen horses.

The hubbub lasted all night, as fathers boasted loudly of their young sons' exploits. The white man was called upon to settle an argument between two fierce boys as to which of them had struck second coup and which must be satisfied with third. After much talk that went over his head, he solemnly pointed at the nearest boy. He didn't know which boy it was and didn't care, but the boy did.

The white man had watched warriors in their triumph. He knew what to do. Modesty about achievements had no place among the Crow people. When a man did something big, he told about it.

The white man smeared his face with grease and charcoal. He walked inside the tepee circle, chanting and singing. He used his own language.

"You heathens, you savages," he shouted. "I'm going to get out of here someday! I am going to get away!" The Crow people listened respectfully. In the Crow tongue he shouted, "Horse! I am Horse!" and they nodded.

He had a right to boast, and he had two horses. Before dawn, the white man and his bride were sheltered beyond a far hill, and he was telling her, "I love you, little lady. I love you."

She looked at him with her great dark eyes, and he thought she understood his English words—or as much as she needed to understand.

"You are my treasure," he said, "more precious than jewels, better than fine gold. I am going to call you Freedom."

When they returned to camp two days later, he was bold but worried. His ace, he suspected, might not be high enough in the game he was playing without being sure of the rules. But it served.

Odl Greasy Hand raged—but not at him. She complained loudly that her daughter had let herself go too cheap. But the marriage was as good as any Crow marriage. He had paid a horse.

He learned the language faster after that, from Pretty Calf, whom he sometimes called Freedom. He learned that his attentive, adoring bride was fourteen years old.

One thing he had not guessed was the difference that being Pretty Calf's husband would make in his relationship to her mother and brother. He had hoped only to make his position a little safer, but he had not expected to be treated with dignity. Greasy Hand no longer spoke to him at all. When the white man spoke to her, his bride murmured in dismay, explaining at great length that he must never do that. There could be no conversation between a man and his mother-in-law. He could not even mention a word that was part of her name.

Having improved his status so magnificently, he felt no need for hurry in getting away. Now that he had a woman, he had as good a chance to be rich as any man. Pretty Calf waited on him; she seldom ran off to play games with other young girls, but took pride in learning from her mother the many women's skills of tanning hides and making clothing and preparing food.

He was no more a horse but a kind of man, a half-Indian, still poor and unskilled but laden with honors, clinging to the buckskin fringes of Crow society.

Escape could wait until he could manage it in comfort, with fit clothing and a good horse, with hunting weapons. Escape could wait until the camp moved near some trading post. He did not plan how he would get home. He dreamed of being there all at once, and of telling stories nobody would believe. There was no hurry.

Pretty Calf delighted in educating him. He began to understand tribal arrangements, customs and why things were as they were. They were that way because they had always been so. His young wife giggled when she told him, in his ignorance, things she had always known. But she did not laugh when her brother's wife was taken by another warrior. She explained that solemnly with words and signs.

Yellow Robe belonged to a society called the Big Dogs. The wife stealer, Cut Neck, belonged to the Foxes. They were fellow tribesmen; they hunted together and fought side by side, but men of one society could take away wives from the other society if they wished, subject to certain limitations.

When Cut Neck rode up to the tepee, laughing and singing, and called to Yellow Robe's wife, "Come out! Come out!'' she did as ordered, looking smug as usual, meek and entirely willing. Thereafter she rode beside him in ceremonial processions and carried his coup stick, while his other wife pretended not to care.

"But why?'' the white man demanded of his wife, his Freedom. "Why did our brother let his woman go? He sits and smokes and does not speak.''

Pretty Calf was shocked at the suggestion. Her brother could not possibly reclaim his woman, she explained. He could not even let her come back if she wanted to—and she probably would want to when Cut Neck tired of her. Yellow Robe could not even admit that his heart was sick. That was the way things were. Deviation meant dishonor.

The woman could have hidden from Cut Neck, she said. She could even have refused to go with him if she had been *ba-wurokee*—a really virtuous woman. But she had been his woman before, for a little while on a berrying expedition, and he had a right to claim her.

There was no sense in it, the white man insisted. He glared at his young wife. "If you go, I will bring you back!'' he promised.

She laughed and buried her head against his shoulder. "I will not have to go,'' she said. "Horse is my first man. There is no hole in my moccasin.''

He stroked her hair and said, *"Ba-wurokee.''*

With great daring, she murmured, *"Hayha,''* and when he did not answer, because he did not know what she meant, she drew away, hurt.

"A woman calls her man that if she thinks he will not leave her. Am I wrong?''

The white man held her closer and lied. "Pretty Calf is not wrong. Horse will not leave her. Horse will not take another woman, either.'' No, he certainly would not. Parting from this one was going to be harder than getting her had been. *"Hayha,''* he murmured. "Freedom.''

His conscience irked him, but not very much. Pretty Calf could get another man easily enough when he was gone, and a better provider. His hunting skill was improving, but he was still awkward.

There was no hurry about leaving. He was used to most of the Crow ways and could stand the rest. He was becoming prosperous. He owned five horses. His place in the life of the tribe was secure, such as it was. Three or four young women, including the one who had belonged to Yellow Robe, made advances to him. Pretty Calf took pride in the fact that her man was so attractive.

By the time he had what he needed for a secret journey, the grass grew yellow on the plains and the long cold was close. He was enslaved by the girl he called Freedom and, before the winter ended, by the knowledge that she was carrying his child. . . .

The Big Dog society held a long ceremony in the spring. The white man strolled with his woman along the creek bank, thinking: When I get home I will tell them about the chants and the drumming. Sometime. Sometime.

Pretty Calf would not go to bed when they went back to the tepee.

"Wait and find out about my brother," she urged. "Something may happen."

So far as Horse could figure out, the Big Dogs were having some kind of election. He pampered his wife by staying up with her by the fire. Even the old woman, who was a great one for getting sleep when she was not working, prowled around restlessly.

The white man was yawning by the time the noise of the ceremony died down. When Yellow Robe strode in, garish and heathen in his paint and feathers and furs, the women cried out. There was conversation, too fast for Horse to follow, and the old woman wailed once, but her son silenced her with a gruff command.

When the white man went to sleep, he thought his wife was weeping beside him.

The next morning she explained.

"He wears the bearskin belt. Now he can never retreat in battle. He will always be in danger. He will die."

Maybe he wouldn't, the white man tried to convince her. Pretty Calf recalled that some few men had been honored by the bearskin belt, vowed to the highest daring, and had not died. If they lived through the summer, then they were free of it.

"My brother wants to die," she mourned. "His heart is bitter."

Yellow Robe lived through half a dozen clashes with small parties of raiders from hostile tribes. His honors were many. He captured horses in an enemy camp, led two successful raids, counted first coup and snatched a gun from the hand of an enemy tribesman. He wore wolf tails on his moccasins and ermine skins on his shirt, and he fringed his leggings with scalps in token of his glory.

When his mother ventured to suggest, as she did many times, "My son should take a new wife, I need another woman to help me," he ignored her. He spent much time in prayer, alone in the hills or in conference with a medicine man. He fasted and made vows and kept them. And before he could be free of the heavy honor of the bearskin belt, he went on his last raid.

The warriors were returning from the north just as the white man and two other hunters approached from the south, with buffalo and elk meat dripping from the bloody hides tied on their restive ponies. One of the hunters grunted, and they stopped to watch a rider on the hill north of the tepee circle.

The rider dismounted, held up a blanket and dropped it. He repeated the gesture.

The hunters murmured dismay. "Two! Two men dead!" They rode fast into the camp, where there was already wailing.

A messenger came down from the war party on the hill. The rest of the party delayed to paint their faces for mourning and for victory. One of the two dead men was Yellow Robe. They had put his body in a cave and walled it in with rocks. The other man died later, and his body was in a tree.

There was blood on the ground before the tepee to which

Yellow Robe would return no more. His mother, with her hair chopped short, sat in the doorway, rocking back and forth on her haunches, wailing her heartbreak. She cradled one mutilated hand in the other. She had cut off another finger joint.

Pretty Calf had cut off chunks of her long hair and was crying as she gashed her arms with a knife. The white man tried to take the knife away, but she protested so piteously that he let her do as she wished. He was sickened with the lot of them.

Savages! he thought. Now I will go back! I'll go hunting alone, and I'll keep on going.

But he did not go just yet, because he was the only hunter in the lodge of the two grieving women, one of them old and the other pregnant with his child.

In their mourning, they made him a pauper again. Everything that meant comfort, wealth and safety they sacrificed to the spirits because of the death of Yellow Robe. The tepee, made of seventeen fine buffalo hides, the furs that should have kept them warm, the white deerskin dress, trimmed with elk teeth, that Pretty Calf loved so well, even their tools and Yellow Robe's weapons—everything but his sacred medicine objects—they left there on the prairie, and the whole camp moved away. Two of his best horses were killed as sacrifice, and the women gave away the rest.

They had no shelter. They would have no tepee of their own for two months at least of mourning, and then the women would have to tan hides to make it. Meanwhile they could live in temporary huts made of willows, covered with skins given them in pity by their friends. They could have lived with relatives, but Yellow Robe's women had no relatives.

The white man had not realized until then how terrible a thing it was for a Crow to have no kinfolk. No wonder old Greasy Hand had only stumps for fingers. She had mourned, from one year to the next, for everyone she had ever loved. She had no one left but her daughter, Pretty Calf.

Horse was furious at their foolishness. It had been bad

enough for him, a captive, to be naked as a horse and poor as a slave, but that was because his captors had stripped him. These women had voluntarily given up everything they needed.

He was too angry at them to sleep in the willow hut. He lay under a sheltering tree. And on the third night of the mourning he made his plans. He had a knife and a bow. He would go after meat, taking two horses. And he would not come back. There were, he realized, many things he was not going to tell when he got back home.

In the willow hut, Pretty Calf cried out. He heard rustling there, and the old woman's querulous voice.

Some twenty hours later his son was born, two months early, in the tepee of a skilled medicine woman. The child was born without breath, and the mother died before the sun went down.

The white man was too shocked to think whether he should mourn, or how he should mourn. The old woman screamed until she was voiceless. Piteously she approached him, bent and trembling, blind with grief. She held out her knife and he took it.

She spread out her hands and shook her head. If she cut off any more finger joints, she could do no more work. She could not afford any more lasting signs of grief.

The white man said, "All right! All right!" between his teeth. He hacked his arms with the knife and stood watching the blood run down. It was little enough to do for Pretty Calf, for little Freedom.

Now there is nothing to keep me, he realized. When I get home, I must not let them see the scars.

He looked at Greasy Hand, hideous in her grief-burdened age, and thought: I really am free now! When a wife dies, her husband has no more duty toward her family. Pretty Calf had told him so, long ago, when he wondered why a certain man moved out of one tepee and into another.

The old woman, of course, would be a scavenger. There was one other with the tribe, an ancient crone who had no relatives, toward whom no one felt any responsibility. She lived on food thrown away by the more fortunate. She slept in shelters that she built with her own knotted hands. She plodded wearily at the end of the procession when the camp moved. When she stumbled, nobody cared. When she died, nobody would miss her.

Tomorrow morning, the white man decided, I will go.

His mother-in-law's sunken mouth quivered. She said one word, questioningly. She said, *"Eero-oshay?"* She said, "Son?"

Blinking, he remembered. When a wife died, her husband was free. But her mother, who had ignored him with dignity, might if she wished ask him to stay. She invited him by calling him Son, and he accepted by answering Mother.

Greasy Hand stood before him, bowed with years, withered with unceasing labor, loveless and childless, scarred with grief. But with all her burdens, she still loved life enough to beg it from him, the only person she had any right to ask. She was stripping herself of all she had left, her pride.

He looked eastward across the prairie. Two thousand miles away was home. The old woman would not live forever. He could afford to wait, for he was young. He could afford to be magnanimous, for he knew he was a man. He gave her the answer. *"Eegya,"* he said. "Mother."

He went home three years later. He explained no more than to say, "I lived with Crows for a while. It was some time before I could leave. They called me Horse."

He did not find it necessary either to apologize or to boast, because he was the equal of any man on earth.

T. V. Olsen has been widely published in the Western field, with credits that include novels and such short stories as this first-rate study of the ways of Sac Indian warriors. His best-known longer work is The Stalking Moon, *for which he wrote the film script. Among his other novels and screenplays are* Red Is the River, The Lockhart Breed, *and* Soldier Blue. *He makes his home in Wisconsin.*

A Kind of Courage

T. V. Olsen

*T*he two men prowled single file along the old game trail where it followed the creekbank, going upstream. They were young men; both were pared down to bone and muscle. They wore rawhide moccasins and leggins of colored stroud, and their calico shirts were removed against the simmering hotness of mid-July. They were armed with hickory bows and quivers of arrows, and each carried a steel-headed tomahawk and a scalping knife. Sweat glistened on the coppery skin of their plucked scalps, bare except for the gaudy scalplocks of Sac warriors.

In these ways the two were alike; otherwise they only differed. Their sorry diet had gaunted both men almost to emaciation, but the man who walked behind was still heavily muscled. Marked by traces of white warpaint, his face was craggy and handsome and held a lurking mischief. He was watchful and swift-eyed.

The youth in the lead was lighter of build, and he wasn't big. His eyes were quiet and indrawn; deep and questing moods glided like quick fish beneath the surface of his face.

The wind made a strange hushing sound through the thick boughs of white pine arching over them. A drift of pine needles, yellowed and dropping in the summer heat, whispered down through the dusty shafts of sunlight. These were the only sounds, for the two Sacs made none. Until the man in the rear suddenly struck his bow against a pine trunk.

The noise was sharp and loud in the quivering sodden air. Tyeema jerked at the sound, then looked back across his shoulder to see the lazy mockery in his companion's face.

Musketabah said sleepily, "One time soon maybe you'll dream yourself into a bird and fly away, and my sister will have no husband."

Tyeema set his face ahead again. There was sweat between his hand and his bow, and he could hear his heart. He was angry at himself for starting at the deliberate noise. Musketabah thought that such tricks were funny.

"Or maybe," Musketabah went on, "you will change into a rabbit. You jump like a rabbit."

Tyeema didn't answer.

"You should have gone with Keokuk and the other women."

"Keokuk is no woman."

"He is an old woman, and so are his friends."

Musketabah's words were soft and very lazy. But the laziness was only a manner of his, for he missed nothing at all. Musketabah, after all, wasn't given to dangerous dreaming; his mind was a fixed point that never strayed by a hair's width from the business at hand.

Maybe this was the way to be at such a time, Tyeema thought, letting his anger turn inward. The gifts for war did not touch each man in like proportion. Some had the stronger arms, the sharper eyes, the quicker brains. Tyeema had never come close to equaling his brother-in-law in any game with lance or bow or in the stalk and kill or in wrestling skills. But then few could outstrip Musketabah in any art of hunting or fighting, and he excelled without half trying. Yet his easy, good-natured arrogance sat on him so lightly that hardly anybody resented it.

Tyeema, on the other hand, was a rather ordinary fellow as Sac braves went, except in one way. And it was not a good way in such times as these. For Tyeema was given to dreaming, not a commendable trait when all of a man's senses and thinking should be keened toward two things only—some sign of the white enemy or a sight of the game that was desperately needed to swell the shrunken bellies of the Rock River people.

There had been a scarcity of game since early spring when they had followed Black Hawk across the Mississippi, returning to Senisepo Kebesaukee, their ancestral homeland at the mouth of the Rock. One bad treaty after another, signed by one weak and ignorant leader after another, had deprived the Sacs of all their former lands east of the big river. It was old Black Hawk, a mere headman of the Rock River Sacs, who at long last, in this white man's year of 1832, had rebelled against the westward-creeping dominion of the whites. He would bring his people back to their old grounds and plant corn in the old way; he did not want trouble with the Americans, but he would not abide by a bad treaty.

Nobody had argued the truth of Black Hawk's words, but the cooler heads among the Sacs knew that his action was no part of wisdom. The Americans were too strong. The Potawatomi and Winnebagoes and Chippewas on this side of the big river had their share of grievances against the whites, but they could spare only halfhearted sympathy for their Sac brothers. *Hoh-hoh*—this was a fool's business Black Hawk had started. Surely the British fathers in Canada had encouraged the old man in his foolishness, but why had he thought they would give him active help? Twenty years ago the British and their Indian allies had been unable to seize this land they called the Northwest Territory from the Americans, and today the Americans were even stronger. Yes, Black Hawk was a *poshi-poshito*, a fool of fools, for even his friend Shabona, the Potawatomi chief, had tried to dissuade him and, failing that, had gone so far as to warn the soldiers and settlers of Black Hawk's intentions.

As to the Sacs themselves, many remained loyal to

Keokuk, chief of all the *Sau-kie-uck* nation, a man whose bitterness toward the whites he had once befriended was tempered by an acid fatalism. He had made the best terms that could be made with the Americans, and hotheads like Black Hawk and his ill-advised counselors, Neapope and The Prophet, would only bring down the badness of the white man's wrath on all the Sacs.

Tyeema knew these things, and the folly of this war was strong in his thoughts long before Black Hawk had made his move. Since he was not of the Rock River tribe and owed them no allegiance, why had he stayed? There was an easy answer: He had married a Rock River woman and had come into her family, according to custom. His wife's father and brother had red war in their minds, and what the women thought did not matter. So they had stayed with Black Hawk, and so did Tyeema.

That was the easy answer, but there was more. At first it had seemed important to change that lazy contempt in Musketabah's eyes, a thing that had made a great knot in Tyeema's guts for so long. If he weren't a great fighter or hunter, at least he was not a fool or a cripple, and he could be as brave as the next man.

The trouble was that Tyeema *was* afraid, and Musketabah knew it. No matter how often Tyeema told himself that his brother-in-law's cool, easy mockery of him should not matter, did not matter, the sting of shame was left festering in him. Staying with Black Hawk had been a mistake, but all he could do now was keep silent and swallow what he must until Black Hawk's great folly reached a bloody end.

Three and a half months ago, when the Sacs had crossed the Mississippi at the Yellow Banks, there had been a prompt reaction from Reynolds, the white chief of Illinois, and from the White Beaver, General Atkinson of the American garrison at Fort Armstrong. In no time at all, fully five thousand regular troops and Illinois militiamen were in the field, picking up the trail of half a thousand Sac warriors and their families. Even Black Hawk, the old fire-eater, had quickly seen the wisdom of a parley. But when a company of militia led by a capering white fool called Stillman had fired on and killed the emissaries sent by Black Hawk under a truce flag, the enraged chief had slaughtered and routed the whole gang, though his party was outnumbered three to one.

Then and afterward, Black Hawk had proved himself an able and wily leader. Swiftly retreating, he and his Sacs were swallowed by the wilderness. Though burdened by their women and children and their animals and belongings, the Rock River people had eluded the white patrols for many weeks. All the while, the Sacs were forging steadily northward toward the bluffs of the Wisconsin River and their final stand—meantime throwing out a swift flurry of raids among the scattered, helpless settlers.

Black Hawk had made an amazing fight—even Tyeema had to admit as much—but in the end it would all be the same. If the whites were paying a terrible price, the misery of the Sacs was threefold. Not in the worst winters recalled by the elders had the people been reduced to the state of near-starvation that now threatened them, thanks to long marches, short sleeps, and whatever snatches of food they could find or take from the whites.

It was not enough. The people were wasting to tottering skeletons. Some were too weak to continue the march; several had already died. All the horses that could be spared had been eaten. Since all food was shared alike, all were now living mainly on a little cracked corn, acorns, elm bark—even grass.

In a valley to the north, the main band was resting over a day; this made a little time for the men to hunt. Maybe Gitchee-Manitou would smile today. Tyeema, thinking of his wife's hollow-eyed face, hoped it might be so. Even a scrawny rabbit would be welcome in the pot. Nan-nah-que, the father, was too sick and weak to go with them, so Tyeema and Musketabah were prowling the streambanks alone.

There was no wind near the ground; the air was heavy with the wet heat of noonday. The sluggish creek flickered with green-gold rays of sunlight. Tyeema thought he was seeing all there was to be seen—the static burring of a drag-onfly above the water, the knotlike lump of a mud turtle on a half-sunk log, a slim greensnake gliding away through the dry cattails. But suddenly Musketabah was at his side, grip-ping his wrist and pointing through the trees.

There was a movement on the creekbank well upstream—one transient spot of color that showed and moved and was gone. That was all, and the two Sacs froze to the spot. When they eased cautiously forward once more, Musketabah brushed Tyeema aside and took the lead. Soon the voices and words of white men reached them. The encampment it-self grew into view on the opposite side of the creek. It was set back off the bank in the trees. There was a rattle of coarse laughter. Tyeema smelled a pinewood fire and roasting meat; his belly ached sorely, and his saliva started to work on nothing.

The two Sacs crept close to the water's edge, for the reeds and willow brush hid them, and they were still many yards downstream from the camp. They watched awhile but could make out little for the trees. Musketabah murmured, "These Long-Knives are a war party, but they are not dressed like the soldiers. How are they called?"

"Militia." The white man's word rolled easily off Tyeema's tongue.

"Mil-lish-ah." Musketabah grunted contemptuously. "Maybe we'll find out how much of a rabbit you are." He peered tightly through the water reeds. "We will go under the water to the other side. That log—there—will hide us. Then we'll be close enough."

"For what?" Tyeema's heart began a dense, almost pain-ful slugging against his ribs.

"To hear what they say, fool. You've gone to the post school at Prairie du Chien; you know their foolish language. Maybe you've also taken a white man's watery heart in your guts, so we'll learn about that too."

Tyeema said, "What does my brother mean?" though he

knew the answer well enough. The spittle had dried on his tongue.

"There will be danger. That close, if we are seen, we won't have time to get away before we're killed or captured." Musketabah's whisper was light. "How brave does my brother feel?"

"It is a foolishness," Tyeema said coldly. "If these Americans are so close to our camp, maybe they'll cross our trail soon. Then they'll find where we are and send word to the White Beaver, and he will bring up troops. The Sacs are not ready to meet the soldiers here. We should go tell Black Hawk to break camp at once and go north swiftly."

"Yes, rabbit, but first we will learn of this mil-lish-ah's plans if we can. That's only wisdom."

It was stupidity, Tyeema knew. The only wisdom was to backtrack as quickly as possible; Black Hawk would want to know at once of a large company of well-armed whites this close to his main camp. If Musketabah wanted to take a senseless risk, that was his business. But even as the thought formed, so did the one bleak flaw in it—and that was Tyeema's own weakness.

He could tolerate no more of Musketabah's taunting charges of cowardice. And if he deserted him now, no matter that his was the wise action, the contempt that only Musketabah had shown would be shared by his wife's family and by many others in the band. And since he really was afraid, he could not be sure how much fear had diluted his wisdom. How could a man leave such a question unanswered and face himself in the night?

He did not show Musketabah another twinge of reluctance; he said only, "I can do this alone. While I remain to hear what the white men say, let Musketabah go without delay to warn Black Hawk."

Musketabah's eyes slitted, the suggestion having obviously touched his pride. "Since when does one trust a rabbit to carry through a man's work?" His whisper was very soft and flat. "I'll see that you do it well. Follow a man, rabbit."

Without another word, he slipped off his quiver and laid it aside with his bow, then crept forward through the reeds and slid noiselessly into the creek. Tyeema did not let himself think. He discarded his bow and arrows, then followed his brother-in-law. The water was warm as he went under, but he felt the instant chilly drag of the current at his legs. Underwater, he opened his eyes and saw Musketabah stroking his way upstream through a golden flood of sunlight.

Tyeema moved after him. A string of bubbles tickled up past his cheeks and ears. A school of minnows swarming past like brown darts nibbled along his shoulders and arms. His lungs were starting to burst. He saw Musketabah swing close to the bank and paddle to the surface.

Fighting his panicked instinct to claw blindly up to air, Tyeema forced himself to break surface lightly, with a faint, neat rustle of water. Then he had to fight to keep from gulping the air; he took it in with shuddering shallow gasps. Close beside him, Musketabah laughed silently.

They were hugging the side of a huge deadfall by the bank; they treaded water, their heads hidden by the rotted trunk. A greenish scum of algae lapped at their chins. Tyeema's heart was pounding more furiously than ever; the weakness of pure hunger had made of that brief submerged swim an agonizing effort. Musketabah showed no sign of exertion.

"And then she said, 'Well, I'll be a son of a bitch,' " one of the white rangers said loudly and clearly. Several of the others laughed. There was a group of them sitting toward this side of the camp, telling stories. Tyeema knew the kind, these being white militia.

He was surprised how easy it was to make out their individual words now. They were still a fair distance away, as the two Sacs could tell by raising themselves till their eyes just topped the log. Tall reeds grew on the creekbank, and beyond it tall grasses and a few birches grew up to the edge of the bivouac. They could make out enough to tell that this was a good-sized company: a large number of rangers were squatting or lying on their backs around a clearing, talking and resting. The several fires were smoking less than most white men's fires. These were a rough and seasoned-looking lot in worn homespuns and buckskins, all of them bearded from many days in the wilderness. But the camp was well ordered and clean; it was clear there was discipline here.

Tyeema took particular notice of three men standing near the center of the camp. Two of them were obviously guides and scouts: one a *métis* half-breed wearing cast-off white man's clothes, the other a full blood in the regalia of a Winnebago chief. The third was a tall white man in a fringed hunting coat; he appeared to be the leader here. His yellow beard chopped slowly up and down as he talked. In answer to a question, the Winnebago, a middle-aged man with a lined and wolfish face, pointed toward the north.

Musketabah murmured close to Tyeema's ear, "I want to hear what that yellow beard says. I'll get nearer."

Tyeema wanted to call him a fool. "If you get nearer, you'll be seen."

"Are these mil-lish-ah different from other whites? Their senses are dead in the woods."

"The Winnebago's senses aren't dead."

"I don't ask you to come, rabbit," Musketabah whispered, and slithered around the log and crawled from the water and past the reed-covered bank. Noiseless as a shadow, he snaked on his belly through the tall grass, which stirred in a slight graceful motion that the mild wind covered.

Suddenly Musketabah halted; his arm whipped up and back. His tomahawk flashed and fell. Tyeema had a glimpse of a huge blacksnake, headless now, thrashing in the grass.

The hearty noise and activity of the whites should have hidden the spare sound and movement Musketabah made killing the snake. Nor did the white men notice anything. But the Winnebago's head promptly turned, his eyes pouncing through the birches and the tall grass. He was leaning on his Kentucky rifle, and now he brought up the long-barreled piece and started across the clearing.

Musketabah knew the game was up. He was on his feet at

once, wheeling back toward the creek in a low, darting run. The rifle made an oddly ringing report, and Musketabah was knocked down, then went somersaulting on his back. He staggered to his feet but almost fell again. By then the militiamen were coming on the run, the yellow beard yelling, "I want that reddie alive!"

Musketabah stumbled on, but the *métis* and three white men were almost at his heels. He swung on them, tomahawk lifted. His arm whipped forward; the war ax made a turning flash of steel that ended in the chest of a white man. No time to get out his knife then, as the *métis* and the other two whites swarmed into Musketabah and carried him to the ground as he fought like a wounded black bear.

Tyeema stayed where he was, not stirring a muscle. If he remained absolutely still, the log and heavy growth of reeds should hide him from anything but a close search.

The rest of the whites came as the three men were wrestling Musketabah to his feet. "*Sacre bleu,*" the *métis* panted. "This one, he is fight like ten t'ousan' devil." The others gathered around the one who was dead in the grass with the tomahawk in his chest; there was a run of ominous talk.

The leader tugged his yellow beard, eying Musketabah. "Well, here's a piece of luck."

"Not so lucky for George," a man growled.

"I mean taking a hostile alive. This 'un has to be a scout and spy for Black Hawk. We was pretty sure the main band wasn't far from here. Seems this proves it. Walking Thunder!"

The Winnebago finished methodically loading and priming his rifle before moving over to the leader.

"I want to know some things. Where the main band is, what its strength is, and what this fellow knows of Black Hawk's plans."

Walking Thunder spoke in the Sac tongue to Musketabah, who did not even look at him. "He not talk now," the Winnebago said then. "You give him me, I take him in woods. By and by he talk."

"I say gut the bastard here and now, Cap'n," a man said softly. "He killed a white man. It's a white man's job."

There was a general clamor of agreement, put harshly down by the captain. "I know how you feel. But any information we can coax out o' him comes first. You boys'll have what's left o' him, you can lay to that."

"My God, Captain Macready." A beardless young man had spoken up, his voice mild with shock. "This is barbarous! You're not actually turning a wounded captive over to this savage?"

"It's their way, boy. They lived by it a long time. I don't aim to preach 'em no different. And we need what this reddie can tell us."

"But you are a white man, sir, and you're permitting this—this dastardly—"

"Listen, sonny." Captain Macready's eyes held a blue glitter. "Some of Black Hawk's bunch got my brother and his family a month back. They skinned my brother alive and left him in the sun. There's plenty men here had things as bad touch them and theirs. You want to ask someone any more about it, here's your chance."

The young man said nothing.

"Maybe a hundred white lives'll be saved if we can run Black Hawk to ground now," Captain Macready went on more quietly. "Once we know what we need to, we'll send a runner back to Colonel Henry, and him and Colonel Dodge'll bring their troops up double quick. I don't aim to abuse no tender ears, so we'll take the redskin off a ways. Walking Thunder, Doucette—lay hold of him. Rest of you get about your business."

The Winnebago and the *métis* caught Musketabah by the arms. His head had dropped to his chest; he was bleeding badly, and for the moment the fight seemed to have run out of him. Captain Macready turned and led the way into the dense pine woods along the creek, followed by the two men supporting the wounded Sac between them. The militiamen were strangely silent, not meeting one another's eyes, as they picked up their dead comrade and carried him back to the camp.

Tyeema waited till they had all cleared away from the area by the bank; even then he didn't move quickly as he pulled himself on his belly from the water. He was undecided. It was more urgent than before that Black Hawk be warned promptly, for even if Musketabah died without talking, the militia was now sure that the Sac encampment was close by; they would scour the region for it.

But there was Musketabah. And suddenly Tyeema quit wondering. Lying flat in the grass, he inched forward into the pines until the forest blocked him from the camp. Then he climbed to his feet and fell into a light jog trot, heading through the woods along the creek on the trail taken by the militia captain.

He was a fool, Tyeema supposed. He had no great affection for his brother-in-law, and his were not the gifts of war. Even if he weren't almost staggering with the weakness of hunger, even if he had the bow and arrows he had left back on the other bank, he would stand little chance against the long rifles of Macready and Walking Thunder, or even the ancient Hudson's Bay musket that Doucette carried. If there were only one instead of three, and if he had a bow or gun, and if he could take the man by surprise . . . but there he was, dreaming. He had none of these advantages; all he had was a bad habit of idle thinking.

Then a faint excitement touched Tyeema, quickening his step a little. At least one of his idle thoughts might have some meat on it. The realization didn't surprise him; just as courage and physical skills came hard to him, so ideas came easily. He turned this one briefly over in his mind and thought it was sound; the simple ideas were always the best ones, and besides, if he thought about it too long, he might lose his nerve. Musketabah, he knew, would be expecting nothing from him in the way of help, and that knowledge tightened his belly.

His senses were quickening now; at last he heard the faint lift of voices that told him the men he was following had stopped not far ahead. Tyeema halted now and squatted, digging his fingers into the forest loam. With a handful of gritty soil, he scrubbed away the traces of white warpaint on his body; he smeared the moist dirt on his skin and then rubbed it on his breechclout and leggins. He trimmed the feathers and porcupine quills from his ornate scalplock with his knife, leaving a ragged tuft of hair.

When these things were done, Tyeema cut a sorry figure that nobody would take for a Sac warrior. Except for one thing—his tomahawk with its whining and wicked blade that would be a useful weapon but also would clash with the picture he wanted to make. He would have to rely on his knife alone. He cached the tomahawk in the crotch of a tree.

Afterward, he partly circled the small cut of clearing to which the militia captain and the other two had brought Musketabah; he wanted to come on it from a direction that would arouse the least suspicion. He had dropped into a languid shuffle, his muscles loose and his mouth pulled into a vacant grin, as he came slowly out of the woods into the clearing.

Walking Thunder saw him first. He also saw at once what Tyeema had relied on him to see. The Winnebago's lips began to move in an uneasy and soundless chant; he kept watching Tyeema. The *métis* was sitting on his haunches, striking flint and steel to make a fire. He glanced up; his eyes narrowed. *"Grâce à Dieu,"* he muttered.

Captain Macready was keeping his eyes on Musketabah, who was sitting on the ground, one fist clamped over his shoulder muscle above the bleeding. At Doucette's low mutter, the captain looked around. He gave an oath and started to swing his rifle up.

Walking Thunder threw out a long arm and said a flat, chopping phrase. Macready paused, looking at Doucette. "What'd he say?"

"Bad—bad to kill." Doucette tapped his head, then stabbed a finger at Tyeema. "Walking Thunder say is bad spirit in this one's head."

Tyeema halted and rolled his eyes from one man to the

next, grinning idiotically. Captain Macready stared at him for a long, suspicious moment. "All right, what of it? Looks Sac to me. Loonie Injuns are bad as any kind. Maybe worse."

"*Non*—you don' comprehen', *Capitaine*. This one, he is touch' in the head by Gitchee-Manitou—he is ver' holy. He is no more of his people; they have turn' him out. Bad luck to kill—big bad luck."

"The hell." Macready was scowling, but he lowered his rifle a little. "You believe that?"

"*Non*, not Doucette." The *métis* laughed, but Tyeema sensed that he was afraid. Grinning, Tyeema walked slowly into the clearing now, reserving a glance for Musketabah. His brother-in-law was eying him with open-mouthed amazement, and Tyeema only hoped he would stay that way and show nothing else.

Tyeema rubbed his belly as he shuffled over to the half-breed. "Food—food."

"Ha, w'at you t'ink? He's hungry, this one." Doucette gave another nervous laugh, and he watched with fearful fascination as Tyeema's hand came up to his shoulder.

Tyeema laughed childishly, patting the *métis*'s shoulder. "Food—food. Friend. You give food."

Captain Macready began to grin. His hands relaxed, letting his Kentucky flintlock slip down through his fingers till the butt touched the ground. "He 'pears to of took a liking to you, Doucette." He was enjoying this now.

"Ha ha," said Doucette. He patted the Sac's shoulder. "What is my brother's name? Eh? Name?"

Tyeema rubbed his belly and said vapidly, "Strawberry," since his name meant that in English. "Strawberry want food."

"Ho ho. M'sieu Strawberry." Doucette laughed loudly, turning his head to wink at the captain. "Strawberry! That is good name for the loonie Injun, eh, *Capitaine*? Strawb—"

The last word was choked off in a gurgling shriek as Tyeema, covered by Doucette's body, yanked his scalping knife now and drove it hard and low into the *métis*'s belly, twisting the blade. Doucette leaned into him, his whole body strung in one hard spasm; he was still on his feet, the dying scream trailing in his throat, as Tyeema wrenched the musket from his hands.

Tyeema leaped away from the falling man, at the same time swinging the musket to bear on Walking Thunder rather than the white man. It was well he did, for the Winnebago's reaction was like lightning. His long rifle was sweeping level even as Tyeema cocked the old musket and shot point-blank, awkwardly, into Walking Thunder's chest. The Winnebago went down, his piece unfired.

In wild haste now, Tyeema spun on his heel to face the white man, both hands clubbed around the empty musket. But Musketabah, as he had hoped, had leaped to time with his expected quickness. Sitting on the ground, he was quite close to Captain Macready; he had simply lunged sidelong and yanked the white man's feet from under him, then grappled him.

Musketabah had a death grip on the man, his back against Musketabah's chest and his own rifle in Musketabah's hands pressed down on his windpipe, crushing it. Captain Macready's mouth sagged open; he was fumbling along his belt for his hunting knife. Tyeema got there first and pulled the knife from its sheath and plunged it into the militia captain's heart.

Musketabah rolled the dead man aside and got to his feet. The others would be coming fast; the musket shot would bring them, Tyeema pointed out, and there was no time to lose.

That didn't trouble Musketabah. The Winnebago was still alive, and Musketabah took the time to remedy that detail. He also took the time to arm himself with Macready's knife and tomahawk, his rifle and powder horn and shot pouch. He insisted that Tyeema take the Winnebago's rifle and accouterments.

"Where is your tomahawk?" he asked.

Wordlessly, resignedly, Tyeema pointed at the woods,

and Musketabah said, "We'll get it. Then go across the creek for our bows and quivers." He slapped Tyeema's shoulder. "You were a smart rabbit to leave the tomahawk before you did your little trick. Even a rabbit can have good brains. Come!"

Less than a minute later, after they had left the clearing, retrieved the tomahawk, and were starting for the creek, a hubbub of men's angry voices was coming from the clearing. There wasn't fifty yards of forest between the clearing and the two Sacs as Musketabah plunged into the water, but he was in no particular hurry. On the other side he paused to plaster his wound with mud, then held Tyeema down to his own leisurely, arrogant trot as they went back to where they had left their bows and arrows.

The tightness in Tyeema's belly did not ease till they were a mile from the creek, moving back in an idle circle toward the main camp, for Musketabah still hoped to scare up some game. Soon they flushed a pair of lean rabbits, and Musketabah knocked one over with an arrow. Tyeema missed his shot.

"You should practice with the rifle," Musketabah told him, scooping up the dead rabbit. "With it, you might do better. Unless the noise should frighten you too greatly."

Tyeema had been staring moodily at the ground, but his patience snapped then. He turned with rage in his heart, and then saw that Musketabah was grinning at him in a lazy, arrogant, and wholly engaging way. And Musketabah tweaked the rabbit's ears. "Well," he said critically, "no brother of this one could have helped me count coup on three enemies. That took a kind of courage, I suppose. Yes, and you have good brains, Tyeema. But you're slow as a turtle. Why, that old Winnebago almost killed you. If Musketabah hadn't been there, the white man would have killed you."

"Yes," Tyeema said. "But—"

"And you missed your rabbit," Musketabah added with satisfaction.

What was the use? "Yes," said Tyeema, "and by the length of a tall man's arm."

"I thought so," Musketabah said agreeably. "But my brother will have a share of my rabbit."

Born on a seventy-two-thousand acre ranch in New Mexico, Tom W. Blackburn began writing for Western pulp magazines in the 1930s, graduated to slick-paper periodicals in the 1940s, and finally turned to writing novels and motion-picture, radio, and television scripts. He was the author of the screenplay for Walt Disney's The Saga of Davy Crockett, *as well as the lyrics for the famous* Ballad of Davy Crockett. *Tense and realistic, "Arrows Fly Westward" is just one example of his sure hand with the Western short story.*

Arrows Fly Westward

Tom W. Blackburn

A *man in bronze astride a painted pony, Longbow rode* into the camp of the hunters. He rode unhurriedly, erect and proud, as was fitting. But there was no leisureliness in his mind. His errand was important.

Among his people, there were two ways a friendly visitor was greeted. If he was known and respected, the chief of the encampment would go forth to meet him. If he was unknown or held in little respect, a younger brave, a boy—even a woman, if need be—met him and escorted him to the lodge of the chief.

But the men in this camp were not of his people. They were of a different kind and were governed by different customs. Therefore he rode without escort nearly to the fire in the center of the camp before he pulled up.

His father would have remained mounted until properly greeted. Longbow did not wait for that courtesy. He swung down and put out his hand to Herman Danby. The hunter met the grip lightly and dropped it at once.

"You wanted to see me?" Longbow suggested.

"How's meat this season?"

"Meat—you mean the buffalo?"

Danby grinned at his companions.

"See?" he asked. "Acts dumb, don't he? Dumb as any Indian. But he's smart. Smart as hell." He turned back to Longbow. "Sure I mean buffalo. Good herds running out here this year?"

Longbow did not like the question, although he had anticipated it. Two seasons past, when the soldiers had last passed through, it had been agreed that as long as there was peace, the buffalo would—as they had since the beginning—belong to Longbow's people alone. Still, the gods had been generous this year and there were many animals upon the grass. This was something Danby and his companions must have already seen. Untruth would accomplish nothing. He nodded.

Danby chafed his hands.

"Won't be for long," he said. "Know that, don't you? Not with them wagons yonder on the Horse Creek bottoms. They'll clean out every hide and bone in a couple of seasons. Take over the water and turn the sod under. What they don't kill for winter meat'll drift off with water and grass gone. What we want to know is what you're going to do about them wagons, Longbow?"

Longbow spread his hands.

"They have come in peace. They make no war. If they plow a few patches of grass and take a few hides, what can be done? There are always the soldiers—"

"Don't play palaver with me," Danby said. "No need for us to go dodging around each other for a couple of hours before we get down to brass tacks. Those settlers on Horse Creek have got your whole tribe backed into a corner. When it comes down to starving—and you know as well as I do that ain't far off—your people'd as soon fight soldiers as anybody else. What you going to do about them wagons?"

"They will leave," Longbow said.

Danby chuckled.

"Or else, eh? So I figured. But they're a strong party. Plenty of men, plenty of guns. Too many for you to run off on your own."

This was fact. Longbow saw no point in denying it. His was no longer a strong tribe. Because it had been agreed with the soldiers, the elders would not permit men of fighting age to trade with smugglers for sufficient powder and guns to arm themselves properly. The elders had promised the soldiers peace, and peace did not prosper when young men had weapons for war.

"You savvy figures," Danby went on. "Got a head on your shoulders. Fact is, way you think you're about the least Indian of any redskin I ever saw."

Longbow did not care for this. It was true he did understand the multiplication of numbers. He had learned this because he could see value in the knowledge. He had learned other matters, as well. And he understood how Danby and some others of his stamp might think him a renegade from his own blood because of that. But they made a great mistake if they believed Longbow, son of a chief for three generations, was not Indian to the last breath of his life.

"Figure it out, Longbow," Danby said. "There's maybe fifty families over there on Horse Creek. And I hear there's another string on the way. Say a buffalo a week for each family, and that don't count carcasses spoilt or killed for hides. Adds up to maybe three thousand head killed off before snow. Add the rumpus clumsy hunters raise with a herd and see what happens to your meat right quick!"

Longbow nodded. The numbers were correct. He had been over them often enough in his own mind. Danby leaned confidentially forward.

"Me and the boys have got an order for five hundred hides. It's a short haul from here, and the herd's easy to get to. Losing five hundred head to hunters that don't stampede the rest don't amount to much. And your people will get what they can use of the meat. And we've got a few extra rifles we might leave behind. A sight less damage than the wagon men.''

"An early blizzard might kill five hundred buffalo," Longbow said.

"At no profit to anyone," Danby agreed. "Give us leave to take our hides, and we'll give you a hand with those wagons. Every man jack of us is worth twenty of the wildest-riding Indians you ever saw. Dig us a little face clay. Give us some feathers and some old robes to wear. We'll ride with you and the young men in your village. We'll paint thick and won't be recognized. Most of your bunch can stay in camp. Make it look like raiders from up north. That way the soldiers won't be able to pin it on you and Horse Creek will be clear again."

Longbow did not think of the soldiers. He did not think of the agreement the elders had made with them. He had seen treaties broken before now when there was injustice which could be remedied in no other way. He did not think of the wagon men and the blood of their families enriching sod no plow would have a chance to touch. The wagon men were intruders, taking that which did not belong to them merely because the land was not marked off with little stakes according to their custom.

He thought only of Herman Danby and his hunters. They were willing to ride against their own kind in masquerade for the right to make a small profit from a few buffalo hides. It was for this that Danby had sent for him, and it was evil. He shook his head.

Danby shrugged.

"All right then, we'll make our peace with the wagons. Don't suppose they much like redskins camped almost in sight of them anyway. They'll like it a lot less when me and the boys get through telling them what kind of redskins you are. We can tell it pretty scary, Longbow. Add our guns to theirs, and we can run you off or wipe you out to the last squaw."

This also was truth. Wagon men would fight for clodded earth as an Indian fought for grass. But they fought the most fiercely when they believed their families were in danger. And the soldiers would believe them when they would not believe an Indian. It was a hard choice, but Longbow shook his head again.

"Suit yourself," Herman Danby said. "Better start your camp moving. We want those hides, and we're going to get them!"

Longbow vaulted astraddle his horse. The animal danced nervously as though this hunters' camp sickened it. Longbow checked the horse a moment, looking down at Danby. There was no need for words. The look alone spoke eloquently. It was a warrior's warning from a man who would not warn twice.

Longbow had not looked into the drain of Horse Creek since the arrival of the wagons. It was in his blood to hate cooking fires whose smoke always rose from the same place. But he rode steadily now toward the encampment of the wagon men.

It appeared Danby had spoken the truth when he said others were expected. The string of clumsy vehicles had outspanned, but they were still in temporary camp, as though waiting for more of their kind. Longbow eyed the scene with a raider's wisdom, measuring its strength. Danby had been right in that also. If Danby's hunters joined the wagons, there would be no standing against them.

He rode straight for the lead wagon, finding it easily by watching the movement of the camp as he approached. This one wagon was the hub to and from which people moved— toward which they all seemed to turn. He saw men reach quietly into tilts for guns as he rode among them. He ignored these. His attention was on the wide, bearded man who sat upon the tongue of the central wagon.

Longbow rode up to him. Because these were strangers and he had not been summoned among them, this time he remained upon his horse.

"I am Longbow," he said.

The bearded man rose to his feet.

"I am John Chandler," he said. " 'Light down."

Longbow swung his leg over and slid down. The bearded man sat back down on the wagon tongue and made a place beside him. Longbow took the offered seat.

"I do not think it is a good time to waste words," he said. "You must leave this valley."

The man beside him smiled a little in his eyes, but his features remained grave under his beard. Longbow understood that this demand, voiced by a single Indian, had amused the chief of the wagons. But the chief of the wagons had a chief's dignity. He did not laugh. This was good.

"We have promised the soldiers there will be no war," Longbow explained. "That is the reason you must leave this valley."

"You are the chief?" the bearded man asked.

"No. My father does not ride to parleys. He makes council only in his own lodge."

The bearded man nodded as though this was reasonable even among his own people. He seemed to understand that the son of a chief was an important envoy.

"This was your land?" he inquired. "You have hunted here a long time?"

"Since the Great Rain. Our children will hunt here after us."

The bearded man shook his head as though he was both weary and sad. He called out, and there was a stir in the wagon behind him. The flap of the tilt opened, and a woman came out. She was young. As she climbed over the boxed seat and stepped to the ground, Longbow saw she had the strength and grace of a woman of his own people before the labors of life among the lodges had coarsened her.

He saw also that she looked at him with a frankness of interest which shocked him. It was his belief that young women should walk with downcast eyes in the company of men. But the interest pleased him. Since he was among her people and must in politeness abide by their customs, he returned it with equal frankness.

The girl smiled. The smile could be meant only for him. Others were not so close as to draw her attention. She carried a fold of paper in her hand. She handed it to the bearded man. He opened it, spread it upon his knee.

"Susan," he said gravely, "this is Longbow. Longbow, my daughter—" He looked up at the girl. "Longbow is from the camp of our neighbors—the camp of the old chief. He tells me that we are on his land and that we must move."

Quick concern rose in the girl's eyes. There was apprehension in them when they touched Longbow again. That made them not as beautiful as they had been. Longbow wished for another smile and tried to bring kindness to his face. The bearded man drew attention to the paper on his knee. Longbow bent over it.

The paper was a map. It was not a good one. Longbow knew this country, and there were many mistakes. Still it was carefully done in ink, and it would have taken a clever craftsman to make lines so clean on whitened buckskin.

For all its mistakes, it would do for parleying. John Chandler put his thick finger down on a place where a square of red lines enclosed the valley of Horse Creek. He put his finger then on some writing in one corner.

"This map was made in Washington," he said. "It says that the land inside this square belongs to the government. It says the government will give a piece of land to every man who will bring his family and make a home on it. It is good land. It is a gift. We want it. That is why we are here."

The bearded man was not angry. He was patient. He was showing courtesy. Longbow was appreciative of these things. He wished to repay in kind.

"It is good land," he agreed. "But not for the plow. It is a good thing to have a gift too. But the government cannot give you this place to make your homes. It does not belong to the government. It belongs to us."

The bearded man looked up.

"We did not make this map. We did not say this land was free for the taking. We are not the government. You should make this talk in Washington."

"What man can make his voice heard across a hundred rivers?" Longbow asked. "I say the truth. I think I can talk with you, but I cannot talk with the government. It sends only soldiers to deal with my people. We do not like the soldiers' words."

John Chandler shrugged and folded up the map. There was sullen distrust in the eyes of some of the men now gathered about the wagon. Longbow saw it, but he hoped he could yet make them understand.

Three or four buckets of water sat under the wagon, carried up from the creek and stored there against need. Longbow bent and lifted two of these. The daughter of the wagon chief was close at hand, watching him with keen interest and near to smiling again. Perhaps she could grasp what others could not.

"You bring plows," he said. "This is not the land of the plow. It is the land of the arrow. It is the land of the grass and the animals which feed on the grass. You would turn that grass under, yet the gods were wise when they planted it here. Look!"

With a quick motion, he upended one of the buckets. The cascade of water struck the mat of grass underfoot, splashed, and ran among the roots almost as clear as it came from the pail.

"That is rain," he said. "However hard it falls, it feeds but does not destroy. But plow under the grass, then see!"

He flung up the other bucket, sending its contents onto a bare patch of ground from which the grass had been worn by the traffic of the camp. The water bit deep into the bare earth, gouging a hole and running off in a thick, mud-laden stream. Longbow pointed his finger at the gouge and the wash of mud.

"When the sun has dried the water, dust is left, waiting for the wind to carry it away. See how it is? It is not land for you. It belongs to my people. You must go!"

The girl looked thoughtfully at the mud, but the bearded man stood up.

"Tell your father we have come to stay," he said. "We

will try to be good neighbors if you will have it that way. But we can be bad enemies, too, if we have to. Tell him that, Longbow.''

Longbow shrugged. He supposed he had known that to expect understanding was to expect too much. These people had a government and they had soldiers. They had also a thirst for land. They could not see justice because of that. They could not see the wisdom of the gods. But it had been a thing he had to do. He had wanted to remember, when ugly times came, that he had done this thing. Well, it was done. And in addition, now, he would have another memory. The daughter of the wagon chief had smiled at him.

It was the burden of old men that they were crotchety and ill of temper, just as it was their value that they were wise. And some retained a hunger for young women beyond their years. The thin-flanked she-coyote who was his father's third wife met Longbow at the fringe of the meadow where he left his horse with the camp herd.

She met him with mockery and unpleasantries, for she resented an unmarried son who was a grown man in her husband's lodge. The old chief was calling for that son, she said. He had been calling and cursing to himself through the whole day. This time, she thought, Longbow would learn that the old man, for all his age and the inactivity of his declining years, was still the chief.

The woman followed Longbow through the village, pouring out her high-pitched harangue, covering him with such embarrassment and humiliation as she could. He would have struck her as she deserved but would not risk further anger at his father's hands. As it was, half the camp was sure to believe he was marching in to punishment for some misdeed.

There was severity and displeasure in the old man's eyes when Longbow entered his father's lodge.

"I believed it was agreed we would not treat with white men," the chief said.

"I rode in peace," Longbow offered.

"Our peace is made with the soldiers," the old man answered shortly. "These hunters come for hides. The wagon men come for land. But we do not have to treat with them."

"It is better to meet with the devils of wind and thunder than to perish in the storm," Longbow said. "We have broken our arrows with the soldiers. But these are not soldiers. We do not have peace with them. I went to talk of that."

Longbow wanted to tell his father about the piece of paper John Chandler had spread out on his knee. He wanted to tell him that Herman Danby knew that whatever the soldier peace, the wagons on Horse Creek were there to stay. He wanted to tell him of the remedy Danby had offered, the threat he had made. But the old man was set in his ways, stubborn in his beliefs. He would say the hunters were renegades whom only a fool would believe. He would say the wagon men were fools who would be made to go away when the soldiers came again. That had been the terms of the peace, and it was the curse of men of honor that they should believe implicitly in the honor of others.

Longbow left his father's lodge and moved unhappily through the encampment. There were smiles. Many had heard the young wife's screeching. There was humor in knowing even the chief's son could be called to task as a boy might be. There was also a quiet ease among the lodges which rubbed the rawness of Longbow's spirit.

These were his people. Legend boasted they had not always been a quiet kind. They had known many enemies, yet they had survived. But now they were upon an evil time. Because of the soldiers' peace of which his father boasted, they smiled among themselves while the worst enemies of all slept upon their grass.

He was not thinking of war. They were too few. Even this enemy was too strong. But Longbow was thinking of battle. It was the nature of white men to do much fighting with their heads. It was their nature to employ trickeries and clever snares. To survive, a man must learn the tricks of any enemy.

Moving back to the meadow, Longbow caught up a fresh horse and rode again into the ridges.

It had not been Longbow's conscious intent to ride again toward the wagons on Horse Creek. It was more that he needed to feed his mind, prod it to greater effort, and sight of the wagons, waiting for the balance of their number to come up before fanning out to take root on the grass, was a powerful stimulant.

He rode in a wide circle to a sandy headland on the far side of the valley. He tethered his horse on the rear slope and went over the crest afoot. He found a screen of brush which gave him shelter and from which he could see the camp of the wagon men. Sitting down here, he gave his thoughts free rein.

Directly a thin plume of dust came up out of a draw and threaded in among the wagons. He recognized the party beneath it as Danby's hunters. Longbow scowled. It was the nature of white men to make no delay. Danby wanted the hides of five hundred buffalo. Alone, his hunters were too few to raid the herds without permission. But allied with the wagon men, no permission would be necessary.

Danby was the kind of man who made war with his own hands. If Danby and his men were not about with talk of danger to the wagons from Longbow's people—if they spread no rumor of taken scalps and swift raids and horrors upon women and children—Longbow thought he might persuade the wagon people to listen to him. The bearded wagon chief had seemed a reasonable man. In a few more talks he might even agree to send for the soldiers so a just settlement could be had between them.

But Danby—Danby wanted no soldiers and would take no chances on such delay. Danby would claim more talk was a trick. An Indian trick. He would talk of white women raped by clay-painted warriors and children's scalps hanging in the lodges of a savage enemy. All this for the right to kill five hundred buffalo!

Longbow was breaking a twig into many small fragments when a horse and rider appeared, skirting a fold in the ridge, quite near at hand. It was the daughter of the wagon chief, and she was alone. She rode well and unhurriedly. Longbow saw she was studying the country, relishing it as he often did. He rose slowly upright.

The girl's horse sensed him first. It danced nervously. The rider checked her mount and began to look about with the unease of one who senses something she does not understand. Longbow did not move. The nervous horse worked much closer before the girl's eyes, sweeping the slope, singled him out.

She started visibly, then rode slowly forward, reining up before Longbow. She smiled and looked back at the country below.

"Beautiful, isn't it?" she said.

Longbow did not make immediate answer.

"Love it, don't you?" she added.

It seemed a curious question. A man did not love land. Love was something else. One was rooted in the land of his birth. One would die on it. One would die for it. But one did not love it. Still, there was beauty, and this woman from the wagons saw it.

"I do, too," she said. "Isn't there room for both of us?"

This Longbow could answer.

"If our peoples were the same," he agreed. "But we are different."

"Yet much alike."

"We breathe alike," Longbow admitted cautiously.

The girl laughed, a warm and friendly thing there in the sun. She nodded, raised her arm in salute, and rode downslope toward the wagons. Longbow watched her go, wondering.

He sat on the slope until dusk. Finally his patience was rewarded. The dust which had filed in among the wagons earlier formed again and trailed out from the camp. Longbow remounted, cut at an angle, and skirted the dust, drawing closer to it with purposeful steadiness.

Darkness came while he rode thus.

Using the noise of their approach to cover his own, Longbow trailed Herman Danby and his companions into stalking distance of their camp. He left his pony in shelter at a safe distance and pressed on afoot. Two of the hunters had remained in camp in the absence of the others. They had supper pots on over the fire. One accosted Danby as he rode into the firelight. Longbow heard the words clearly.

"How did you do, Manny?"

Danby's answer was a sullen, angry blurring of sound. Longbow made no meaning from it. He judged, however, that Danby had not fared as well as he had anticipated among the wagons. Before he would let them at their meal, the hunter gathered his whole crew before him and spoke in swift, low tones. The whole attitude of the crouching circle of men was that of a council of war.

If Longbow could have approached closer, he might have overheard. But Danby's men were skillful enough hunters. They had been careful in selecting their camp. There was no shelter behind which an eavesdropper could crouch.

Danby left a guard posted and turned the rest of his crew in. Longbow began to feel hunger and a desire to sleep himself. This increased as the night wore on, but duty remained. Three hours short of dawn, obviously at an agreed time, the guard woke his companions. They dressed and saddled in the darkness. With Danby in the lead, every man filed out of the camp.

Longbow gave them suitable lead, then followed, silent and unseen as the soft dawn wind. The hunters rode steadily in a sweeping circle. In half an hour Longbow realized they were taking this course to avoid the village of his people. In another half hour it was plain they were driving for a buffalo herd on the slopes to the north.

For a little he wondered if Danby, having run against luck

in stirring the wagon people against his father's village, had determined to make his buffalo kill and risk getting out. If so, it was folly. Longbow knew his people. At the first sound of slaughter among the herds, they would know the peace was broken. Soldiers or no soldiers, they would arm and ride in swift retribution. There would be no escape for Danby and his hunters. Surely the man knew that.

But Danby did not intend to kill the hides he wanted this morning. Only enough for bait. When they reached the grazing herd, a few of the hunters cut in, firing with practiced speed. When half a dozen of the animals were down, Danby shouted and the hunters withdrew. Danby issued orders. Most of the hunters, riding abreast and allowing their ponies to leave plain tracks on the sod, rode straight and hard toward the wagon camp. Three of their number, keeping to firm and trackless ground, headed back toward their own camp.

Longbow was briefly puzzled, then understood. Flattening along the back of his pony, he raced these three for their destination. If he could reach their camp ahead of them— A tight smile pulled at his lips.

Danby was forcing the issue, but white men were not the only ones who understood trickery. The main force of the hunters was leaving a wide track for Longbow's people to follow from the slaughtered and abandoned buffalo to the wagons. It would be believed that the wagon men had ridden into the herd for wanton dawn sport. And for such useless, wasteful killing there must be payment. The men from the village would believe the wagon men guilty unless it could be proved to them the hunters had been absent from their camp at a time when they could claim they all had been sleeping.

Longbow's pony ran like an antelope. He kept a fold in the ridges between himself and the three hunters hurrying back to their blankets to establish an alibi for the others. Little by little he forged ahead of them. But he had no great lead upon them when he flung down beside the ashes of their nearly dead fire.

Working furiously, he seized bedding rolls, extra saddle gear, flaying equipment, spare ammunition—everything upon which he could lay his hands. He piled all onto the smoldering coals. A blanket began to smoke, a piece of leather curled from the heat. But flame would not catch.

Glancing up, Longbow saw Danby's three men lope out of a cut, stare at the thin column of smoke above the camp, and come on hard. Dropping to his knees, Longbow blew frantically at the smoldering heap, trying to fan it to consuming flame. But the coals were ash-laden and stubborn. The foremost of the three hunters jerked his rifle up and fired. The ball gouged dust a yard from Longbow. He flinched but continued to blow like a madman.

Another shot plowed into the camp. A third came so close Longbow could feel its lethal tug. Suddenly the rolling smoke exploded into flame. Fire leaped from the whole heap of camp gear, the flames burning indelible proof onto every piece of gear that none of the hunters had been in their camp to protect their possessions from a single raider.

Bounding to his feet, Longbow raced for his horse. The well-trained animal swung obediently so that he could make a vaulting mount. Reckless satisfaction pulsed in Longbow. But one of the hunters had pulled up in sudden immobility. From motionless saddle, the man fired his rifle again.

Longbow saw the flash of flame. He also thought he saw the missile which struck him. It was not possible to see a bullet. He knew this. Yet certainly a great black thing flung through the air, blocking his vision, and struck him a savage, crushing blow on the head which flung him limply into a great pit of oblivion.

After an interminable time, Longbow became aware of painful motion. His head throbbed, and he appeared to be bound in such a way that circulation was impeded in a dozen places. But it was a trait among his people that pain could not override caution.

The blow on his head must have been a glancing strike

from the hunter's shot. He had fallen, been taken prisoner, bound securely. All this some hours past. It had barely been dawn when he fired the gear in the hunters' camp. The heat of the sun against his body spoke of noonday now.

He was doubled loosely across the cantle of a saddle. A man rode the seat before him. He could hear leather creak with the rider's weight. He could hear the sound of other horses moving along nearby. He opened his eyes cautiously.

The countryside reeled a little, then steadied. The party bearing him was following a draw into the Horse Creek bottoms. He caught a glimpse of the wagon camp below. It had altered since he had last seen it. The irregular previous pattern was gone. The wagons had been moved into a tight defensive circle. All save one wagon, apart. A patch of burned grass surrounded the charred remnants of its charred wheels and body timbers. He could see alert guards posted about the camp.

Watching carefully from under nearly closed lids, Longbow studied the riders escorting him. They were Herman Danby and his crew of hunters. And they were men well satisfied with themselves. Why not? They had turned his own raid on their camp to good use. It was a fortune of war, Longbow supposed, and Longbow accepted it as such, waiting for a better time to betray a sign of returning consciousness.

Danby's party was challenged at the edge of the wagon camp. Danby demanded to see John Chandler and was permitted to lead his company and its prisoner into the circle of wagons. There they faced Chandler, his daughter, and the outraged wagon people.

"You set yourself up great shakes at reading the sign those Indians left when they fired that wagon on you this morning," Danby said. "Took the word of the kid supposed to be watching your horses that it was whites instead of sneaking redskins. Made it pretty plain you figured we might have done the job to stir up trouble with the Indians so we'd have a clean shot at their buffalo. We didn't like that, Chandler!"

"Didn't expect you to," the wagon chief said. "Nor to have the gall to come back here. State your business, Danby."

"Them redskins wasn't just against you," the hunter said. "Aimed to clear us all out. Hit our camp, too. Only we got one, in spite of the bad light. That do for proof?"

Chandler came forward, turned Longbow's head, and looked at him.

"He's wounded," the wagon chief said. "You lugged him across the hills, trussed like that?"

"Won't matter, when you've had your look," Danby said. "Only one way to handle raiding redskins. Still think we lied?"

There was a long pause.

"No," John Chandler said finally.

"Then maybe you'll listen to joining up with us and taking the fight out of those Indians before they take another swipe at us."

A number of the wagon men spoke up, angrily in agreement. Listen—they'd be damned fools not to. And so would Chandler. As train captain he had a duty to every soul with him. The Indians had struck first. The peace he had been talking about—the peace they had made with the cavalry— plainly didn't amount to a hoot in hell. The thing to do was to strike back at once, seize the initiative, and hold it. Not that anybody held with renegades like Danby and his hunters, but they had good guns and they could shoot. And they were white.

"You know how I feel," the wagon chief said. "I'd send a good man on a fast horse for the cavalry. I'd take a stand here and wait for them to show up and straighten this out. I came here to raise walls and turn a furrow, not to fight. But I'm one man. What the rest of you want, I'll order. You got a plan, Danby?"

The hunter dismounted.

"Get that carcass down and roll it under a wagon, out of the way," he ordered his men. "We'll get to it later."

He moved away with John Chandler. Callous hands lifted

Longbow from the saddle. They dumped him roughly on the ground and rolled him under a wagon with carelessly prodding boot-toes. The harsh treatment set his head to throbbing again. He fought that until thought began to move steadily in his skull again.

He stirred in his helplessness. A quick, indrawn breath sounded, near at hand. He opened his eyes a little. Susan Chandler, her skirts caught up in one hand, was running toward another wagon. He realized she had been standing close, watching him. He thought she was running to her father and Danby to tell them the Indian under the wagon was far from dead.

Longbow tensed, waiting for the alarm. It did not come. The girl came back quickly, a rag of clean cloth and a basin in her hands. She crawled under the wagon to him. There was outraged kindness in her eyes. A touch of the smile he had seen before was about her whitened lips. He closed his eyes again.

While cloth and cleansing water gently explored his wound, he thought swiftly. It was good to keep his eyes closed. If they were open, they must look deep into the eyes of this woman. That would bring further trouble for both. They were of different peoples. There was no hope for what either might see in the mind of the other.

He knew he must not think of her as a woman. Her hair was the color of the sun. Among his kind a woman's hair was raven black. He must remember this was not a matter of a man and a girl. At best it was an omen. It was proof to him and to his people that among these wagons were some who were not like Herman Danby. It was proof there were some who were not altogether like the wagon chief too.

The wagon chief was a fair man, but he was a worshiper of land. And his justice was tempered by the safety of his own kind. But there was compassion in this woman who was his daughter. Therefore there would be compassion in others, even when more wagons came. There was hope then. Not among them all. Not all at once. But in some coming day there could be the peace of which the soldiers talked. And it would be for his own people as well as these people of the plow.

Longbow clung to that hope. It was the first he had known. As these people changed, so would his own. They had but to understand also. They had but to learn, to see that this grass had once been a place for Sioux and Blackfoot and Crow and could in time become a place for Indian and wagon man. If he could look at this woman as he had done and she at him, perhaps that time was no great space away. This he thought. This he believed.

The bathing of his wound refreshed him. Longbow stirred again in a gesture of gratitude. The girl spoke softly.

"Can you ride?"

He nodded.

"Then go quickly when I tell you. My horse is behind this wagon. Go to your camp. Get your people away. When it is dark, they intend to burn you out. They are afraid. There must be another valley, other buffalo. Go there. Wait. Do not fight. Someday they will pay you for the harm. They are good people, but they listen to the hunters because they are afraid. Make your people understand that."

"I do not know," Longbow said. "My father—"

"Make him see. Make him!"

The woman crawled from beneath the wagon and was gone. There was much activity in the camp, much talk and gathering of guns. In the bustle, Longbow lay forgotten beneath the wagon. The sun set, and a clanging bar of iron called the wagon people to their evening meal. The woman returned then.

"Now," she whispered. "Go!"

Longbow rolled over. He could see behind the wagon the hoofs of the horse she had promised. He crawled to them, slipped the tie, and pulled himself up. He felt awkward in the unaccustomed saddle, built for a small woman and with the stirrups set for her. Longbow was not a saddle man. He bore the galling of the tree and disdained the shortened stirrups, riding with his feet hanging straight down, after the fashion of his people.

He eased toward the perimeter of the camp, passing within yards of a guard, unheard as a shadow and unseen because the man was not on guard against danger at his back. In a brief handful of minutes, Longbow was over a sheltering rise and riding like the wind.

The fire in the chief's lodge burned low. There was silence when Longbow finished his tale and the urging of his plea. Here and there an old head nodded. The chief's son sang a tale so that it lived before one's eyes. He pleaded a counsel with the tongue of the wise. But the thing he urged. Ai! It was against the old laws. It stung the old pride. Was that the road to wisdom?

The young men held their tongues, but their eyes were hot. The old men had fought in their time. Were they children—women, even—that they could not fight now in their own time? The low embers of the fire snapped to themselves, and all heads turned toward the thin, straight-backed figure of the old chief. Each man believed himself wise, but the old man was the wisest of them all.

Longbow watched his father's face with the others. At length the chief spoke.

"We have heard," he said to Longbow. "You tell what you have seen and heard in a straight way. You were brave in injury, cautious in danger. You risked your life for your people and dealt honorably with the foreign woman. These are the marks of a man. But they do not make you wise. Only the years do that."

The old man paused and looked about the council.

"I have seen many years, many times. I have seen great days, listened long to wise men. But after all this, I know but little. We have lived long here. We have fought enemies and endured hardships and fathered children and hunted beyond any memory. But we have not grown fat, nor are there as many lodges among us as there were in the old times. Not as many children. Not as many warriors. Our pony herds grow smaller, and there is one buffalo where once there were ten.

"I think then that the old ways are not the best. I think the bravest man is not always the first in battle. I think there is courage in galling honor with the sting of running when the enemy cries fight. I think there is strength in the patience to wait when the blood is hot for revenge. It is easy to cry war. Only the strong can cry peace."

The old man rose stiffly to his feet. He faced Longbow and placed his hands upon his shoulders.

"My son, I cannot weigh your counsel, but we have taken mine long enough. I only know one thing. We win no victory if we grow less every season. Speak. Your words are mine."

In his turn, Longbow looked about the council. He saw some who would stand against him, now and at later times. He saw some who believed him a fool. But they were his own kind. They were not the enemy he feared. He could deal with them. And time would make even that easier. More wagon men would come. He understood that. But in time they also would grow wiser. In time there would be more among them like the woman whose eyes had told him so much and so little.

He raised his voice with the authority of a chief.

"Break camp," he said. "Strike the lodges. We go westward, toward the mountains. That way lies peace. We fight still, but let patience be our arrow!"

A potlatch was a unique contest among the Alaskan Indians in which one chief would try to give away or destroy more of his belongings than an enemy chief could give away or destroy of his belongings. Edward Wellen's suspenseful tale of just such a contest between a white trapper and a Kwakiutl chief offers full particulars. Wellen has published many short stories over the past twenty-five years, most of them mystery/suspense and science fiction, with occasional excursions into the Western. His work, as "Potlatch" proves, is consistently fresh and inventive.

Potlatch

Edward Wellen

*E*rnie Emmett stabbed his paddle savagely into the stream and glared back. Hard in his wake, Chuckaluck Gaines was cutting the silky water delicately, letting the current do most of the work. The stream widened and Emmett thrust even more fiercely into the flow, more to vent his rage than to lengthen water between their canoes.

Ripples warned of rocks and Ernie Emmett threw aside his rage for the moment to ride this stretch of the river safely. The canoe answered poorly but Emmett wore a hard grin as he shaved through. It was the top-heavy load of furs that made the canoe unwieldy. Then his eyes smoldered and he looked back.

The pile of furs in Chuckaluck's canoe came to barely half that in Emmett's—but it was Ernie who had set out all the traps, snowshoed around and around the trapline all winter, skinned all the pelts. Chuckaluck showed when the winter's catch was just about in; he traveled awfully light for an Alaskan winter but Ernie Emmett had more manners than to ask what led Chuckaluck to quit the gold camp in such obvious haste.

Warming his neat hands, Chuckaluck stayed close to the stove in Emmett's cabin; he sipped Ernie's coffee and watched approvingly while Ernie's rough hands mended traps, cut firewood, skinned. He watched, and weighed the mounting pile of skins with his eyes, then offhandedly suggested a friendly game of cards to pass the long night—and somehow won a third of Ernie's catch before Ernie caught on that they were playing for keeps.

Chuckaluck had negotiated the ripples and now looked up. He met Emmett's glance and gave a friendly wave. Ernie Emmett scowled and faced forward.

They broke out into the open water of the fjord and Emmett prowed toward Totem. Shortly the settlement would round into sight and Emmett's sense of excitement quickened. He wondered how much Totem had grown. Whatever its size, brawling Totem would be a ghost town if Yukon Flo weren't waiting. He felt his beard—he'd have to trim that fur some. He grinned. Chuckaluck had skinned him; still, Emmett could afford to cut up twice as many didoes as his old rival Chuckaluck—and nothing could change that in the mile they had yet to cover.

Ernie Emmett shivered in a sudden cold wind and faced about. Chuckaluck smiled and plunked at his paddle as if at a banjo; it dripped golden notes in the lowering sun. But Emmett was looking beyond Chuckaluck Gaines. The sky seemed all at once menacing. The water was whitening behind them. Williwaw. A squall, rushing seaward down the slope, was bearing swiftly down on them.

One dip of the paddle told Emmett it was worse than useless to try cutting across the line of the williwaw toward shore. He barely kept from capsizing. Best try to ride it out—a poor best. One thing might work, though.

He back-paddled to let Chuckaluck pull abreast and even

so had to shout, "Let's lash canoes together. Might keep us from turning over."

Chuckaluck's face had paled but it gleamed wetly in a smile. "Sure—for a dozen skins."

Emmett stared in outrage. "It's your only chance too."

Chuckaluck turned a shiver into a shrug. "You know me. I'm a gamblin' man."

Voice tight, Ernie Emmett said, "Half dozen."

"What skin you tryin' to save? Them or your own?"

"Both."

Chuckaluck Gaines held his canoe steady with difficulty and yelled, "Done."

Emmett cut the thongs tying a bundle of furs and fastened the canoes together, lashed paddles holding them squarely apart, forming an outrigger. He paused for one instant when lightning showed Chuckaluck laughing. Emmett damned himself to eternal torrential darkness, like that which had fallen over them, for letting Chuckaluck skin him again. He finished the lashing, then huddled in the lee of his furs and swore mightily that no one and no thing should strip him of one skin more—if he came out of this with a whole one of his own.

He came out of it on a gravelly shore, out of a dream of unending bailing to keep from swamping. He raised up and his aching arms told him the dream was memory.

His furs. He looked around wildly.

The rocky shore had staved in the canoes but the precious cargoes seemed intact. Then it struck him that Chuckaluck was missing and, strangely, he had a feeling of loss. At heart, Chuckaluck hadn't really been too bad.

Then the soul-warming smell of boiling coffee drew Emmett to the sheltered side of a huge boulder. Chuckaluck Gaines grinned up from a driftwood fire.

" 'Bout time," Chuckaluck said.

Ernie Emmett scowled. Chuckaluck's grin widened. Chuckaluck stretched, grimacing comically, and handed Ernie the pot. Emmett downed searing coffee gratefully and after a moment followed Chuckaluck back to the wreckage.

He stopped and stared disbelievingly. Chuckaluck was kneeling. It restored Emmett's faith in human nature—in Chuckaluck's nature, rather—when he saw the attitude was not one of thanksgiving, at least not for deliverance from danger. Chuckaluck was reverently selecting skins from Emmett's pile.

He grew aware of Emmett and put on a hurt look to answer Emmett's glare. "I waited till you come to, didn't I? The six you owe me, remember?"

Ernie Emmett remembered and winced. "All right." He watched, tight-lipped, then shouted, "Not that one. I'm savin' that ermine for Yukon Flo." He bit his lip; he hadn't meant to say it.

But Chuckaluck wasn't laughing. "What *I* had in mind. Sure is a beauty." He stroked it, then sighed at the implacable furrowing of Emmett's brow and set the ermine down and chose a silver fox.

A shadow fell. Emmett snapped his head up, looked around. Indians.

The smoke, furling and unfurling, had drawn them. Ernie's hand furtively reached for his knife, then relaxed. Kwakiutl, by the look of them. Not dangerous except when in mourning, and he saw no signs of mourning.

So the night and day of blow had swept them down through Hecate Strait and dashed them on the northern coast of Vancouver Island. A far cry from Totem.

The Indians had grouped like an arrowhead aiming at Ernie Emmett and Chuckaluck Gaines. An old man with the bearing of a chief was the flinty tip. He eyed Emmett, Chuckaluck, the furs, and the canoes with insolent curiosity. A slender girl peered over his shoulder, warmth and a strange hope in her brown eyes.

Ernie Emmett made the sign of peace.

The old man's face didn't change. He spoke. The girl translated haltingly, her voice a waterfall.

She tried to soften the chief's words but Emmett felt their sting. "My father the great chief Wakiash does not like the ways of the white man. But he feels pity for you." Two old squaws came forward and threw a heavy blanket each at Emmett's feet. "He sees your blood is thin that you need many skins. He gives you these to help warm you."

Blood rushed to Emmett's face but he said nothing.

"My father wishes to speed you on your way back to where you belong." The other Indians were smiling; some laughed openly as two braves came bearing a magnificently carved and painted canoe. The braves set it down at Emmett's feet, careless of the blankets. This readiness could only mean that the Indians had watched the whites for a time before coming to encounter them. The old man's face cracked in a scornful smile and he spoke to his daughter.

"My father gives you his best canoe. He does not look for anything in return," she said.

By the time Emmett felt he had hold of his voice, and was ready to use it to mutter thanks, the Indians were gone.

Chuckaluck was grinning and rubbing his hands together. He froze and raised an eyebrow on seeing the look on Emmett's face. "What's wrong? Something for nothing—couldn't want a better deal."

Ernie Emmett shook his head and spoke slowly. "The old fox was baiting us, trying to trap us into a potlatch."

"Potlatch?"

"A Kwakiutl contest. You win when you give away or destroy more of your belongings than your enemy gives away or destroys of his."

Chuckaluck laughed. "I'd sure let my enemy win." He sobered quickly. "What makes you so positive the old man's our enemy?"

"Didn't you hear his talk? He was shaming us in front of his people." Ernie Emmett nodded. "He hates whites, all right."

"Why?"

Emmett shrugged. "We come in with steel traps, and some of us with poison, and the big game dies out. The Indian traps just to meet his wants. No, the chief knows our ways are the doom of his ways."

Chuckaluck Gaines glanced about uneasily. "Maybe we best load up and shove off."

Emmett shook his head, smiling wryly. "Comes to that, we're too wore out to outdistance them. No, he's won. He won't bother us. We can rest up till tonight—or even till morning if there's no stars tonight."

Emmett squatted and picked up a pebble. "Let him crow. I sure wasn't gonna let him badger me into letting loose of my furs." He threw the pebble into the water, winced, and rubbed his shoulder.

They didn't see any Indians the rest of the day. But at twilight, as they were bedding down, soft footfalls jerked them alert. It was the daughter of Wakiash.

She put up a hand for silence, looked around, and listened, then stole nearer. "You leave in the morning?"

Ernie Emmett nodded.

"Take me with you."

Ernie Emmett stared at her.

Chuckaluck was quick to step forward and play the gallant. "Why, my dear?" He held his head at a fawning, preening tilt.

"There is a young man of our tribe on the mainland."

Emmett hid a smile as Chuckaluck's face fell.

The girl, after a slight pause, went on half shyly, half boldly, "We wish to wed, but he is poor. My father knows how my heart is and has set a watch on the canoes so that I will not paddle away. I will hide under the skins and no one will know I go with you."

Emmett read in her eyes that this was no trick. But his head had started to shake no before she finished. Her eyes appealed. Doggedly, Emmett shook his heavy head no. He fumbled for words; they seemed to catch on his furred tongue.

"We can't betray your father's hospitality," he said. A slight smile showed him the girl knew as well as he did that hospitality was the wrong word—hostility was more like it, perverse hostility. But the end was the same; the chief had put the two white men in his debt.

Too proud for tears or further entreaty, she eyed him with scorn. "The white man fears to risk losing his furs." Her eyes dulled and her voice deadened. "My father tells us the old ways are best. It may be he is right." But there was spirit in her yet; her eyes blazed.

Ernie Emmett had steeled himself to suppress shame and rage at the father's words. Now, blinking a little, then rallying, Emmett bit down on the iron in his soul to take a tongue-lashing from the daughter. But she looked past him at Chuckaluck and remained silent. More than her words, it was her silence that troubled Emmett. Then she was gone, one with the gloom.

Chuckaluck eyed Emmett quizzically, then yawned. "Me for the hay." He rolled up in his blankets.

Emmett followed suit but was restless.

Chuckaluck rose on an elbow. "Got under your skin?"

Ernie Emmett said nothing but got up and walked the phosphorescent rim of the sea, kicking furiously at pebbles. He didn't know why he was letting the girl bother him. She had nothing to do with him and he had nothing to do with her.

Then why should he feel guilty? He told himself he didn't, and returned to where Chuckaluck lay snoring and turned in. Chuckaluck snored himself awake for a moment, then fell asleep once more. Soon Emmett himself lay sleeping. He dreamed; in his dream, voices were whispering, and he read into the whispering accusing words. But he said *No*, and the whispering stopped.

After wolfing down a soggy breakfast, Ernie Emmett and Chuckaluck shoved off. To Emmett's relief, the Indians, if they were watching, didn't show themselves. Surprisingly, Chuckaluck Gaines did his share of the paddling, if not more, and the shore thinned and faded.

They made toward the mainland, to take advantage of the eddy Emmett knew ran up the coast, and were well out on the Sound, when Chuckaluck glanced around, lost his smile, and redoubled the energy of his stroke.

Emmett looked back and his heart leaped like an uprivering salmon. Three canoes were speeding after them and he saw amid the flashing of paddles the flashing of weapons.

There was no hope of outstripping them and he told Chuckaluck so. They shipped their paddles and waited. Ernie Emmett edged his rifle to hand. "Wonder what they want?"

"I wonder," Chuckaluck said, forcing a smile.

His voice sounded strange but there wasn't time for Emmett to wonder at that. The lead canoe was drawing alongside. Wakiash stood in the bow.

Wakiash spoke. Emmett made a gesture of not understanding and looked for the girl but didn't see her in any of the boats. The chief spoke over his shoulder and a brave leaned forward and thrust a harpoon in among the furs. Emmett's face tightened and his hand curled to sweep up his rifle. Then his mouth flew open as the harpoon produced a yelp and the furs trembled alive.

The girl crept out from under and looked around. Wakiash spoke quietly. The girl shrank back momentarily, then recovered, and with the stiff grace of pride stepped into her father's canoe.

Eyeing Ernie Emmett narrowly, Wakiash spoke again to his daughter. She answered, her voice barely audible. Wakiash grunted, his eyes remaining on Emmett.

Her voice expressionless, the girl said, "I have told my father you did not know I had hidden under the skins."

Emmett knew the surprise on his face when the girl emerged had been too real for Wakiash to mistake it for acting. But what a man knows to be so and what he chooses to acknowledge to be so are often at variance.

Wakiash gave a sudden contemptuous wave of dismissal and the three canoes turned as one. Emmett felt himself at one and the same time relaxing in relief and flushing with anger. Then he forgot himself as he caught the despairing look the girl threw back at him, at the mainland, toward the lover she would never join. The canoes dwindled.

Chuckaluck Gaines breathed out, self-consciously breaking the silence. "Well, we got out of that all right. We've had our share of hard luck. From here on out it'll be cream.''

He watched Emmett out of the corner of his eye. Emmett remained gloomily unresponsive. Chuckaluck drew out a whistle carved in the likeness of an open-mouthed mask and softly lilted the melody of a ballad Yukon Flo often rendered.

''Where'd you get that?'' Emmett asked indifferently.

Chuckaluck held the wooden whistle out for Emmett to see. Emmett's interest quickened. It was Kwakiutl work. He eyed Chuckaluck with dawning suspicion. He had a shadowy notion of what had happened.

Chuckaluck hesitated, then said, ''Syah-an-cu-ti gave it to me.''

''Who?''

''The girl. If you have to know, we made a deal to stow her away, while you were sleeping.''

Ernie Emmett remembered the dream whispering.

Chuckaluck grew defensive under Emmett's gaze. ''I didn't do it just for the whistle. It was the romantic in me.''

Emmett stared at Chuckaluck unseeingly. The girl's despairing look backward rose before him. He told himself the sensible thing to do was to forget that look, to remember instead the joys of Totem that Chuckaluck had sought to conjure up with the whistle, the joys that were waiting, the joys that the furs would make his. But he knew he would never forget that look.

He knew a wiser man would shrug off the burden of that look, as a wiser man would laugh off the shame Wakiash had put on him. But he was what he was, and he swung the canoe around.

Chuckaluck paled in alarm. ''I don't know what you're aiming to do but don't drag me into it.''

Emmett eyed him briefly. ''I won't. Don't worry.''

Chuckaluck couldn't help worrying, angrily, bewilderedly, plaintively. ''Why the devil you heading back into sure trouble? Why you playing the fool? Why?''

* * *

Ernie Emmett entered the long house of Wakiash. Chuckaluck Gaines stumbled, on following him, for the Kwakiutl dug away the earth floor to a depth of one foot. Wakiash, sitting on a mat on one of the low wooden couches surrounding the fire, glanced up. His eyes widened slightly on the white men as though they had come down through the roof like Winter Dancers.

The slate pipe he was smoking, carved to represent a man in a canoe, didn't waver in his hand. His face remained fixed as the great faces carved on the stout posts supporting the ridgepole.

The air was close, fishy, rank, pungent with cedar smoke. Emmett's eyes accommodated to the smoke and the play of light and shadow and he made out Syah-an-cu-ti. "Tell Wakiash to raise the potlatch pole."

The girl caught her breath and translated the words; they struck fire in the chief's flinty eyes. The girl gave his answer. "Good. I will break your name. I will flatten you. You will die of shame."

Emmett smiled crookedly and made three trips to the canoe and back, fetching his possessions and heaping them beside the seat he took across from Wakiash. Chuckaluck sat on the sidelines, making it plain he was simply an interested observer. His share of the fur catch remained safely stowed aboard the canoe.

Wakiash spoke and four young men ladled vast quantities of valuable candlefish oil on the fire. The flames roared up, yet no one, Chuckaluck saw, moved back—that would have been to lose face—and he remained where he was, lost part of an eyebrow, and grinned at his neighbors.

Wakiash was smug as if he had just done a good stroke of business. "Do not ask for mercy."

Emmett saw Chuckaluck eyeing him with a pitying smile. His courage almost failed him. Then he nerved himself. He counted out his three dozen steel traps and thrust them under the fire. While the blaze wasn't hot enough to melt the metal, it was hot enough to ruin the temper; in any case, Emmett was sacrificing them.

Wakiash smiled scornfully. "Do not think you can put out my fire." A brave counted out eighty blankets and fed them to the flames. Wakiash eyed Emmett arrogantly. "Do not ask for mercy."

Emmett wasn't ready to ask for mercy but he felt like asking Wakiash to call it off. It hurt him to see sound goods go to waste. He knew the thought and sweat and care that went into the gathering and making and tending of things. He had made his gesture, he could call it quits now, he would let Wakiash have his triumph.

Instead he found himself hefting his rifle. He unloaded it, gave it a caressing look, then slung it into the fire. Even Wakiash drew in his breath a trifle. But Emmett did not look away from the charring stock.

Wakiash sent braves to break into pieces seven canoes and bring the pieces to heap upon the fire. The fire blazed but Wakiash, being a true chief, did not have his men remove the roof boards it threatened. "Do not ask for mercy."

Ernie Emmett buckled down to divesting himself of his riches—blankets, axe, knife, coffee pot, frying pan, grub, snowshoes. Then the furs. He deposited them on the fire by fifties, retaliating for every pouring of candlefish oil and immolating of blankets.

As the first of the furs began to scorch, Emmett unwillingly found himself thinking with furious jealousy of Chuckaluck, his share of furs intact, returning to Totem and Yukon Flo. He tried to put that thought away from him but found himself turning to face Chuckaluck.

Chuckaluck was eyeing him strangely, almost with compassion, it seemed to Emmett. But he couldn't be sure he had read it right, for Chuckaluck's face quickly woodened.

Emmett withdrew his gaze. He would show them all. "Do not ask for mercy," he told Wakiash.

Wakiash, when Syah-an-cu-ti translated it for him, laughed scornfully and came back with a punishing one hundred blankets.

At some time during the proceedings, and in spite of the

heat, Emmett felt a shiver of something like ecstasy. Some spirit was lifting him up and showing him that on the larger scale he was in a sense really sacrificing nothing—naked he had come into the world, naked he would go out. He had been led by an invisible hand to a point beyond regret. Then he grew aware that some other spirit was leading him past even that—destroying had become dangerously exhilarating. He came down to earth and held himself to matching Wakiash. It was no longer a matter of proving himself in Chuckaluck's eyes or the girl's eyes or even in the eyes of Wakiash. It was a matter of proving himself in his own eyes.

Wakiash had exhausted his candlefish oil, his blankets, his canoes. Emmett still had a dozen or so furs. Three copper sheets, each unique, each having its own name, each sacred in the history of the tribe, were the dearest possessions of Wakiash. His people valued these etched sheets of native copper at more than ten thousand blankets apiece. Wakiash made ready to destroy them.

The people stirred. The sound of shifting broke the flame-crackling silence. It was an uneasy moment, a moment of unvoiced protest if not of revolt. All knew that Wakiash had gone far already, knew that he had gone farther than any chief in the memory of the oldest of them. But all knew the pride of Wakiash.

The flames furbished the coppers, then consumed them.

Wakiash sat haughtily and smiled insultingly at Ernie Emmett.

Emmett could never match that—not that he had hoped to win. But he felt suddenly weary, sweaty, empty. Might as well wind it up right, he thought dully. He tossed his furs one by one to the flames, then held up the ermine. It was lovely. Looking at it now, Emmett knew he never again would go fur trapping. He might try his hand at gold mining or lumber jacking—but never again fur trapping. He turned with a wry smile to where Chuckaluck sat.

But Chuckaluck Gaines was missing. Emmett felt cast down but not bitter at this desertion. He couldn't blame Chuckaluck. If he had been in Chuckaluck's shoes and

Chuckaluck had been in his, Emmett believed he too might not have been able to stomach this insane destroying. But he was in his own shoes, and he smiled inwardly looking at them, a fine pair of Lapland reindeer boots.

Emmett set the ermine aside for last and pulled off the boots and tossed them onto the fire. Then he lifted the ermine and with a silent apology to Yukon Flo drew it back to throw it after the boots. He froze.

Chuckaluck was back, staggering under his furs. He dropped them beside Emmett and jerked a thumb at him. "These are his."

Wakiash didn't move but he seemed to shrink in upon himself. Then his shoulders bowed.

Ernie Emmett and Syah-an-cu-ti paddled the canoe toward the mainland. Chuckaluck lolled in the empty bottom, tootling his whistle. The sky was a robin's-egg blue and Emmett dreamed. The whistling stopped for a moment. Chuckaluck glanced back at Emmett with a grin.

It seemed to Ernie Emmett that Chuckaluck eyed the ermine at Emmett's shoes with a gleam. Emmett took one hand from the paddle and drew the ermine nearer. He'd better not dream anymore till he was really in Totem or Chuckaluck Gaines would skin him out of it.

During the 1950s, no one wrote better popular Western novels and stories than Steve Frazee. Testimony to this fact is a highly impressive record of eighteen published novels; first prize in an annual contest conducted by Ellery Queen's Mystery Magazine *for a modern Western story, "My Brother Down There" (see number two in this series of anthologies,* The Outlaws*); one collection; such film adaptations as* Many Rivers to Cross, Running Target, *and* The Alamo*; and such stories as "Great Medicine," the strong tale of a Crow Indian named Little Belly who believed he could defeat the white man if he could only steal the white man's "medicine"—all this written between 1951 and 1960!*

Great Medicine

Steve Frazee

Deep in the country of the Crows, Little Belly squatted in the alders, waiting for his scouts. The Crows were many and angry in the hills this summer, and there was time to think of that; but since Little Belly was a Blackfoot who had counted five coups he could not allow his fear, even to himself.

He waited in the dappled shadows for more important news than word of Indians who did not love the Blackfeet.

Wild and long before him, the ridges whispered a soft, cool song. In shining steps, beaver ponds dropped to the great river flowing east toward the land of those with the mighty medicine. Dark and motionless, Little Belly waited.

He saw at last brief movement on a far hill, a touch of sun on the neck of a pony, the merest flash of a rider who had come too close to the edge of the trees.

That was No Horns and his appaloosa. No Horns, as ever, was riding without care. He was a Piegan and Little Belly was a Blood, both Blackfeet; but Blackfeet loved no one, sometimes not even each other. So Little Belly fingered his English knife and thought how easily small things caused one to die.

He saw no more of No Horns until the scout was quite close, and by then Whirlwind, the other scout, was also on the ridge. They came to Little Belly, not obliged to obey him, still doubtful of his mission.

Little Belly said to No Horns, "From a great distance I saw you."

"Let the Crows see me also." No Horns stretched on the ground with a grunt. Soon his chest was covered with mosquitoes.

Whirlwind looked to the east. Where the river broke the fierce sweep of ridges there was a wide, grassy route that marked the going and coming of Crows to the plains. Whirlwind pointed. "Two days."

"How many come?" Little Belly asked.

Whirlwind signaled fifty. "The Broken Face leads."

No white man in the mountains was greater than the trapper chief, Broken Face, whom the white men knew as Yancey. He took beaver from the country of the Blackfeet and he killed Blackfeet. The Crows who put their arms about him in his camps thought long before trying to steal the horses of his company. If there was any weakness in Broken Face it was a weakness of mercy.

So considering, Little Belly formed the last part of his plan.

Half dozing in the deep shade where the mosquitoes whined their hunting songs, No Horns asked, "What is this medicine you will steal from the white trappers?"

It was not muskets. The Blackfeet had killed Crows with English guns long before other white men came from the east to the mountains. It was not ponies. The Blackfeet traded with the Nez Perces for better horses than any white trapper owned. It was not in the pouches of the white men, for Little Belly had ripped into the pouches carried on the belts of dead trappers, finding no great medicine.

But there was a power in white men that the Blackfeet feared. Twice now they had tried to wipe the trappers from the mountains forever, and twice the blood cost had been heavy, and the white men were still here. Little Belly felt a chill, born of the heavy shade and the long waiting, but coming mostly from the thought that what he must steal might be something that could not be carried in pouches.

He stood up. "I do not know what it is, but I will know it when I see it."

"It is their talk to the sky," Whirlwind said. "How can you steal that?"

"I will learn it."

No Horns grunted. "They will not let you hear."

"I will travel with them, and I will hear it."

"It is their Man Above," Whirlwind said. "He will know you are not a white man talking."

"No," Little Belly said. "It is something they carry with them."

"I did not find it," No Horns said, "and I have killed three white men."

"You did not kill them soon enough," Little Belly said. "They hid their power before they died."

"If their medicine had been strong, I could not have killed them at all." No Horns sat up. He left streaks of blood on the heavy muscles of his chest when he brushed mosquitoes away. "Their medicine is in their sky talk."

Whirlwind said, "The Nez Perces sent chiefs to the white man's biggest town on the muddy river. They asked for a white man to teach them of the Man Above, so that they could be strong like the white men. There were promises from the one who went across these mountains long ago. The chiefs died. No white man came to teach the Nez Perces about the sky talk to make them strong."

"The Nez Perces were fools," Little Belly said. "Does one go in peace asking for the ponies of the Crows? It is not the sky talk of the trappers that makes them strong. It is something else. I will find it and steal it."

Whirlwind and No Horns followed him to the horses. Staying in the trees, they rode close to the river, close to a place where the trappers going to their summer meeting place must pass.

Little Belly took a Crow arrow from his quiver. He gave it to Whirlwind, and then Little Belly touched his own shoulder. Whirlwind understood but hesitated.

He said, "There are two days yet."

"If the wound is fresh when the trappers come, they will wonder why no Crows are close," Little Belly said.

No Horns grinned like a buffalo wolf, showing his dislike of Little Belly. He snatched the arrow from Whirlwind, fitted it to his bow and drove it with a solid chop into Little Belly's shoulder.

With his face set to hide his pain, Little Belly turned his pony and rode into the rocks close by the grassy place to wait for the coming of the trappers. The feathered end of the shaft rose and fell to his motion, sawing the head against bone and muscle.

He did not try to pull the arrow free while his companions were close. When he heard them ride away on the long trip back to Blackfoot country he tried to wrench the arrow from his shoulder. The barbs were locked against bone. They ground on it. The pain made Little Belly weak and savage, bringing water to his face and arms.

He sat down in the rocks and hacked the tough shaft off a few inches from his shoulder. He clamped his teeth close to the bleeding flesh, trying with strong movements of his neck to draw the iron head. Like a dog stripping flesh from a bone he tugged. The arrow seemed to loosen, dragging flesh and sinew with it; but the pain was great. All at once the sky turned black.

Little Belly's pony pulled away from the unconscious man and trotted to join the other two.

When Little Belly came back to the land of sky and grass he was willing to let the arrow stay where it was. It was bet-

ter, too, that the white men would find him thus. But that
night he was savage again with pain. He probed and twisted
with the dull point of his knife until blood ran down and
gathered in his breech clout. He could not get the arrow out.
He thought then that he might die, and so he sang a death
song, which meant that he was not afraid to die, and therefore, could not.

He dozed. The night was long, but it passed in time and
the sun spread brightness on the land of the Crows. Hot and
thirsty, Little Belly listened to the river, but he would not go
to it in daylight. It was well he did not, for seven long-haired
Crows came by when the sun was high. Three of them saw
his pony tracks and came toward the rocks. Others, riding
higher on the slope, found the tracks of all three horses.
They called out excitedly.

A few seconds more and the three Crows coming toward
Little Belly would have found him and chopped him up, but
now they raced away to join the main hunt.

All day the wounded Blackfoot burned with thirst. The
sun was hotter than he had ever remembered; it heaped coals
on him and tortured his eyes with mist. When night came he
waded into the tugging current of the river, going deep,
bathing his wound and drinking. By the time he crept into
the rocks again he was as hot as before. Many visions came
to him that night, but they ran so fast upon each other afterward he could not remember one of them clearly enough to
make significance from it.

Old voices talked to him and old ghosts walked before
him in the long black night. He was compressed by loneliness. The will to carry out his plan wavered. Sometimes he
thought he would rise and run away, but he did not go.

From afar he heard the trappers the next day. He crawled
to the edge of the rocks. The Delaware scouts found him,
grim, incurious men who were not truly Indians but brothers
of the white trappers. Little Belly hated them.

Without dismounting, they watched him, laughing. One
of them tipped his rifle down.

Little Belly found strength to rise then, facing the Delawares without fear. The dark, ghost-ridden hours were gone. These were but men. All they could do to Little Belly was to kill him. He looked at them and spat.

Now their rifles pointed at his chest, but when the Delawares saw they could not make him afraid, they dismounted and flung him on the ground. They took his weapons. They grunted over his strong Nez Perce shield, thumping it with their hands. Then they threw it into the river. They broke his arrows and threw away his bow. One of them kept his knife.

When they took his medicine pouch and scattered the contents on the ground, Little Belly would have fought them, and died, but he remembered that he had a mission.

The big white man who came galloping on a powerful horse was not Broken Face. This white man's beard grew only on his upper lip, like a long streak of sunset sky. His eyes were the color of deep ice upon a river. Strong and white, his teeth flashed when he spoke to the Delawares. Little Belly saw at once that the Delawares stood in awe of this one, which was much to know.

The white man leaped from his horse. His rifle was strange, two barrels lying one upon the other.

"Blackfoot," one of the Delawares said.

Curiously, the white man looked at Little Belly.

A Delaware took his tomahawk from his belt and leaned over the Blackfoot.

"No," the white man said, without haste. He laughed. From his pocket he took a dark bone. A slender blade grew from it quickly. With this he cut the arrow from Little Belly's shoulder. He lifted Little Belly to his feet, looking deep into the Blackfoot's eyes.

Little Belly tried to hide his pain.

"Tough one," the white man said.

The Delaware with the tomahawk spoke in Blackfoot. "We should kill him now." He looked at the white man's face, and then, reluctantly, put away his tomahawk.

Broken Face came then. Not far behind him were the mules packed with trade goods for the summer meeting. Long ago a Cheyenne lance had struck Broken Face in the corner of his mouth, crashing through below his ear. Now he never spoke directly before him but always to one side, half whispering. His eyes were the color of smoke from a lodge on a rainy day, wise from having seen many things in the mountains. He put tobacco in his mouth. He looked at Little Belly coldly.

"One of old Thunder's Bloods," he said. "Why didn't you let the Delawares have him, Stearns?"

"I intended to, until I saw how tough he was."

"All Blackfeet are tough." Broken Face spat.

Little Belly studied the two men. The Broken Face was wise and strong, and the Blackfeet had not killed him yet; but already there were signs that the weakness of mercy was stirring in his mind. It was said that Broken Face did not kill unless attacked. Looking into Stearns's pale eyes, Little Belly knew that Stearns would kill any time.

"Couldn't you use him?" Stearns asked.

Broken Face shook his head.

Stearns held up the bloody stub of arrow. He smiled. "No gratitude?"

"Hell!" Broken Face said. "He'd pay you by slicing your liver. He's Blackfoot. Leave him to the Delawares."

"What will they do?"

"Throw him on a fire, maybe. Kill him by inches. Cut the meat off his bones and throw the bones in the river. The Bloods did that to one of them last summer." Broken Face walked to his horse.

"Couldn't you use him to get into Blackfoot country peacefully?" Stearns asked. "Sort of a hostage?"

"No. Any way you try to use a Blackfoot he don't shine at all." Broken Face got on his horse, studying the long ridges ahead. "Likely one of the Crows that was with us put the arrow into him. Too bad they didn't do better. He's no good to us. Blackfeet don't make treaties, and if they did, they wouldn't hold to 'em. They just don't shine no way, Stearns. Come on."

Not by the words, but by the darkening of the Delawares' eyes, Little Belly knew it was death. He thought of words to taunt the Delawares while they killed him, and then he remembered he had a mission. To die bravely was easy; but to steal powerful medicine was greatness.

Little Belly looked to Stearns for mercy. The white man had saved him from the Delawares, and had cut the arrow from his shoulder; but those two deeds must have been matters of curiosity only. Now there was no mercy in the white man's eyes. In one quick instant Little Belly and Stearns saw the utter ruthlessness of each other's natures.

Stearns was greater than Broken Face, Little Belly saw, for Stearns made no talk. He merely walked away.

The Delawares freed their knives. "Is the Blackfoot a great runner?" one asked.

In his own tongue Little Belly spoke directly to Broken Face. "I would travel with you to my home."

"The Crows would not thank me." Broken Face began to ride away, with Stearns beside him.

"Is the Blackfoot cold?" A Delaware began to kick apart a rotten log to build a fire.

"I am one," Little Belly said. "Give me back my knife and I will fight all of Broken Face's Indians! Among my people Broken Face would be treated so."

"What did he say?" Stearns asked Broken Face.

Broken Face told him. He let his horse go a few more paces and then he stopped. For an instant an anger of indecision twisted the good side of Broken Face's mouth. "Let him go. Let him travel with us."

The ring of Delawares was angry, but they obeyed.

It had been so close that Little Belly felt his limbs trembling; but it had worked: deep in Broken Face was softness that had grown since his early days in the mountains because he now loved beaver hides more than strength. Now he was a warrior with too many ponies.

Little Belly pushed between the Delawares and began to gather up the items from his medicine pouch. It shamed him, but if he did not do so, he thought they might wonder too much and guess the nature of his cunning.

Jarv Yancey—Broken Face—said to Stearns, "You saved

his hide in the first place. Now you can try to watch him while he's with us. It'll teach you something.''

Stearns grinned. ''I didn't know him from a Crow, until the Delawares told me. You know Blackfeet. Why'd *you* let him go?''

Broken Face's scowl showed that he was searching for an answer to satisfy himself. ''Someday the Blackfeet may catch me. If they give me a running chance, that's all I'll want. Maybe this will help me get it.''

''They'll break your legs with a club before they give you that running chance.'' Stearns laughed.

There was startled shrewdness in the look the mountain man gave the greenhorn making his first trip to the Rockies. ''You learn fast, Stearns.''

''The Scots are savages at heart, Yancey. They know another savage when they see him. Our wounded friend back there has a heart blacker than a beaten Macdonald trapped in a marsh. I took several glances to learn it, but I saw it.''

The Delawares rode by at the trot, scattering to go on ahead and on the flanks as scouts. Neither Stearns nor Yancey looked back to see what was happening to Little Belly.

Ahead, the whispering blue of the mountains rose above the clear green of the ridges. There were parks and rushing rivers yet to cross, a world to ride forever. Behind, the mules with heavy packs, the *engagées* cursing duty, the wool-clad trappers riding with rifles aslant gave reason for Jarv Yancey's presence. As Stearns looked through the sun-tangled air to long reaches of freshness, a joyous, challenging expression was his reason for being here.

Just for a while Yancey thought back to a time when he, too, looked with new eyes on a new world every morning; but now the ownership of goods, and the employment of trappers and flunkies, gave caution to his looks ahead. And he had given refuge to a Blackfoot, which would be an insult to the friendly Crows, an error to be mended with gifts.

Stearns spoke lazily. "When he said, 'I am one,' it touched you, didn't it, Yancey? That's why you didn't let the Delawares have him."

Jarv Yancey grunted.

The Blackfoot walked with hunger in his belly and a great weakness in his legs, but he walked. The horses of the trappers kicked dust upon him. The *engagées* cursed him, but he did not understand the words. He could not be humble, but he was patient.

And now he changed his plan. The Broken Face was not as great as the other white man who rode ahead, although the other was a stranger in the mountains. The cruel calmness of the second white man's eyes showed that he was protected by mighty medicine. Little Belly would steal greatness from him, instead of from Broken Face.

There would be time; it was far to the edge of Blackfoot country.

The one called Stearns took interest in Little Belly, learning from him some Blackfoot speech through talking slowly with the signs. Little Belly saw that it was the same interest Stearns took in plants that were strange to him, in birds, in the rocks of the land. It was good, for Little Belly was studying Stearns also.

It was Stearns who saw that Little Belly got a mule to ride. Also because of Stearns the Delawares quit stepping on Little Belly's healing shoulder and stopped stripping the blanket from him when they walked by his sleeping place at night.

There was much to pay the Delawares, and there was much to pay all the white men, too, but Little Belly buried insults deep and drew within himself, living only to discover the medicine that made Stearns strong.

By long marches the trappers came closer to the mountains. One day the Crows who had ridden near Little Belly when he lay in the rocks came excitedly into the camp at nooning, waving scalps. The scalps were those of No Horns and Whirlwind. Little Belly showed a blank face when the Crows taunted him with the trophies. They rode around him, shouting insults, until they had worked up rage to kill him.

Broken Face spoke to them sharply, and their pride was wounded. They demanded to know why this ancient enemy of all their people rode with the friends of the Crows. They were howlers then, like old women, moaning of their hurts, telling of their love for Broken Face and all white trappers.

Broken Face must make the nooning longer then, to sit in council with the Crows. He told how this Blackfoot with him had once let him go in peace. The Crows did not understand, even if they believed. He said that Little Belly would speak to his people about letting Broken Face come into their lands to trap. The Crows did not understand, and it was certain they did not believe.

Then Broken Face gave presents. The Crows understood, demanding more presents.

Dark was the look the white trapper chief gave Little Belly when the Crows at last rode away. But Stearns laughed and struck Broken Face upon the shoulder. Later, the Blackfoot heard the Delawares say that Stearns had said he would pay for the presents.

That was nothing, Little Belly knew; Stearns gave the Delawares small gifts, also, when they brought him plants or flowers he had not seen before, or birds they killed silently with arrows. It might be that Stearns was keeping Little Belly alive to learn about his medicine. The thought startled him.

Now the mountains were losing their blue haze. At night the air was like a keen blade. Soon the last of the buffalo land would lie behind. There was a tightening of spirit. There were more guards at night, for the land of the Blackfeet was not far ahead. With pride, Little Belly saw how the camp closed in upon itself by night because his people were not far away.

And still he did not know about the medicine.

Once he had thought it was hidden in a pouch from which Stearns took every day thin, glittering knives to cut the hair from his face, leaving only the heavy streak across his upper lip. On a broad piece of leather Stearns sharpened the knives, and he was very careful with them.

But he did not care who saw them or who saw how he used them; so it was not the knives, Little Belly decided. All day Stearns's gun was busy. He brought in more game than any of the hunters, and since he never made sky talk before a hunt, the Blackfoot became convinced that his powerful medicine was carried on his body.

At last Little Belly settled on a shining piece of metal which Stearns carried always in his pocket. It was like a ball that had been flattened. There were lids upon it, thin and gleaming, with talking signs marked on them. They opened like the wings of a bird.

On top of it was a small stem. Every night before he slept Stearns took the round metal from his pocket. With his fingers he twisted the small stem, looking solemn. His actions caused the flattened ball to talk with a slow grasshopper song. And then Stearns would look at the stars, and immediately push the lids down on the object and put it back into his pocket, where it was fastened by a tiny yellow rope of metal.

This medicine was never farther from Stearns's body than the shining rope that held it. He was very careful when the object lay in his hand. No man asked him what it was, but often when Stearns looked at his medicine, the trappers glanced at the sky.

Little Belly was almost satisfied; but still, he must be sure.

One of the *engagées* was a Frenchman who had worked for the English fathers west of Blackfoot country. Little Belly began to help him with the horses in the daytime. Broken Face scowled at this, not caring for any kind of Indians near his horses. But the company was still in Crow country, and Little Belly hated Crows, and it was doubtful that the Blackfoot could steal the horses by himself, so Broken Face, watchful, wondering, allowed Little Belly to help the Frenchman.

After a time Little Belly inquired carefully of the *engagée* about the metal ball that Stearns carried. The Frenchman named it, but the word was strange, so Little Belly soon forgot it. The *engagée* explained that the moon and stars and the sun and the day and night were all carried in the metal.

There were small arrows in the medicine. They moved and the medicine was alive, singing a tiny song. The *engagée* said one glance was all Stearns needed to know when the moon would rise, when the sun would set, when the day would become night and the night would turn to day.

These things Little Belly could tell without looking at a metal ball. Either the Frenchman was a liar or the object Stearns carried was worthless. Little Belly grew angry with himself, and desperate; perhaps Stearns's medicine was not in the silvery object after all.

All through the last of the buffalo lands bands of Crows came to the company, professing love for Broken Face, asking why a Blackfoot traveled with him. The trapper chief gave them awls and bells and trinkets and small amounts of poor powder.

He complained to Stearns, "That stinking Blood has cost me twenty dollars in goods, St. Louis!"

Stearns laughed. "I'll stand it."

"Why?"

"He wants to kill me. I'd like to know why. I've never seen a man who wanted so badly to kill me. It pleases me to have an enemy like that."

Broken Face shook his head.

"Great friends and great enemies, Yancey. They make life worth living; and the enemies make it more interesting by far."

The mountain man's gray eyes swept the wild land ahead. "I agree on that last." After a while he said, "Besides wanting to kill you, like he said, which he would like to do to any white man, what does he want? There was three of them back there where the Delawares found him. He didn't have no cause to be left behind, not over one little arrow dabbed into him. He joined us, Stearns.''

''I don't know why, but I know what he wants now.'' Stearns showed his teeth in a great streaking grin. ''I love an enemy that can hate all the way, Yancey.''

''If that makes you happy, you can have the whole damned Blackfoot nation to love, lock, stock and barrel.'' After a time Yancey began to laugh at his own remark.

Little Belly was close to Stearns the evening the grizzly bear disrupted the company, at a bad time, when camp was being made. There was a crashing on the hill where two *engagées* were gathering wood. One of them shouted. The other fired his rifle.

The coughing of an enraged bear came loudly from the bushes. The *engagées* leaped down the hill, throwing away their rifles. Little Belly looked at Stearns. The big white man was holding his medicine. He had only time to snap the lids before grabbing his rifle from where it leaned against a pack. The medicine swung on its golden rope against his thigh as he cocked his rifle.

Confusion ran ahead of the enormous silver bear that charged the camp. The mules wheeled away, kicking, dragging loosened packs. The horses screamed and ran. Men fell over the scattered gear, cursing and yelling as they scrambled for their guns. There were shots and some of them struck the bear without effect.

Thundering low, terrible with power, the grizzly came. Now only Stearns and Little Belly stood in its path, and the Blackfoot was without weapons. Little Belly fought with terror, but he stayed because Stearns stayed. The white man's lips smiled, but his eyes were like the ice upon the winter mountains.

Wide on his feet he stood, with his rifle not all the way to his shoulder. Tall and strong he stood, as if to stop the great bear with his body. Little Belly covered his mouth.

When Stearns fired, the bear was so close Little Belly

could see the surging of its muscles on the shoulder hump and the stains of berries on its muzzle. It did not stop at the sound of Stearns's rifle, but it was dead, for its legs fell under it, no longer driving. It slid almost to Stearns's feet, bruising the grass, jarring rocks.

For a moment there was silence. Stearns poured his laugh into the quiet, a huge deep laugh that was happy, wild and savage as the mountains. He looked at his medicine then, solemnly. He held it to his ear, and then he smiled and put it back into his pocket. He stooped to see how his bullet had torn into the bear's brain through the eye.

There was still confusion, for the mules and horses did not like the bear smell, but Stearns paid no attention. He looked at Little Belly standing there with nothing in his hands. Stearns did not say the Blackfoot was brave, but his eyes said so. Once more he laughed, and then he turned to speak to Broken Face, who had been at the far end of camp when the bear came.

One of the *engagées* shot the bear in the neck. Broken Face knocked the man down for wasting powder and causing the animals more fright.

Quickly Little Belly left to help with the horses, hiding all his thoughts. Truly, this medicine of Stearns's was powerful. Little Belly could say that Stearns was brave, that he shot true, standing without fear, and laughing afterward. All this was true, but still there was the element of medicine which protected a brave warrior against all enemies.

Without it, bravery was not enough. Without it, the most courageous warrior might die from a shot not even aimed at him. In the round thing Stearns carried was trapped all movement of the days and nights and a guiding of the owner in war and hunting.

Now Little Belly was sure about the object, but as he pondered deep into the night, his sureness wore to caution. He could not remember whether Stearns listened to the talk of his medicine before the bear made sounds upon the hill or after the shouts and crashing began.

So Little Belly did not push his plan hard yet. He watched

Stearns, wondering, waiting for more evidence. Sometimes the white man saw the hard brown eyes upon him as he moved about the camp, and when he did he showed his huge grin.

Three days from the vague boundary of ridges and rivers that marked the beginning of Blackfoot lands, the Delaware scouts reported buffalo ahead. At once the camp was excited. Broken Face looked at the hills around him, and would not let more than a few ride ahead to hunt.

Stearns borrowed a Sioux bow and arrows from one of the Delawares. He signaled to Little Belly. Riding beside Stearns, the Blackfoot went out to hunt. With them were the Delawares, Broken Face and a few of the trappers. When Broken Face first saw the weapons Little Belly carried he spoke sharply to Stearns, who laughed.

Little Belly's mule was not for hunting buffalo, so the Blackfoot did not go with the others to the head of the valley where the animals were. He went, instead, to the lower end, where he would have a chance to get among the buffalo when the other hunters drove them. The plan was good. When the buffalo came streaming down the valley, the startled mule was caught among them and had to run with them, or be crushed.

In the excitement Little Belly forgot everything but that he was a hunter. He rode and shouted, driving his arrows through the lungs of fat cows. He could not guide his mount, for it was terror-stricken by the dust and noise and shock of huge brown bodies all around it. When there was a chance the mule ran straight up a hill and into the trees in spite of all that Little Belly could do to turn it.

He saw Stearns still riding, on through the valley and to a plain beyond where the buffalo still ran. Little Belly had one arrow left. He tried to ride after Stearns, but the mule did not like the valley and was stubborn about going into it. By the time the Blackfoot got steady movement from his mount, Stearns was coming back to where Broken Face and some of the other hunters were riding around a wounded bull that charged them in short rushes.

Down in the valley, Stearns said to Yancey, "That bull has a dozen bullets in him!"

"He can take three dozen." Yancey looked up the hill toward Little Belly. "Your Blackfoot missed a good chance to light out."

Stearns was more interested in the wounded buffalo at the moment. The hunters were having sport with it, running their horses at it. Occasionally a man put another shot into it. With purple blood streaming from its mouth and nostrils, rolling its woolly head, the bull defied them to kill it. Dust spouted from its sides when bullets struck. The buffalo bellowed, more in anger than in pain.

"How long can it last?" Stearns asked, amazed.

"A long time," Yancey said. "I've seen 'em walk away with a month's supply of good galena."

"I can kill it in one minute."

Yancey shook his head. "Not even that gun of yours."

"One shot."

"Don't get off your horse, you damned fool!"

Stearns was already on the ground. "One minute, Yancey." He looked at his watch. He walked toward the bull.

Red-eyed, with lowered head, the buffalo watched him. It charged. Stearns fired one barrel. It was nothing. The bull came on. Stearns fired again. The buffalo went down, and like the bear, it died almost at Stearns's feet.

"You damned fool!" Yancey said. "You shot it head-on!"

Stearns laughed. "Twice. For a flash, I didn't think that second one would do the work."

Little Belly had seen. There was no doubt now: Stearns had made medicine with the round thing and it had given him power to do the impossible.

The hunters began to butcher cows. Fleet horses stood without riders. Little Belly had one arrow left, and Stearns was now apart from the others, examining the dead bull. But when the Blackfoot reached the valley, Broken Face was once more near Stearns, with his rifle slanting toward Little Belly.

"Take that arrow he's got left," Yancey said.

Stearns did so. "I was going to give him his chance."

"You don't give a Blackfoot any chance!" Yancey started away. "There's other arrows sticking in some of the cows he shot. Remember that, Stearns."

Little Belly did not understand the words, but the happy challenge of Stearns's smile was clear enough.

They went together to one of the cows Little Belly had killed. The white man cut the arrow from its lungs. He put the arrow on the ground and then he walked a few paces and laid his rifle on the grass. He looked at Little Belly, waiting.

The white man still had his medicine. It was too strong for Little Belly; but otherwise he would not have been afraid to take the opportunity offered him. He tossed his bow toward the mule. The white man was disappointed.

They ate of the steaming hot liver of the cow, looking at each other while they chewed.

That night the company of Broken Face feasted well, ripping with their teeth the great, rich pieces of dripping hump rib as they squatted at the fires. Little Belly ate with the rest, filling his belly, filling his mind with the last details of his plan.

When the stars were cold above, he rose from his blanket and went to the fire. He roasted meat, looking toward the outer rim of darkness where Stearns slept near Broken Face. Then, without stealth, Little Belly went through the night to where the French *engagée* guarded one side of the horse corral.

The Frenchman saw him coming from the fire and was not alarmed. Little Belly held out the meat. The man took it with one hand, still holding to his rifle. After a time the guard squatted down, using both hands to hold the rib while he ate. Little Belly's hand trailed through the dark, touching the stock of the gun that leaned against the man's leg.

The *engagée* smacked his lips. The meat was still against his beard when Little Belly snatched the gun and swung it. Quite happy, the Frenchman died, eating good fat cow. Little Belly took his knife at once. He crouched, listening. The rifle barrel had made sound. Moments later, the horses shifting inside their rope enclosure made sound also.

Little Belly started back to the fire, and then he saw that two trappers had risen and were roasting meat. He put the knife at the back of his belt and went forward boldly. He picked up his blanket and threw it around him. He lay down near Stearns and Broken Face.

One of the trappers said, "Was that Blackfoot sleeping there before?"

Grease dripped from the other trapper's chin as he looked across the fire. "Don't recall. I know I don't want him sleeping near me. I been uneasy ever since that Blood took up with us."

After the white men had eaten they went back to their blankets. The camp became quiet. For a long time Little Belly watched the cold star-fires in the sky, and listened to the breathing of Stearns.

Then, silent as the shadows closing on the dying fire, the Blackfoot moved. At last, on his knees beside Stearns, with the knife in one hand, Little Belly's fingers walked beneath the blanket until they touched and gripped the metal rope of Stearns's great medicine. To kill the owner before taking his medicine would mean the power of it would go with his spirit to another place.

Little Belly's fingers clutched the chain. The other hand swung the knife high.

Out of the dark came a great fist. It smashed against Little Belly's forehead. It flung him back upon the ground. The white stars flashed in his brain, and he did not know that he held the medicine in his hand.

Stearns was surging up. Broken Face was out of his blanket in an instant. The hammer of his rifle clicked. Little Belly rolled away, bumping into packs of trade goods. He leaped up and ran. A rifle gushed. The bullet sought him.

He heard it tear a tree. He ran. The medicine bumped his wrist. Great was Little Belly's exultation.

Stearns's rifle boomed twice, the bullets growling close to Little Belly; but now nothing could harm him. The great medicine was in his hand, and his legs were fleet.

The camp roared. Above it all, Little Belly heard Stearns's mighty laugh. The white man had not yet discovered his terrible loss, Little Belly thought. Stearns and maybe others would follow him now, deep into the lands of his own people.

When day came Little Belly saw no signs that Stearns or any of the white men were pursuing him. It occurred to him that they were afraid to do so, now that he had stolen their greatest power.

The medicine was warm. All night he had carried it in his hand, sometimes listening with awe to the tiny talk it made. It frightened him to think of opening the lids, but he knew he must do so; this medicine that lived must look into his face and know who owned it now. He pried one lid open. There was another with a carved picture of a running horse and talking signs that curved like grass in the wind.

Now Little Belly knew why Stearns's horse had been more powerful and fleeter than any owned by other members of Broken Face's company.

Little Belly opened the second lid. His muscles jerked. He grunted. Golden talking signs looked at him from a white face. There were two long pointing arrows, and a tiny one that moved about a small circle. The song of the medicine was strong and steady, talking of the winds that blew across the mountains, telling of the stars that flowed in the summer sky, telling of the coming and going of the moon and sun.

Here was captured the power of strong deeds, held in the mysterious whispering of the medicine. Now Little Belly would be great forever among the Blackfeet, and his people would be great.

The age-old longing of all men to control events that marched against them was satisfied in Little Belly. He pushed the lids together. He held the medicine in both hands, looking at the sky.

In his pouch was his old medicine that sometimes failed, the dried eye of a mountain lion, a blue feather that had fallen in the forest when Little Belly had seen no bird near, a bright green rock shaped like the head of a pony, the claw of an eagle and other things.

When the sun was straight above, the Crows were on his trail. He saw all three of them when they rode across a park. His first thought was to run hard, staying in the heavy timber where their ponies could not go. He had learned that on his first war party against the Crows long ago.

One of the enemies would stay on Little Belly's trail. The others would circle around to keep him from reaching the next ridge. It was a matter of running fast. Little Belly started. He stopped, remembering that he had powerful medicine.

He took it from his pouch and looked at it, as Stearns had done before he killed the bear, before he killed the great buffalo. The medicine made its steady whisper in the silent forest. It told Little Belly that he was greater than all enemies.

So he did not run. He went back on his own trail and hid behind a log. No jay warned of his presence. No squirrel shouted at him. His medicine kept them silent. And his medicine brought the Crow, leading his pony, straight to Little Belly.

While the Crow was turning, Little Belly was over the log with his knife. Quickly, savagely, he struck. A few minutes later he had a scalp, a heavy musket, another knife and a pony. He gave fierce thanks to his medicine.

Little Belly rode into the open below one end of the ridge. The Crow circling there saw him and came to the edge of the trees. Little Belly knew him at once, Thunder Coming, a young war chief of the Crows. They taunted each other. Little Belly waved the fresh scalp. Thunder Coming rode into the open to meet his enemy. Out of rifleshot, they ran their ponies around each other, yelling more insults.

At last they rode toward each other. Both fired their rifles and missed. At once Thunder Coming turned his horse and rode away to reload.

Little Belly would have done the same, except that he knew how strong his medicine was. He raced after Thunder Coming. The Crow was startled by this breach of custom, but when he realized that he was running from one who chased him, he started to swing his pony in a great circle to come back.

The Blackfoot knew what was in Thunder Coming's mind then. The Crow expected them to try to ride close to each other, striking coup, not to kill but to gain glory.

Little Belly allowed it to start that way. Then he swerved his pony, and instead of striking lightly and flashing past, he crashed into Thunder Coming, and swung the musket like a war club.

Thunder Coming died because he believed in the customs of war between Blackfeet and Crows; but Little Belly knew he died because of medicine he could not stand against. There was meat in Thunder Coming's pouch. That, along with his scalp, was welcome.

For a while Little Belly stayed in the open, waiting for the third Crow to appear. The last enemy did not come. Although the Blackfoot's medicine was great this day, he did not care to wait too long in Crow country. He went home with two Crow scalps and two Crow ponies.

The young men called him brave. The old chiefs were pleased. Little Belly boasted of his medicine. With it, he sang, the white men could be swept from the hills. The Blackfeet became excited, ready for battle. The women wailed against the coming bloodshed.

Each night when the first stars came Little Belly talked to his medicine, just as he had seen Stearns do; but the Blackfoot did not let others see him when he twisted the small stalk that protruded from the flattened ball. The medicine made a tiny whirring noise to show that it was pleased.

While the Blackfeet made ready for war, sending scouts to report each day on the progress of Broken Face and his company, Little Belly guarded his medicine jealously. It was living medicine. It was what the white men would not reveal to the Nez Perces who had sent chiefs down the muddy river. Little Belly had not gone begging white men to tell what made them powerful; he had stolen the secret honorably.

Now he had the strength of a bear and the wisdom of a beaver. His fight against the Crows had proved how mighty was his medicine. With it he would be great, and the Blackfeet would be great because he could lead them to victory against all enemies.

It was right that he should begin by leading them against the trappers. Let the old chiefs sit upon a hill. Every day the scouts returned, telling how carefully the white men held their camps. The scouts named men they had seen in the company, strong warriors who had fought the Blackfeet before.

Thunder and the old chiefs were thoughtful. They agreed it was right for Little Belly to lead the fight.

At last the Blackfeet rode to war.

For several days Jarv Yancey had been worried. The Delaware outriders were not holding far from the line of travel now; they had seen too much spying from the hills, and this was Blackfoot country.

"How do they usually come at you?" Stearns asked.

"When you're not looking for 'em," Yancey said.

"Would they hit a company this big?"

"We'll find out."

Stearns laughed. "Maybe I'll get my watch back."

"Be more concerned with holding on to your hair."

The trappers camped that night in a clump of timber with open space all around it. Yancey sent the guards out into the open, and they lay there in the moonlight, peering across the wet grass, watching for movement from the black masses of the hills. The silence of the mountains rested hard upon them that night.

Cramped and wet, those who stood the early-morning watch breathed more easily when dawn came sliding from the sky and brought no stealthy rustling of the grass, no shrieks of bullets.

All that day, the Delawares, on the flanks and out ahead and on the back trail, seemed to be crowding closer and closer to the caravan. They knew; they smelled it. And Yancey and the other trappers could smell it too. Stearns was quieter than usual, but not subdued. His light blue eyes smiled into the fire that night before he went out to take his turn at guard.

The trappers watched him keenly. They knew how joyfully he risked his neck against big game, doing foolish things. The Bloods were something else.

Mandan Ingalls was satisfied. He said to Sam Williams, "He don't scare for nothing. He's plumb anxious to tackle the Bloods. He'd rather fight than anything."

"He come to the right country for it," Williams said.

That night a nervous *engagée* fired his rifle at a shadow. Without shouting or confusion, the camp was up and ready in a moment. Then men cursed and went back to bed, waiting for the next disturbance. The old heads remembered the war cries of the Blackfeet, the ambushes of the past and friends long dead. Remembering, the veterans slept well while they could.

When the moon was gone Little Belly led four young men in to stampede the white men's horses. They came out of a spit of timber and crawled to a winding stream. Close to the bank, overhung with grass, they floated down the creek as silently as drifting logs.

They rose above the bank and peered fiercely through the darkness. The smell of animals close by told Little Belly how well his medicine had directed him. A guard's rifle crashed before they were among the horses. After that there was no more shooting, for Broken Face himself was at the corral, shouting orders.

In addition to the rope enclosure around the animals, they were tied together and then picketed to logs buried in the earth. So while there was a great kicking and thumping and snorting, Little Belly and his companions were able to run with only the horses they cut loose.

But, still, it was good. The raiders returned to the main war party with ten animals.

Remembering the uproar and stumbling about when the bear charged the trappers as they prepared to rest, Little Belly set the attack for evening, when Broken Face would be making camp. Two hundred warriors were ready to follow the Blackfoot war chief.

The scouts watched the trappers. The Blackfeet moved with them, staying on the trees on the hills. A few young men tried to surprise the Delawares, but the white men's scouts were wary. In the afternoon Little Belly thought he knew where the trappers would stop, in an open place near a small stand of trees. They did not trust the dark forest, now that they knew the Blackfoot were watching.

Little Belly went to make his medicine.

He opened the lids to look upon the white face with the shining talking signs. Upon the mirror of the medicine was a drop of water, left from last night's swimming in the creek. Little Belly blew it away. His face was close to the medicine. The tiny arrow was not moving. Quickly, he put the round thing to his ear.

There was no whispering. The medicine had died.

Little Belly was frightened. He remembered how Stearns had laughed through the darkness when Little Belly was running away with the round thing. There was trickery in the medicine, for it had died as soon as Little Belly sought its strength to use against white men.

The Blackfoot let the medicine fall. It struck the earth with a solid thump. He stared at it, half expecting to see it run away. And then he saw the tiny arrow was moving again.

Little Belly knelt and held the round thing in his hands. It was alive once more. He heard the talking of the power inside, the power of white men who smiled when they fought. Once more that strength was his. Now he was warm again and his courage was sound.

Even as he watched, the arrow died.

In desperation, with all the memories of Blackfoot sorrows running in his mind, Little Belly tried to make the medicine live. He talked to it by twisting the stalk. For a time the medicine was happy. It sang. The tiny arrow moved. But it died soon afterward. Little Belly twisted the stalk until the round thing choked, and the stalk would not turn anymore.

He warmed the medicine, cupping it in his hands against his breast. Surely warmth would bring it back to life; but when he looked again there was no life.

He was savage then. This was white man's medicine, full of trickery and deceit. Little Belly hurled it away.

He went back to the Blackfoot warriors, who watched him with sharp eyes. Wind Eater said, "We are ready."

Looking through a haze of hate and fear, Little Belly looked below and saw that Stearns was riding with the lead scouts. "It is not time yet." The spirit of the medicine had fled back to Stearns.

"We are ready," Wind Eater said.

Little Belly went away to make medicine, this time with the items in his pouch. He did many things. He burned a pinch of tobacco. It made a curl of white smoke in the shape of death.

Yesterday, it would have been death for Blackfoot enemies. Now, Little Belly could not read his medicine and be sure. After a while he went back to the others again. They were restless.

"The white men will camp soon."

"Is not Little Belly's medicine strong?"

"The Broken Face will not be caught easily once he is camped."

"Is not Little Belly's medicine good?" Wind Eater asked.

"It is strong," Little Belly boasted, and they believed him. But his words struck from an emptiness inside. It seemed that he had thrown away his strength with the round thing. In desperation he considered going back to look for it. Maybe it had changed and was talking once more.

"We wait," Wind Eater said. "If Little Belly does not wish to lead us—"

"We go," Little Belly said.

He led the warriors down the hill.

The length of Little Belly's waiting on the hill while dark doubts chilled him was the margin by which the Blackfoot charge missed catching the trappers as the bear had caught them. Little Belly saw that it was so. The thought gave fury to his movements, and if he had been followed to where he rode, the Blackfeet could have overrun the camp in one burst.

They knocked the Delawares back upon the main company. Straight at the camp the Blackfeet thundered, shrieking, firing muskets and arrows. The first shock of surprise was their advantage. The *engagées* leaped for the clump of timber, forgetting all else. The trappers fired. While they were reloading Little Belly urged his followers to carry over them.

He himself got into the camp and fired his musket into the bearded face of a trapper standing behind a mule to reload his rifle. But there was no Blackfoot then at Little Belly's back. All the rest had swerved and were screaming past the camp.

Little Belly had to run away, and he carried the picture of Stearns, who had stood and watched him without firing his two-barrelled rifle when he might have.

Broken Face gave orders. His men ran the mules and horses into the little stand of trees. They piled packs to lie behind. Broken Face rallied the *engagées*.

It was a fort the Blackfeet tried to ride close to the second time. The rifles of the trappers slammed warriors from the backs of racing ponies.

There would never be a rush directly into the trees, and Little Belly knew it. The fight might last for days now, but in the end, the white men, who could look calmly on the faces of their dead and still keep fighting, would win. They would not lose interest. The power of their medicine would keep them as dangerous four days from now as they were at the moment.

The Blackfeet were not unhappy. They had seen two dead white men carried into the trees, and another crawling there with wounds. There were four dead warriors; but the rest could ride around the trees for a long time, shooting, yelling, killing a few more trappers. And when the Indians tired and went away, it would take them some time to remember that they had not won.

All this Little Belly realized, and he was not happy. True, his medicine had saved him from harm even when he was among the mules and packs; but if the white man's medicine had not betrayed him before the fight, then all the other warriors would have followed close upon him and the battle would be over.

He rode out and stopped all the young men who were racing around the trees, just out of rifleshot. He made them return to the main body of warriors.

"I will kill the Broken Face," Little Belly said.

Wind Eater smiled. "By night?"

"Now. When it is done the others will be frightened with no one to lead them. They will be caught among the trees and we will kill them all." His words were not quite true, Little Belly realized. The men who rode with Broken Face would not fall apart over his death, but an individual victory would prove how strong the Blackfeet were; and then they might go all the way in, as Little Belly had fought Thunder Coming, the Crow war chief.

Cold-seated in Little Belly's reason was the knowledge that one determined charge into the trees would end everything; but a voice whispered, *If the medicine is good.*

Signaling peace, Little Belly rode alone toward the trees. Broken Face came alone to meet him.

"Before the sun dies I will fight Broken Face here." Little Belly made a sweeping motion with his hand. He saw blood on the sleeve of the white man's shirt, but Broken Face held the arm as if it were not wounded. Little Belly knew that fear had never lived behind the maimed features of the man who watched him coldly.

"When you are dead the Blackfeet will go away?" Broken Face asked.

"If the white men go away when you are dead."

Broken Face's mouth was solemn, but a smile touched his eyes briefly. "There will be a fight between us." He went back to the trees.

When Stearns knew what had been said, he grinned. "High diplomacy with no truth involved."

"That's right," Yancey said. "But killing Little Belly will take a heap of steam out of the rest."

"If you can do it."

Yancey was surprised. "I intend to."

"Your arm is hurt. Let me fight him," Stearns said.

Yancey bent his arm. The heavy muscles had been torn by a hunting arrow, but that was not enough to stop him. He looked at his packs, at mules and horses that would be fewer when the Bloods swept past again. Something in him dragged at the thought of going out. It was foolish; it was not sound business.

Casually he looked at his trappers. No matter what he did, they would not doubt his guts. Jarv Yancey's courage was a legend in the mountains and needed no proving against a miserable riled-up Blackfoot war chief. The decision balanced delicately in Yancey's mind. A man died with his partner, if the time came; and a man in command fought for those he hired, or he should not hire good men.

Yancey shook his head. "I'll do it."

"I thought so." Stearns put his arm around Yancey's shoulder in friendly fashion, and then he drove his right fist up with a twist of his body. Yancey's head snapped back. He was unconscious as Stearns lowered him to the ground.

"It's my fault that Little Belly is still alive," Stearns said. He looked at Mandan Ingalls. "You might take a look at Yancey's arm while things are quiet."

Ingalls spat. "For a while after he comes to, you're going to be lucky to be somewhere with only a Blood to pester you. If you don't handle that Blackfoot, Stearns, you'd just as well stay out there."

Stearns laughed. He took his horse from the timber with a rush. Once in the open, looking at the solid rank of Blackfoot cavalry across the grass, he leaped down and adjusted his cinch. He waved his rifle at them, beckoning. He vaulted into the saddle and waited.

The song of the dead medicine was in Little Belly's ears. It mocked him. Once more he had been tricked. Stearns, not Broken Face, was down there waiting. The power of the stolen medicine had gone through the air back to the man who owned it, and that was why the great one who laughed was waiting there, instead of Broken Face.

Silent were the ranks of Blackfeet and silent were the rifles of the trappers. Little Belly hesitated. The fierce eyes of his people turned toward him. In that instant Little Belly wondered how great he might have been without the drag of mystic thinking to temper his actions, for solid in him was a furious courage that could carry him at times without the blessing of strong medicine.

He sent his pony rushing across the grass. He knew Stearns would wait until he was very close, as he had waited for the bear, as he had faced the wounded buffalo. Riding until he estimated that moment at hand, Little Belly fired his musket.

He saw Stearns's head jerk back. He saw the streak of blood that became a running mass on the side of the white man's face. But Stearns did not tumble from his horse. He shook his head like a cornered buffalo. He raised the rifle.

Stearns shot the pony under Little Belly. The Blackfoot

felt it going down in full stride. He leaped, rolling over and over in the grass, coming to his feet unharmed. The empty musket was gone then. Little Belly had only his knife.

There was a second voice to the white man's rifle. The silent mouth of it looked down at Little Belly, but the rifle did not speak. Stearns thrust it into the saddle scabbard. He leaped from his horse and walked forward, drawing his own knife. The shining mass of blood ran down his cheek and to his neck. His lips made their thin smile and his eyes were like the ice upon the mountains.

It was then that Little Belly knew that nothing could kill the white man. It was then that Little Belly remembered that his own medicine had not been sure and strong. But still the Blackfoot tried. The two men came together with a shock, striking with the knives, trying with their free hands to seize the other's wrist.

Great was Stearns's strength. When he dropped his knife and grabbed Little Belly's arm with both hands, the Blackfoot could do nothing but twist and strain. The white man bent the arm. He shifted his weight suddenly, throwing his body against Little Belly, who went spinning on the ground with the knife gone from his hand and his shoulder nearly wrenched from its socket.

A roar came from the trees. The Blackfeet were silent. Stearns picked up Little Belly's knife.

Then, like the passing of a cloud, the cold deadliness was gone from Stearns. He held the knife, and Little Belly was sitting on the ground with one arm useless; but the white man did not know what to do with the knife. He threw it away suddenly. He reached out his hand, as if to draw Little Belly to his feet.

The trappers roared angrily. Stearns drew his hand back. Little Belly was no wounded buffalo, no charging bear; there was no danger in him now. Stearns did not know what to do with him. Seeing this, the Blackfoot knew that the greatest of white men were weak with mercy; but their medicine was so strong that their weakness was also strength.

Stearns went back to his horse.

"Shoot the stinking Blood!" a trapper yelled.

Stearns did nothing at all for a moment after he got on his horse. He had forgotten Little Belly. Then a joyful light came to the white man's eyes. He laughed. The white teeth gleamed under the streak of red beard. He drew his rifle and held it high. Straight at the Blackfeet ranks he charged.

For an instant the Bloods were astounded; and then they shouted savagely. Their ponies came sweeping across the trampled grass. Stearns shot the foremost rider. Then the white man spun his horse and went flying back toward the trees, laughing all the way.

Wild with anger, the Blackfeet followed too far.

They raced past Little Belly and on against the rifle fire coming from the island of trees. They would crush into the camp, fling themselves from their ponies and smash the white men down! But too many Blackfeet rolled from their ponies. The charge broke at the very instant it should have been pressed all the way.

Little Belly saw this clearly. He knew that if he had been leading there would have been no difference.

His people were brave. They took their dead and wounded with them when they rode away from the steady fire of the trappers' rifles. They were brave, but they had wavered, and they had lost just when they should have won.

For one deep, clear moment Little Belly knew that medicine was nothing; but when he was running away with the rest of the warriors old heritage asserted itself: medicine was all. If the power of Stearns's round object, which could not be stolen for use against white men, had not turned Little Belly's bullet just enough to cause it to strike Stearns's cheek instead of his brain, the fight would have been much different.

Little Belly knew a great deal about white men now. They laughed because their medicine was so strong, so powerful they could spare a fallen enemy. But he would never be able to make his people understand, because they would remember Little Belly was the one who had been spared.

As he ran from the field he knew it would have been better for him if Stearns had not been strong with mercy, which was medicine too.

Comanche Woman

Fred Grove

A *brazen sun beat down on the figures strung out across*
the yellow prairie, their long travois poles raising puffs of
smoky dust. They rode warily, on horses worn thin, as
strangers in a land they had once known and claimed. They
followed a single warrior toward the company of cavalry
drawn up outside the stone fort.

"Think they mean trouble?" the young lieutenant in
charge said nervously, turning to the weathered man whose
ragged moustache drooped in its white oxbow over broad
lips, whose getup struck the lieutenant as extremely outland-
ish for a government scout—greasy blue britches, calf-hide
vest, calico shirt and that ridiculous floppy hat banded with
frayed beaver skin, worn as though a special mark or badge.

The old man—far older than he would admit to the officers at the fort—was shading one hand against the glare,
squinting. He grew more intent, stiffly erect. His eyes

weren't much by now, but he knew this band, these Antelope people! He watched the warrior leading them in. The broad, high-boned Comanche face, and the hair as fair as corn silk.

"No trouble," he replied after some moments, stifling the disgust he longed to express. "They wouldn't bring their families along an' start a fight. You're lookin' at the last Comanche band, Lieutenant. Remember that. Buff'lo's gone. The war's over." And a good deal more, he thought, his mind retreating suddenly to dwell on dim shapes and sunlit buttes and curly grasses that rolled away like an ocean, on these same whirlwind people and the dreaming white woman who had lived among them so long ago.

It was late afternoon, while the women gathered mesquite wood for the supper fires, before Emily could approach the small white girl brought in that morning as Kill Bears' captive.

The girl whirled, an instant fear climbing high in her small, taut face. "Let me be!" she cried and shrank away. Her skin, too light for the Texas sun, had peeled on her nose and cheeks. Her hair was the color of flax and needed washing; even so, it managed to curl softly along the temples. But what held Emily rigid and aching was the terror she saw blazed in the thin face, in the enormous blue eyes that seemed too large for the rest of her. She was only nine or ten.

"No hurt . . . you," Emily said, forming the awkward words. Over the years she had made herself speak English so she would not forget how her people at the stockade had talked.

She put out a tentative hand, and wasn't surprised when the girl struck it aside.

"No hurt . . . no hurt."

"Git away—you dirty Injun!" The girl snatched up her bundle of wood and ran.

Emily caught her easily. The captive whimpered and

twisted, and in that brief struggle Emily felt a sickening knowledge. This little white girl wasn't strong enough for camp work. Not as Emily had been when captured. Once winter came she would die like a young quail caught in a blizzard.

"Me white—me white," Emily said, desperate to be understood, holding her firmly, but not hurting. She pointed to her own blue eyes and yellow hair. "See? Me white—like you."

The captive dropped her sticks. Some of her terror edged away, then suddenly all of it, as she seemed to notice Emily's features for the first time. Her mouth twisted and she came sobbing into Emily's arms, and Emily was murmuring words she hadn't said in years.

"Your name, child?" she asked after a bit.

"Mary . . . Mary Tabor."

"Where is your home?"

"Down river from Fort Belknap."

"That's on the Salt Fork of the Brazos."

Mary displayed a small, pleased, wet-eyed smile. "You've been there?"

"A long time ago," Emily lied, wanting to humor her.

"My folks . . ." Mary began and trailed off, lips quivering.

Emily shook her head. "Don't talk now. Go back to camp. Don't let the Indians see you crying. Be brave."

That evening she spoke to Jumping Bull. "The little *Tejano* girl Kill Bears captured. I want her for a slave in our lodge."

"She is not strong. You would have to take care of her."

"She's not strong now because Kill Bears is mean to her. She goes hungry. She longs for her people. I could teach her many things. She will grow strong. She will be like a little sister to me."

Across the soft gloom in the tipi, Emily saw her husband's dark gaze play over her; it gave her a warm feeling. She could not forget how he had paid Runs Antelope, her captor, many horses for her. She was proud of him, in a

way. Jumping Bull was a rising warrior who never lacked
followers when he led war parties against the Utes or
Tejanos. And even when she knew he was raiding the settlements, she wanted him to return. She wondered why, as a
wealthy man who had only one son, he hadn't taken another
woman into his lodge. A skilled hunter, he could provide for
several wives and many children.

But for her, always, between them, lay the wedge of her
massacred people, so distant and lost in time they might
never have existed save in a dream, even though he had been
too young to go on that raid.

He didn't answer and she, wanting this as nothing she had
asked before, wisely forced down her eagerness.

Two days passed. Then she noticed that Jumping Bull's
horse herd appeared smaller. Certain swift buffalo runners
were missing. She said nothing and waited.

On the third day Mary Tabor came to live in the lodge.

"Now tell me about your kinfolks," Emily said.

Mary stared at the toe of her rawhide moccasin. "Wiped
out. 'Less Uncle Amos got away." She shuddered and Emily saw the fear again, livid as a quirt slash in the pale face.

"Some day you will go back," Emily said gravely, sad
for her. "Don't ever quit hopin'. I ain't."

Mary's large eyes showed a searching, inquisitive look,
older than her years. "Mean you'd leave Jumping Bull if
you could?"

Emily averted her eyes, somehow annoyed and surprised.

"He's mighty good for an Injun," Mary went on. "Gave
good horses for me. He ain't mean like Kill Bears, who
beats his womenfolks. Reckon I'm lucky; I know that. And
you—you're so good to me, Emily. Now you show me how
to do Injun chores. I got to earn my keep. I can sew a mite. I
can cook. I can make cornbread."

"There's no corn meal," Emily said, smiling, knowing
Mary would be no bother. First, she washed and braided
Mary's light hair; by that afternoon she had lost the driven
look. Soon Emily dressed her in buckskins, after working
the hides until they were soft and smooth and buff in color,

and adding bright bead designs and fringes on sleeves and hems.

Having Mary close and hearing her speech awakened in Emily sleeping words and expressions. Homesickness seized her. She saw as never before the cool spring beyond the stockade where the children had played, the red plum bushes heavy with fruit, the sweet, dim faces of her mother and the neighbor women. She thought of her father, away when the Indians struck. Was he alive? Had he searched for her or offered ransom? She felt the strength of a new determination. She spent more time instructing Yellow Bird, her son.

"Peace is better than war," she would say when Jumping Bull wasn't around. "It is not right to kill."

"*Tejanos* kill us," the boy said. He was brown as any Comanche and he had the proud, high cheekbones of his father, but you couldn't mistake the white cast of his mouth, or the blue eyes and yellow hair. Trouble was, he thought like a Comanche.

"It takes a brave man to follow the peace road," she said, "when the others howl to fight."

The boy looked puzzled. "My father is brave. He fights."

When they reached a stopping place in their discussions, he would leap up with relief and run out. Emily, left to her dreaming, could see him grown up as a white man and living in a wooden house with windows.

By the time the band trailed out on the vast prairie floor of the Staked Plains for summer trading, she was thinking of home with an increasing sick desperation. Her resolve deepened.

They drew up to a place called *Casas Amarillas*—the Yellow Houses—a high bluff in which caves had been cut. There the *Comancheros* waited with their familiar high-wheeled *carretas*.

Emily's usual excitement was missing. She moved dully. Mary helped her raise the long cedar tipi poles and lift the cover of dressed buffalo skins against the framework, fasten the small wooden pins and pound the pegs. That done, Mary joined the other youngsters curiously observing the trade people and the many bright goods.

Soon she came flying back. "There's a white man out there!"

"White man!" Emily looked up. "No white man has ever come here." She shook her head; it wasn't possible.

"He's a trader," Mary insisted, impressed, and her hands framed the shape of a large man. "Black boots . . . buckskins and a big round hat with beaver skin around it. The children call him Beaver Hat."

Emily got up. "He's white? You're certain?"

"I heard him talkin' to Jumping Bull. I saw him as close as I am to you."

"Then he will come here," Emily said, more to herself. There would be much palavering and smoking and feasting before Jumping Bull, who owned more horses than any warrior in the band, struck his trade. Excitement swept her.

To her disappointment, Jumping Bull returned alone. He looked pleased and secretive as he reached inside his blanket and held out something that shone.

She caught her breath. It was a silver necklace, turquoise set in each link, very bright and pretty in the sun; his first real gift for her, worth many horses. She considered it longingly, in confusion. She took the necklace and spread it out in her hands, and started to slip it over her head. As she did, a thought arrested her. Jumping Bull didn't know she was going to tell the white trader about her people. Therefore, it would be unseemly for her to wear his gift. Yet she couldn't refuse it.

"It's too pretty to wear now," she said, instead, and saw the flicker of hurt deep in his brown eyes before he walked away.

Afterward, she placed the necklace among her things—with the hand mirror, the colored beads left over from making Mary's dress, awls and needles of sharpened bone, a pair of thin, shell earrings obtained from the *Comancheros*, and a broken comb found in the litter of an old camp ground.

Near evening the next day she took a buffalo paunch to the water hole below the yellowish cliffs. Coming back, she looked about and stopped suddenly. Tiny tremors raced through her.

A rawboned white man in a broad hat was walking beside Jumping Bull. She delayed, until they passed her and entered the lodge. Had the white man noticed her pale skin? Her yellow hair?

She hung up the water paunch and when she came to the lodge door, carrying a kettle of meat, she paused desperately so Beaver Hat could see her framed there in the full light. Going in, she saw her husband on his robes, facing the door. Beaver Hat sat on his left, in the place of honor. She lingered so long while placing the kettle and wooden bowls and spoons that Jumping Bull threw her a questioning look.

Beaver Hat seemed not to notice.

She stood outside, slumped in dejection. As a Comanche woman she couldn't approach the white man in camp. People would laugh at Jumping Bull, whose wife talked to strangers. Yet why should she, a captive, think of him and his reputation as a warrior? She didn't understand herself.

Yellow Bird ran in to eat. She fed him and watched him run off into the dusky light. She sent Mary to play and sat motionless, listening to the murmuring voices inside the tipi. A thought settled; it kept growing, stirring her. She emptied the paunch into a large kettle and went unhurriedly to the spring and opened the bag, letting it fill slowly while she watched.

When she could wait no longer, when evening's haze masked the brown land and her long absence would be noted, she saw a figure leave the lodge and start toward the trader's camp.

She rose at once, the water bag forgotten, and stepped away, striding to intercept him. But the fine feeling of anticipation with which she had begun deserted her suddenly. She slowed her step, uncertain. What if he pretended again not to see her?

She could hear his bootsteps, heavy, steady. Not once did

his head turn in her direction. His gaze seemed fixed afar. His beaver hat made him look taller.

She walked faster and turned to stand across his path. He couldn't miss her now! She saw his eyes stray over her, and she waited for some sign that she existed. He came on, just a few steps away. Still, he gave no awareness of her.

Her head lifted. She was white, not Comanche! She posted herself squarely. Facing him, she saw him swing his glance right and left. To her astonishment and relief, he halted and said, low, "I know, ma'am . . . you're white." She heard nothing but pity as he spoke, pity and helplessness.

She touched her breasts. "Me Emily—Emily Bragg," she said, and suddenly she became angry with herself. She had thought so long over the impressive way she would speak, the rehearsed white man's words. Now, in her anxiety, she was falling back on the old, halting, Indian-camp English, which she'd come to despise since Mary came.

"Bragg? Bragg?" He pulled on his chin and mulled the name around on his tongue. He shifted one high shoulder and inclined his head in the manner of one who listens. A tawny moustache fell down the slopes of his broad mouth. His eyes, almost white against the brownness of his face, squinted in at the corners. The eyes were wise, but missing was the shrewd glint of a *Comanchero*.

"My father's name was Josiah Bragg. He built a fort on a river." She could never think of him as dead; at last the words were rising off her tongue. "The settlers called it Fort Bragg. There was a massacre—ever'body killed—"

"On the Navasota, wasn't it?" he interrupted, and nodded reminiscently, in sympathy. "I recollect that. You been all this time with the Antelope-Eaters?"

"Since I was ten."

He hesitated, not meeting her eyes. "They didn't swap you off none . . . nor trade you around to other bands or tribes?"

"No," she replied and drew herself straighter.

He appeared relieved, though his pity slid back as he said, "Now you're Jumping Bull's woman?"

"His wife," she said, surprised at her instant sharpness. "Listen to me! I still have people. I know. They'll pay ransom."

"Thought you said everybody was rubbed out?"

"My father wasn't there. He was east in the settlements." She spoke in a torrent, in confusion, and a pang of guilt pressed her. She'd meant to tell him first about Mary. "Listen! There's a little *Tejano* girl here—Mary Tabor. Her folks lived on the Brazos Salt Fork. Maybe she's got kin left—somebody. The pony soldiers at Fort Belknap will know. Somebody'll remember that raid . . . just last summer. Her folks had stock." Emily didn't know whether Mary's people possessed wealth or not; as she remembered, everybody on the frontier was poor. She'd said that on impulse; anything to stir up the greed in this white trader who didn't look or act like a *Comanchero*. "Her people, my people, I know will pay ransom. Many guns, many blankets."

"What about your boy?" he asked. "Figure Jumping Bull'd give up you an' the boy together?"

She shook her head evasively and touched his arm with a pleading gesture. "All I know I've dreamed about goin' home ever since they took me. You will take word?"

She waited, feeling her throat muscles tighten. Waves of purple twilight thickened across the open land and lay banked in darker shadows against the foot of the bluff. Camp sounds fell away.

"Ma'am," he said, finally, "true, I brought some trade goods. But no guns. I ain't a real *Comanchero*. I'm a scout for the state of Texas. There's a big war comin' between the states." When her brows knitted in puzzlement, he tried to explain and pointed. "Americans agin Americans. North and South. A brother-killin' war. Mighty bad. Texas wants to keep the Comanches peaceful. That's why I'm here."

"You take word?" she said, slipping into the sparse, hated camp lingo.

He didn't answer at once. "I'll try. Maybe I can locate

somebody. If I can, I'll send a rider back. My man can say the *Tejanos* are lookin' for two whites like you an' Mary. That there'll be ransom goods.'' She was thanking him with her eyes, her throat too full for speech. ''Ma'am, you're a mighty brave woman. Only don't get your hopes too high now. If I can't find anybody—well. Could be, too, the band won't let you go.''

''I am Jumping Bull's *wife*,'' she said. ''Not *their* slave.''

Beaver Hat's eyes looked thoughtful, but Emily no longer saw pity. He had that expression as he walked off.

Emily clung to it, trusting it, as the slow days wore away and the fickle band shifted from one scattered watering to another. By late summer, as restless as the whirlwinds that played across their shimmering world, the Antelope-Eaters had returned to the Yellow Houses, where the constant *roo-roo-oo* of bellowing buffalo bulls meant winter meat ranged nearby.

That was when the dark-skinned rider found them. Emily felt the hot clutch of excitement as she gave him food and fought down her questions. Was her father alive? Was Mary's uncle?

The rider and Jumping Bull talked, and then the man went to his picketed horse and waited.

It seemed a long time before Jumping Bull called her, before she stood in the gloom of the lodge. She had never feared him. Except now she had to will herself to meet his eyes.

''Beaver Hat,'' he said, expressionless, ''sends me word from the *Tejano* chiefs. They want to buy you and the little white slave.''

She stared into her hands, ashamed for him to see her naked elation.

''Your home is here,'' he told her.

''I am not Comanche,'' she said, looking up. ''I want to go back to my people.''

''It would not be the same. Your skin is white, but your heart is Comanche.''

"I am a white woman. I want my son to live as a white man."

His dark eyes flashed a baffled anger.

"My father is rich. He will pay much for me."

He flinched as if struck. His eyes locked on her, in them something she had never seen until now. He strode past her, gone.

White-faced, standing in the lodge door, she saw him go out and speak to the rider. What was he saying?

He told her nothing, and the following morning, taking only his medicine bundle, he rode off alone. He returned after three days, lean and hollow-eyed.

Soon she heard the camp crier calling: "You friends of Jumping Bull—come to his lodge tonight. He will lead a war party against the Utes."

Emily's heart turned cold. In that moment she became a Comanche woman again, fearing for her warring husband. She watched with dread as the warriors hung up their shields to absorb the powerful sun medicine and readied weapons. All except Jumping Bull, who chose only his long *bois d'arc* lance, which only the bravest carried. A war-lance man never retreated, and the feeling spread through her that he would not return.

All during the hot afternoon she heard him singing and drumming songs in the lodge. Near sundown the war party paraded through the village. They would leave tonight, for it was bad to go in daylight. As darkness fell, the old men beating the drums struck up a throbbing song.

Now the departing warriors began choosing women partners for the dance.

Emily waited. Always before he had danced with her.

His gaze brushed her, just once. He wheeled swiftly by. That was all. He danced on and she knew that he had shut her out of his heart.

Living was dreading and dreaming and instructing young Yellow Bird. *Is it good to see friends in their grief slashing themselves? Is it good to see old people without sons, no one to kill meat for them? Is the war way good?*

Several times a day she climbed the bluff to catch the first signs of distant movement, hoping to see low puffs of dust, or dark figures crawling through the glazy heat waves.

On the afternoon that she sighted the bobbing shapes in the west, she thought first of the war party. She watched a long time; they were so far away and the sun burned her eyes.

Of a sudden she dropped her head. There was no war party. The figures out there were mainly mules pulling high-wheeled carts. But, remembering Mary, she felt a warm triumph and she ran toward camp.

They stood outside the lodge and waited for Beaver Hat to make his way through the Comanches swarming around the carts. He came quickly. As he approached, Emily took Mary's hand.

"It's all right," he announced, displaying the engulfing smile of one bringing good news. "Got plenty of things—blankets, calico, tobacco, coffee, kettles."

Mary uttered a small cry and Emily held her harder.

"Ma'am," Beaver Hat said, his eyes fixing Emily alone, "your father is still living. There's a little town growed up there now close to the fort."

Emily felt her throat lump. A mist crossed her eyes. She fought a sudden trembling. "Is . . . is he old?" she asked, and the fort and its phantom people and the Navasota and its post-oak hills swam in a sweet haze. "I mean . . . does he look old?" In truth, she didn't know what she meant.

"His hair is snow white. A hardy man for his age, though. Handles stock. Raises cotton. He's well to do."

"Did he . . . is he . . . ?" Again, Emily faltered.

"He never married again, if that's what you mean. Lives by himself. He wants you back, ma'am. Says you're all he's got. He's never quit lookin' for you." His voice changed. "I figure we'd better pull out tomorrow."

Emily didn't understand. She stared into his face. "Pull out? My husband is making war on the Utes." She hesitated even more and when she spoke, her voice sounded other than her own. "And my son?" Her gaze broke away from his.

"Mean Jumping Bull didn't tell you?" he demanded, astonished. "Why, he gave his word to my man last summer. You can go home now. You an' Mary. With me. As for the boy, it's his choice to go or stay. What's more, Jumping Bull didn't want any ransom goods. Your father sent 'em just the same—for good will."

"My husband is gone," she said again, dully. "I can't go now. His war party's been out a long time."

Beaver Hat pulled on his beard, and she could see the wise eyes thoughtfully upon her. He said, "That's not all. About that fight on the Salt Fork, ma'am. All Mary's kin got wiped out. I'm mighty sorry."

Mary's fingers were clawing into Emily's palm. But Mary didn't whimper as she would have months ago.

"Now, ma'am," he said earnestly, "set your mind to this. I can wait a few days. No longer. I won't ever be back here again." He turned away.

Emily heard shouts on the afternoon of the second day after Beaver Hat's arrival. She ran out to the shrillness of wailing voices and, hurrying to the camp's edge, she recognized a warrior who had traveled with the war party. His face was painted black. Scattered behind him trailed a small band of riders. Sixteen men had gone to war; not half that many were returning. Jumping Bull, she saw, wasn't among them.

She stumbled. The sky was spinning. As she swayed upward, she noticed, just now, the cedar-pole travois.

Running, running, she found him upon it. His long spear lay beside him, unbroken. A red, wicked slash ran crookedly across his chest. His dark eyes, open, took no notice of her even when she bent over him. She heard a warrior say:

"He counted many coups with the war lance before he went down. He told us to leave him, but we put him on the drag. His spirit wants to stay in his body, but his heart is on the ground."

She followed them, holding herself tightly, as if she

might fall apart if she did not, followed as they carried him inside the lodge. Seeing him on the buffalo robes, she thought, "He tried to die; only he was too strong, too brave." And she was proud.

Yellow Bird sat at his warrior father's feet to watch and worship. Mary Tabor, big-eyed, silent, slipped to Emily's side, intent on the rise and fall of Jumping Bull's heavy breathing. And in the wide eyes Emily saw again the fear that Mary had when she first came to the Indian camp.

In a little while Emily felt Mary touch her arm. She turned to find Beaver Hat standing back from the doorway. Emily stepped outside, Mary close on her heels.

"I saw them bring him in," Beaver Hat said, nodding his regret. He paused. "I'll have to know now, ma'am. Hard time for you to decide. I understand that."

Emily felt Mary's hand creep inside hers, and the calling images of her father and the fort and the people seemed to float again before her, revealed in soft sunlight, forever there, forever secure. She could see each face, each remembered woodland path and hill shape.

"No harder," she said then, shaking her head. "Guess I decided the other day; just didn't know. My home is here." And suddenly: "But Mary will go! My father is old—she will make him a good daughter."

At that, Mary sobbed and Emily felt her fierce, small grasp.

Beaver Hat's jaw hung. His broad lips opened, closed. His eyes ran over her, thoughtfully, a blend of sadness behind them. And he did a strange thing. He swept off his hat. For her, she knew, some *Tejano* sign she didn't remember. But she sensed it was good, and without pity.

Mary couldn't stop sobbing. "Emily, don't make me leave you!"

Emily grew firm. She took Mary's arm, just as she had that first day, and led her the few steps to Beaver Hat.

"Go now—be brave," Emily said, and kissed one wet cheek. "Don't look back. I don't think I could stand that."

She watched them walk off. Once Mary seemed to lag, to falter, to cry. But she didn't look back.

Emily turned. She went inside and searched among her scant possessions and found the necklace, which she looped around her neck.

She saw Jumping Bull look up as she faced around. His dark, warm gaze came over her.

"There will never be another woman in this lodge," he said.

She inclined her head, indicating approval. The faces in the old dream had gone. Only those of her husband and son were real. Yet, for Yellow Bird, because he was young, she could dream of the peace road.

The sons of famous fathers usually have a difficult time find-
ing themselves and moving out of the shadows cast by their
parents. Not Stephen Overholser, whose dad, Wayne D.
Overholser, is one of the best practitioners of the modern
Western. Not only has the younger Overholser established a
name for himself, but he has done so in the same field in
which his father works. Steve won a Spur Award from the
Western Writers of America for Best Western Novel of
1974 for A Hanging in Sweetwater, and he has published a
string of other well-received Western books. ''Captive in
Paradise'' is one of his best short stories, a stunning tale
about a kidnapped Arapahoe Indian boy.

Captive in Paradise

Stephen Overholser

*T*he fight on the main street of Paradise raised so much
dust that the dozen onlookers stood upwind in a tight, quiet
crescent. Behind them, three dogs paced back and forth in
the rutted street, nervous as the gusting prairie wind.

Young Eagle, an Arapahoe boy of eight summers, sat in
the bed of a farm wagon, watching the fight between his
bearded captor and the cowboy. The farm wagon was
stopped across the street from the one establishment with any
claim to prosperity, the Shoo-fly Saloon.

Paradise was an eastern Colorado Territory town whose
life had been drained by a route change in the Union Pacific
rail line. False-fronted buildings along the narrow main
street stood empty. Clapboard houses that clustered around
what was meant to have been the heart of a new Western

town were now stripped of all furnishings and most doors and windows.

Young Eagle was naked beneath the tattered wool blanket that he pulled around himself against the wind. These prairie winds smelled of snow. The blanket also covered Young Eagle's broken right leg, a leg that was now swollen and dark below the knee.

Young Eagle watched the fight without knowing the sense of it. He spoke no words of the white man's language. He understood only a few cuss words that he had heard at the Indian agent's store, enough to make him believe that white men despised their women. Young Eagle could often guess the whites' meaning by their exaggerated gestures or by their tone of voice, but this fight made no more sense to him than why he had been brought here.

Fourteen days ago, the bearded man had stolen Young Eagle from Soaring Eagle's camp on the reservation. For the first five days of his captivity, Young Eagle was bound hand and foot in the back of the farm wagon. The bearded man traveled only by night, leading Young Eagle to believe that he was the spirit of death. By day, the bearded man concealed the wagon in trees or in heavy brush while he ate jerked venison, drank from one of the jugs he kept beneath the wagon seat, or slept.

On the evening of the sixth day, Young Eagle had managed to work the ropes off his feet. He tried to escape, but was in such a weakened condition that the bearded man easily caught him. With muttered cuss words, the bearded man threw Young Eagle to the earth and stomped on his shin with one hobnailed boot.

When they reached the open prairie, they traveled by day. The first town they came to was Paradise. Young Eagle felt mystified here, and frightened. Most of the whites' frame dwellings, squat and ugly to his eye, were obviously abandoned. Even on the street where the bearded man stopped the team of horses, Young Eagle saw few signs of life. Aside from the Shoo-fly Saloon and one store, the buildings were dark-windowed and empty.

Young Eagle had watched the bearded man enter the saloon. Half a dozen saddled horses were tied at the rail outside, all branded Circle B. As the bearded man opened the saloon door, Young Eagle heard a woman's shrill laughter, but that one human sound was cut off by the closing door.

Presently, the bearded man came outside, followed by six cowboys and an equal number of townspeople. The cowboys were slender men who wore boots with pointed toes, chaps over their trousers, dark flannel shirts, and large, sweat-rimmed hats. The six townspeople, all men, looked different. One was pudgy and red-faced; another was very thin, wearing a dark suit and a derby hat. Another, with a bulging stomach, wore patched clothes and no hat.

In the open doorway of the saloon stood a huge white woman. Young Eagle stared at her. She wore bright red coloring on her cheeks and lips. She met his gaze, and their eyes held until Young Eagle looked away.

Young Eagle saw no sign of anger in any of the white men, only silent determination. Was this the secret of their strength? he wondered as he watched the bearded man and one thick-necked cowboy face one another, circling, their fists raised.

The cowboy, hatless now, was quick and agile. He feinted, then quickly punched the bearded man in the face. The bearded man was rocked back but kept his footing.

Charging, the bearded man swung both fists in wide arcs. Even though the cowboy managed to slug the bearded man once, he was driven back by the attack. The bearded man pressed his advantage and punched the cowboy in the nose, with all of his weight behind the blow. A gasp came from the onlookers, as though they themselves had been struck.

The cowboy went down but quickly scrambled to his feet. His nose bled. The bearded man, sensing victory, charged again, but this time the cowboy sidestepped and slugged him on the temple as he stumbled past.

Every time the fighting whites came together, Young Eagle noticed, their feet stirred powdery dust in the street as if the men had plunged their boots into dry puddles. Gusts of wind took the dust away in a brown streak, away from the silent onlookers, and away from the dogs.

The cowboy had lost none of his quickness from being knocked to the ground. He rapidly punched the bearded man with his right fist, followed by a left. The bearded man tried to rush him, but the cowboy eluded him.

For a time, the fight became a pursuit of the cowboy by the bearded man. The onlookers, maintaining a safe distance, followed the fighters as they came close to the farm wagon, then moved back across the street near the boardwalk in front of the Shoo-fly Saloon.

Even though the bearded man was the pursuer, he got the worst of the fight. The cowboy chose openings and punched his adversary with smooth combinations of rights and lefts before ducking away.

Then the bearded man, his face puffy and bleeding, stepped close to the cowboy and planted his hobnailed boot on the cowboy's foot. The bearded man drew his right fist back and swung, underhanded. He struck the cowboy below his belt buckle, very hard.

The cowboy fell to the street, writhing. Aiming for the crotch, the bearded man kicked him. The cowboy's mouth stretched open and he cried out hoarsely.

Several cowboys cursed the bearded man. The oldest among them, a cowman whose hair streamed out from under the brim of his hat like fine silver, spoke in a low, growling voice: "Let him up. Don't kick him no more."

Breathing raggedly, the bearded man backed away, warily watching the cowboy struggle to his feet. His friends shouted encouragement, but the cowboy was clearly hurt. He straightened up and tried to raise his fists but could bring them no higher than his waist.

The bearded man lunged toward him. Half turning, he drew his right arm back and swung. His fist came around in a great, wind-ripping arc, striking the cowboy squarely on the jaw.

The blow sent the cowboy tumbling to the street. He rolled through the dust and came to rest against the hind legs of the horses tied at the rail. One speckled gelding squealed in panic and reared. The horse beside him, a muscular buck-skin stallion whose eyes rolled wide, lashed out with his hoofs at the prone man. One shod hoof struck the cowboy's head with a report that Young Eagle heard over the sound of the wind.

The fat woman in the doorway of the saloon shrieked. All of the onlookers, until then hushed in a moment of shock, rushed to the fallen cowboy. They pulled him away from the horses. Young Eagle caught a glimpse of the cowboy's face and saw that it was open-mouthed and still.

The silver-haired cowman knelt beside the cowboy, then stood. He snatched his hat off his head and slapped it against his thigh. "Skull's smashed in."

The bearded man, standing spread-legged in the street, wiped a hand through his shaggy beard. The hand came away red. "Is he dead?" he asked in a blurred voice.

Several of the cowboys nodded, but none spoke. They stared down at the fallen cowboy.

"I whupped him," the bearded man said, coming a step closer. "You seen me whup him. The bet's still good."

All of the cowboys and townspeople ignored the bearded man. In a louder voice, he went on: "We had twenty-five dollars riding on this fight—"

The silver-haired cowman whirled and faced the bearded man. "Shut your mouth, mister. The man's dead. Show some respect."

"Wasn't my fault he got kicked," the bearded man said. "All I'm saying is that I got twenty-five dollars coming to me."

The cowman switched his hat from his right hand to his left and drew his revolver from the holster on his hip. He aimed the gun at the bearded man's chest. "Goddamn it, I told you to shut your mouth. You shut it, or I'll shut it for you—permanent."

A tense moment passed while the bearded man and the cowman stared at one another. Then the bearded man turned away abruptly and walked across the street to his wagon.

Behind him, the cowman holstered his revolver. The four cowboys gathered around him, and the townspeople moved toward the boardwalk in front of the Shoo-fly Saloon.

Muttering to himself, the bearded man reached under the wagon seat. He tried to lift out a brown jug with his right hand but winced with pain. He brought the jug out with his other hand and pulled the cork with his teeth. Young Eagle saw blood on the cork when he spat it out.

Young Eagle watched the bearded man tip the jug over his forearm. He filled his mouth and spat reddened whiskey into the street. Then he tipped the jug to his mouth and drank.

Young Eagle turned his gaze to the cowboys. They listened intently to the silver-haired cowman, then all of them walked slowly to the fallen cowboy. They lifted the body and placed it over the saddle of one of the horses.

The silver-haired cowman ran a lariat over the body and beneath the horse, tying the ends to the saddle horn. Then all the men swung up into their saddles. Young Eagle saw that the silver-haired cowman rode the stallion that had kicked the cowboy.

The five men of the Circle B ranch rode out of Paradise, leading the horse that carried the body of the cowboy.

Watching them go, the bearded man cursed softly. He drank from the jug again. Across the street, the fat woman had moved out of the doorway to the boardwalk, looking in his direction. The men of the town stood a short distance away, and near them the three dogs sat with their backs against the wind.

The bearded man called across the street to the woman. "Well, I just got robbed out of twenty-five dollars. Ain't there law in Paradise?"

The fat woman replied, "I'd be surprised if you had two dollars to your name, mister. What would you have done if you'd lost that fight?"

"That ain't what I asked you, woman," he said. "I said, ain't there law here?"

"Ought to be a law against a man like you being alive,"

the fat woman said. She glanced at the knot of townspeople. "I reckon every man here would vote in favor of that."

"I ain't asking you to like me," the bearded man said. He added, "You don't have to stand there gawking at me, neither."

"I'm not looking at you," she said. "I'm looking at that boy in your wagon. Full-blood Indian, isn't he?"

The bearded man looked at Young Eagle, then nodded once in reply.

"What are you doing with him?" she asked.

"You look after your business, woman," the bearded man said, "and I'll look after mine."

The fat woman came striding off the boardwalk with surprising speed and grace, her laced-up shoes sending up clouds of dust before her.

"Don't use that kind of talk on me, mister," she said. "I asked you a question. I want an answer."

Under her glare and threatening bulk, the bearded man backed against the farm wagon. "That boy's off the reservation down south. I brung him up here."

"What for?" she demanded.

"Reasons of my own," the bearded man said.

The woman turned away from him and moved down the length of the wagon bed. She lifted a corner of the tattered blanket.

"Hell, he don't have a stitch on!" she exclaimed.

"Don't matter," the bearded man said. "Injun's skin is thick as buffalo hide."

Young Eagle was frightened. He tried to pull away from the woman and cover himself. He heard her speak soothingly to him, then she lifted the edge of the blanket that covered his right leg.

"Oh, my God, he's hurt," she said softly.

The bearded man set the jug down on the wagon seat. "Leave him be."

The fat woman quickly bent down and pulled up her long skirt, exposing one thick white leg. Above her calf, a small holster was strapped to her leg. She pulled out a double-barreled derringer and straightened up, pointing the weapon at the bearded man's face.

"I can see there's only one language you understand, mister," she said. "I've never killed a man before, but I know I could blow a hole in your face and never lose a minute's sleep over it."

The bearded man swallowed. He stared at her.

The fat woman called over her shoulder to the townspeople, then motioned downward with the derringer. "Mister, sit down right there. Sit up against the wheel of your wagon."

The bearded man silently dropped to one knee and sat. He looked up sullenly as the men of the town gathered around the fat woman.

"Take that rope," she said, pointing to a length of rope in the wagon bed, "and tie this gent to the wheel. Maybe that'll keep him out of trouble for a while."

She held her derringer aimed at the bearded man while the man wearing the derby hat lifted the rope out of the wagon.

Young Eagle watched while the rope that had been used to bind his hands and feet was now looped around the bearded man's chest and run through the spokes of the wagon wheel. When the rope was knotted, the fat woman raised her skirt, to the great interest of all the men, and shoved the derringer back into its holster.

At first, Young Eagle fought when the fat woman tried to lift him out of the wagon. But she spoke softly to him and calmed him. She lifted him slowly and carefully so that none of his weight rested on the injured leg. She turned and carried him across the street to the Shoo-fly Saloon.

Inside, the saloon was long and narrow with a high ceiling. Lanterns were suspended overhead on wires. Young Eagle saw a potbellied stove in the middle of the room. A bar with a dully gleaming brass rail at its base ran the length of the wall. In front of the bar, all the way to the opposite wall and to the back of the saloon, were round gaming tables, captain's chairs, and a roulette wheel.

Young Eagle's eyes were caught by the roulette wheel.

He wondered if it was a symbol of the whites' spiritual beliefs, as he had been told the cross was.

Young Eagle felt a glow of warmth from the stove when the fat woman set him down on a felt-covered table nearby. She pulled the blanket off him, then poked his swollen leg. Young Eagle struggled against the pain, but tears streamed from his eyes as the fat woman probed and pressed her hands against the sides of his leg.

"Leg's swolled up so bad that I can't tell if it's busted," she said. She thought a moment. "Better put a splint on it. If the bone's busted, it'll heel straight." Rummaging through a kindling box beside the potbellied stove, she pulled out two short boards and set them on the table beside Young Eagle's leg.

She walked behind the bar. Bending down, she came up with a dark blue flannel shirt and a piece of torn bar towel. When she returned to the table, she put the big shirt on Young Eagle and buttoned it. The man-sized shirt reached to his knees.

He watched as the fat woman tore the towel into strips. With the help of one of the men, she placed the boards on either side of Young Eagle's leg and pressed them tightly together.

Pain brought sweat to Young Eagle's face. He stared at the high ceiling while the boards were tied into place with the strips of towel. He was hot, then chilled. When the whites were done, he felt warm and drowsy.

The fat woman picked up the tattered blanket and walked out of the saloon through the front door. Outside, the three dogs intercepted her and followed her across the street. The bearded man scowled as he looked up at the fat woman. His beard was caked with drying blood. The dogs bounded ahead of the woman, sniffing cautiously around the bearded man. They slunk away when he spoke. "You ain't going to get away with this."

"I'll turn you loose," she said, dropping the blanket at his feet, "after you answer some questions."

"Such as what?" he demanded.

"When was the last time that boy had anything to eat?" she asked.

"I fed him regular," he replied in a low voice.

"You didn't overfeed him," she said. "He's thin as wire."

When the bearded man shrugged in reply, she said, "You never did answer my question. Why did you take that boy off the reservation? Is he yours?"

"Hell, no," the bearded man said, offended. He added, "I had my reasons. That's all you need to know."

The fat woman looked at the team of horses harnessed to the farm wagon. "Be a real shame if someone spooked that team while you're tied to the wheel."

The bearded man stared up at her. "Goddamn, you're a hard one."

"Answer my question," she said, "and I'll be easier to get along with."

After a long moment, the bearded man said, "Hand that jug down to me."

The fat woman took the jug from the wagon seat and gave it to him. She watched him tip it over his forearm and drink. His right hand was swollen now and appeared to be immobile.

"Savages killed my brother," the bearded man said. He drank again. "I was out hunting and came back to camp and found him. They cut him something fierce. Cut his balls off and stuffed them in his mouth.

"Savages," he muttered, staring at the jug. "I knew where their camp was. I watched it for two days, figuring a way to get my revenge. Then I seen this boy swimming in a water hole. All by hisself." He looked up at the fat woman. "I grabbed him and brung him north."

"What were you doing on the reservation, anyway?" the fat woman asked.

"Prospecting," he said. He added defensively, "It's a free country. My brother and me, we never done those savages harm—"

He was interrupted by the drumming sounds of running

horses. The fat woman turned her head and looked up the street. The cowboys from the Circle B ranch were coming at a gallop. The last horse carried the flopping body of the dead man. A cloud of dust swirled up behind the riders like a dark ghose in pursuit.

The silver-haired cowman was in the lead. He pulled his stallion to a sliding halt near the farm wagon.

"The country's crawling with Indians," he said, breathing hard. "Must have broke the reservation. We saw a war party of maybe fifty, sixty braves headed this way. Take cover. Between us, maybe we can hold them off."

"Cut me loose," the bearded man said, struggling against the rope around his chest. "Cut me loose!"

"That war party must be tracking him," the fat woman said to the cowman.

"What for?" he asked.

"He stole a boy off the reservation," she replied.

The bearded man stared up at them, then yelled, "Ain't you white, too? Cut me loose!" He strained against the rope. "Give me a running chance!"

"You kidnapped that boy?" the cowman demanded. "What'd you do a fool thing like that for?"

"I aimed to let him go," the bearded man said. "Set him loose now. The savages will take him and go. They won't bother you folks."

Across the street, one of the cowboys shouted, "I seen one! An Indian ran between those buildings!"

The cowman turned and looked up the empty street where his rider pointed. "A scout, likely. They're coming."

"Cut me loose!" the bearded man cried.

The cowman ignored him and called to his men. "Grab up your rifles and get into the saloon. We'll fort up there." Turning to the fat woman, he said, "Come on."

They ran across the street. Behind them, the bearded man pleaded with them to release him. He sobbed, then cursed them as they entered the saloon.

Three mounted Indians appeared at the far end of the street. They rode slowly toward the saloon. Behind the leaders, forty Arapahoe warriors came on foot. They were armed with bows and arrows, war clubs, and a few rifles. All were painted and stripped for combat.

The tallest of the three mounted warriors wore a single eagle's feather in his hair. He carried a repeating rifle, a rare prize among this tribe. The man was Soaring Eagle, leader of this war party.

"Here they come!" shouted a cowboy who leaned his head out of the saloon door.

The silver-haired cowman had positioned his riders and all the men of Paradise at the front and rear doors and windows of the saloon. They were well armed but had little ammunition. The cowman had told them not to shoot until the Indians were very close. An immediate, devastating show of force might rout them.

The fat woman strode across the saloon to the table where Young Eagle lay. Despite the commotion, he had not awakened. When the fat woman scooped him up into her fleshy arms, Young Eagle blinked and opened his eyes.

"What's happening?" he asked in Arapahoe.

The question was echoed in English by the silver-haired cowman. "What the hell are you doing?"

The fat woman did not reply. She pushed her way past a cowboy stationed at the front door, shoved the door open with her foot, and went outside.

The fat woman crossed the boardwalk and stepped down to the street. The advancing Arapahoes, less than a hundred feet away now, stopped. Across the street, the bearded man sobbed and babbled senselessly.

"Father!" Young Eagle exclaimed to the warrior wearing the single eagle's feather.

Soaring Eagle nodded once at his son but made no move to dismount. He looked thoughtfully at the bearded man, then at the saloon windows. Behind the glass, white men peered out. Another aimed a rifle at him through the open front door.

Soaring Eagle asked his son, "What has happened to you? Did this white woman injure your leg?"

"No, Father," Young Eagle said. He pointed over her shoulder to the bearded man. "That man took me. He hurt my leg. Father, he is the spirit of death who travels by night."

The fat woman approached Soaring Eagle and held out the boy. "Here, take him."

Soaring Eagle swung a leg over his pony and slid to the ground. He handed his rifle to the mounted warrior who rode next to him and walked to the fat woman. First he examined the splint, then took his son in his arms. He carried the boy to his horse and placed him on the war pony's back.

Soaring Eagle moved to one of the warriors who carried a war club. The club was a fist-sized stone wrapped in tanned hide and attached to a length of tree limb. Soaring Eagle took the club and strode to the bearded man.

The bearded man hung his head and sobbed as Soaring Eagle stood over him. The Indian paused a moment, then raised the war club over his head. He brought it down swiftly, striking the bearded man's outstretched leg below the knee. The bearded man cried out.

Soaring Eagle turned and walked away. He returned the war club to its owner, then mounted his pony behind his son. The warrior beside him tossed the repeating rifle to him. Soaring Eagle turned his pony and, with a single motion of his arm, signaled the war party to follow.

The fat woman stood in the middle of the street, watching the Indians go. The three dogs, tails buried behind their legs, came out of hiding and sniffed the ground the Indians had trod.

Moments later, the silver-haired cowman came out of the Shoo-fly Saloon. He was followed by his riders and the men of Paradise. They stood together on the boardwalk. The only sounds were the bearded man's low moans and the gusting prairie wind.

A short distance away from the white man's village, Soaring Eagle halted and gathered his warriors around him. He asked Young Eagle to tell what had happened to him and to describe what he had seen during his captivity. Soaring Eagle listened while his son spoke, looking back at the cluster of square buildings on the prairie.

When Young Eagle finished, Soaring Eagle spoke.

"Listen while I tell what I have learned. Many summers ago, the white tribes came to the land of our fathers. The whites fought us and defeated us with their weapons and their diseases. They dug into the sacred earth. They brought the fearsome iron horse and the singing wires. They sent us to barren lands where we were told we must live forever.

"But look. See what has happened to the white tribes. All but a few have gone away. The whites left behind fight among themselves. Soon all the whites will be gone, victims of their own cruelty. The lands of the Arapahoe will be ours once again."

A deceptively simple story about a group of Southwestern Indians, "Bank Holiday" is one of the fourteen that comprise Edwin Corle's first published work, Mohave: A Book of Stories *(1934). Such subsequent volumes as* People on the Earth, Burro Alley *and* An American Dream *firmly established Corle as a provocative storyteller and one of the leading chroniclers of life—especially desert life—in the great Southwest.*

Bank Holiday

Edwin Corle

*T*om Lobo, whose real name was Gray Wolf, walked up to the door and looked in. The door, which he had learned was always open at certain hours, was locked. Tom Lobo's unimaginative mind found nothing exciting in this unexpected order of events. He stood still in the bright sunlight and did nothing. He was thinking, "This place is not open: therefore I cannot go in." He walked to the curb and stood looking at the building.

He thought it was a nice white building. He thought it had pretty gold letters on the windows. He thought it was a pretty hot morning. He thought he would like a glass of beer.

And so Tom Lobo stood before the First National Bank of the little desert town of Coachella and waited. Several merchants and ranchers went by and some commented about the bank. If Tom Lobo had cared to listen he might have caught phrases—"Until they get things straightened out"—"Checks ain't worth a whoop"—"Roosevelt"—"Congress"—

"Scrip money"—"Be open in three days"—"Won't be open in three months"—but he didn't listen. He was thinking that it was a nice white building.

Charley Joe came down the street. He and Tom Lobo said good morning by looking at each other and not by speaking. Then Charley Joe went to the door of the bank. He wasn't very surprised to find it closed. He didn't try to peek in the way the white men did. He walked to where Tom Lobo was standing. Charley Joe wore a pair of blue overalls and a gray shirt with no tie. Tom Lobo wore an old pair of dark blue trousers and a gray shirt with no tie. There was little or no difference between them, except that Tom Lobo wore a dirty white hat of the "Panama" variety, while Charley Joe wore no hat at all. Presently Charley Joe took a pipe from a shirt pocket and began to pack it with tobacco.

"Closed," said Tom Lobo.

"Mmm," agreed Charley Joe.

He struck a match and lit the pipe.

"Good terbacker," said Tom Lobo.

"Mmm," agreed Charley Joe.

They stood in silence for some minutes. They both seemed perfectly at ease and there was no attempt at small talk. After a while it became clear to both of them that the white men, who came to the bank and found it closed, went away more excited than they had come. Many of them raised their voices and asked questions and talked fast.

"Why bank closed?" asked Charley Joe.

"Don't know," replied Tom Lobo.

"Maybe John Whitewater know," said Charley Joe.

"Maybe," agreed Tom Lobo.

That ended the banking situation for the moment. After another minute of smoking Charley Joe said, "Got new horse."

"Where old horse?" inquired Tom Lobo.

"Dead," said Charley Joe.

Then Black Eye, who had been sitting in the shade by the freight station, came down the street. Black Eye was a very old Indian with a wrinkled face and gray hair. He wasn't quite as tall as Tom Lobo and Charley Joe. But he was thought to be very wise. The three men greeted each other without words. Black Eye didn't go to the door of the bank. He simply looked at it and at two passing ranchers who were jokingly and nervously reassuring themselves that "everything was O.K." The ranchers climbed into a Ford truck and drove off. Other white men appeared. They rattled the doors and even peered in the windows.

"Bank no work," said Black Eye.

"Mmm," agreed Tom Lobo and Charley Joe.

"Charley Joe got new horse," said Tom Lobo.

"Old horse dead," added Charley Joe.

"Mmm," said Black Eye.

The three of them stood in silence. They turned and faced the citadel of the white man's economic system. Townspeople were talking in groups and rushing up and rushing away. They seemed frightened. "The First National Bank of Coachella," spelled the gold letters on the windows. The information was hardly necessary. It was the only bank in Coachella, or in the entire Coachella Valley. It was the only bank within a radius of seventy-five miles. But the Indians weren't reading the imposing title, or the names of the executives printed on the door. They were just looking at the bank.

"Why bank close?" asked Charley Joe.

"Why, Black Eye?" asked Tom Lobo.

"Don't know," admitted Black Eye.

"Bank got money. Saw money there yest'day," said Tom Lobo.

"Sure, bank got money," said Charley Joe. "I put money there."

"Maybe John Whitewater know," said Black Eye.

"Maybe," agreed Tom Lobo.

"Wait see," said Black Eye.

And so they waited as the morning went on, and the brilliant desert sun became hotter toward the middle of the day. John Whitewater did not arrive. But Tony Gee did. Tony Gee was working at a date ranch, or date "garden" as they are locally called, not far from Indio. Tony Gee was a prosperous Indian, but he was not the authority that was John Whitewater. John Whitewater had been a friend of old Fig Tree John, and Fig Tree John had been the wisest Indian in the methods of the white men in all the Colorado Desert. Fig Tree John was reputed to have been one of Frémont's scouts, and to have killed five men. Nobody knew if that were true, and nobody cared anymore because old Fig Tree was dead. But his wisdom lived after him in the person of John Whitewater. Whenever anybody wanted to learn anything he looked up John Whitewater. So naturally John Whitewater would know why the bank was closed and why the ranchers were excited. The thing to do was to wait for John Whitewater. Nevertheless, the arrival of Tony Gee at noon brought a shred of explanation.

Tony Gee drove into town in his rattly old Ford. It sputtered up the street and nosed into the curb. Tony Gee sat very erect in the seat and held the steering wheel with both hands, and with elbows wide apart. He drove his rattletrap car with ridiculous dignity. He abandoned it at the curb and walked to the door of the bank. Tony Gee wore dirty corduroy pants, a gray shirt with no tie, and a straw hat. He looked at his friends and they looked their greeting back to him.

Tony Gee stopped at the door of the bank and gave serious consideration to a sign on the door. None of the others had looked at the sign.

"Bank H-O-L-I-D-A-Y—" he spelled out. "Until next M-O-N-D-A-Y. By order of the G-O-V-E-R-N-O-R."

Tony Gee thought about the message. He turned the significance of it over in his mind. The white man's governor had said to close the bank. His money was in this bank. The governor had said he couldn't have his money. Vaguely he wondered why. He wasn't belligerent, but he was curious. He had worked for a white man and had earned money. He had been told to put this money in a white man's bank. Now the G-O-V-E-R-N-O-R said he couldn't have the money he had earned. Tony Gee couldn't quite puzzle it out. He turned to the three men at the curb. They were looking at him. He knew they couldn't read the sign.

"Bank closed," said Tony Gee.

"Why?" asked Tom Lobo.

Tony Gee waited a long time. He wanted to get it all clear to his own satisfaction.

"Bank closed because man says so."

"What man?" asked Charley Joe.

"Big man say close bank."

"Why close bank?" asked Black Eye.

Tony Gee was not used to questions. He was not at all sure of his ground. He was a little bit afraid of Black Eye.

"Bank closed," he insisted. Then he said no more, but proceeded to roll himself a cigarette. The other three men said nothing. A white man in Tony Gee's place would have felt embarrassed and would have made some excuse and left. But Tony Gee found refuge in stoicism. The bank was closed. His friends knew it was closed. He knew it. He told them the sign said so. That took care of all that could be said about it. He smoked his cigarette in silence. The four of them stood together and waited.

"John Whitewater know," said Tom Lobo after a long wait.

"Maybe," said Tony Gee.

"One time Fig Tree John know, now John Whitewater know," remarked Charley Joe in an unusually complex line of thought.

"Maybe," said Black Eye.

For several days John Whitewater had been camping near La Quinta. He had been cutting mesquite wood and working hard at it. He arrived in Coachella about two o'clock in the afternoon. He saw the group before the bank and he gave the men no immediate thought. He had business in town. He wanted to buy a new shovel, and a small ax to chop away the short stubborn desert mistletoe that was parasitic to the profitable mesquite. But first he had to go to the bank and get some cash. He was very rich with almost a hundred dollars in the bank, and was very proud of it. He liked going to the bank. It was beyond mere vanity. It was pride and self-esteem. The group watched him approach and they saw him stop at the door. Not even John Whitewater could go any further.

He read the sign.

"Bank Holiday until next Monday by order of the Governor."

He went over it several times. Beyond the fact that the bank was closed, it didn't mean very much to him. He wanted a shovel and a small ax. His money was in the bank, and if he could just get inside, he knew what he had to do to get the clerk to give him money. But there was no clerk inside. The bank was empty. His money was locked up. It was something that had never happened before. He really didn't understand it.

Thinking hard, he turned to the men who awaited him. They didn't ask him any questions. They respected his experience and they waited to hear from him. He knew that he was expected to explain the situation. But first he had to explain it to himself. They stood together in a little group and looked at one another and at the bank.

"Bank closed," began John Whitewater as if he were bringing a new truth to the world. There was a slight pause while they waited. John Whitewater did not seem to be disposed to speak further.

"Why?" asked Black Eye. He enjoyed this, and his question was almost accusatory. He was the only one of them who had no money in the bank. He had no money at all.

"Why?" he repeated.

"Bank closed because gov'ment close him up. Gov'ment say bank close, so he close. Gov'ner of gov'ment close bank up because he can. So he did until Monday."

"Why he close bank?" asked Tom Lobo.

John Whitewater considered. He had vaguely heard of bank failures.

"Maybe bank close because no money. Don't know. Maybe no money in bank."

Tony Gee didn't agree with this.

"Money in bank," he said. "I got money in bank. Tom Lobo got money in bank. Charley Joe got money in bank. Plenty money in bank."

"Sure, money in bank," added Black Eye.

John Whitewater's first theory was blasted. He had no creative imagination so he was unable to think of a second. They all stood and waited for him to go on. John Whitewater did not mind. If he couldn't answer a question, that was the fault of the question. He shrugged his shoulders and simply remarked, "Bank closed."

His friends were disappointed. They expected more information. For over three hours they had known that the bank was closed. And all this business of the governor and the government sounded like a lot of words, and no more. Still, John Whitewater was John Whitewater, and if he couldn't explain any better than that, possibly there was no other explanation. John Whitewater had been the friend of Fig Tree John, and that was authority enough. They stood helplessly and waited for further ideas. They watched ranchers and townspeople become nervous and panicky, and they watched them scurry to and fro using many words.

John Whitewater was turning the course of events over in his mind. He felt that it was reasonable that the bank must have money, for, as his friends had pointed out, they had all put money in it except Black Eye. So money was there. That was one point.

Now John Whitewater went from the general to the particular. He took up his own case. Before he could do any more work he wanted a shovel and an ax. That was a point. To get these he wanted his money which was in the bank. That was another point. To get the money he had to transact certain business within the bank. So that was the basic point, and everything evolved from that. Everything depended upon the opening of the bank.

The other Indians had similar lines of thought, but their ideas were not as clean-cut and as orderly as John Whitewater's. They supposed that some step had to be taken, but just what it was to be they did not know. But with the advent of John Whitewater things reached a crisis. His opinion would be their opinion.

"What we do, John?" asked Black Eye, speaking for the majority.

John Whitewater considered. He thought, without any change of expression coming over his face. He thought of the mesquite, the shovel and the ax, the money, and the opening of the bank. All depended upon the opening of this bank. The ways of the white man were often an enigma. There was no accounting for some of his devices. Acceptance and patience seemed the method of least trouble. Sometime the white man must open his bank. Perhaps in an hour, perhaps next Monday, perhaps next year. Just now the white men, and many of their women, were coming and going to and from the closed door of the bank. They were all talking all the time. There were many words John Whitewater didn't understand. There seemed to be a great deal of excitement and gesticulating and a lot of unnecessary perspiring. There was nothing for John Whitewater to do about it. He wasn't at all sure of what was going on in the white man's world, and a noncommittal acceptance of whatever the white man wanted to do seemed to be the only solution. Then he reached the conclusion that was to determine their policy.

"Maybe sometime bank open," said John Whitewater. "We wait."

And so all five Indians sat down on the curb in the warm sunshine and waited.

You have already read a story in these pages by Clay Fisher since he is the same Henry Wilson Allen who writes as Will Henry. As Clay Fisher, he has published many notable works, including the collection, The Oldest Maiden Lady in New Mexico and Other Stories, *and "The Tallest Indian in Toltepec," which won a Spur Award from the Western Writers of America for Best Short Story of 1965 and is arguably this writer's finest story.*

The Tallest Indian in Toltepec

Clay Fisher

Where the wagon road from Toltepec, in the State of Chihuahua, came up to the Rio Grande, the fording place was known as the old Apache Crossing. This was because the Indians used it in their traffic into and out of Texas from Old Mexico. It was not a place of good name and only those traveled it who, for reasons of their own, did not care to go over the river at the new Upper Crossing.

This fact of border life was well understood by Colonel Fulgencio Ortega. He had not forgotten the Indian back door to El Paso. That is why he had taken personal charge of the guardpost at this point.

A very crafty man, Colonel Ortega. And efficient. It was not for nothing that the *descamisados*, the starving shirtless poor, called him the Executioner of Camargo. Chihuahua had no more distinguished son, nor another half so well known in the ranks of the irregular *rurales*, which is to say the stinking buzzards, of the border.

210

Now, with his men, a score of brutes so removed from decency and discipline that only their upright postures stamped them as human beings, he lounged about the ashes of the supper fire. Some of the bestial soldiers bickered viciously over the cleaning of the filthy mess kits. Others sat hunched about a serape spread on the ground, belching and complaining about the foulness of their luck with the cards, and with the kernels of shelled corn that passed for money among them. The heat of the evening was stifling. Even with the sun now down at last beyond the Rio, it was still difficult to breathe with comfort. The horseflies from the nearby picketline still buzzed and bit like rabid foxes. It was a most unpromising situation. In all of the long daylight they had wasted at the ford, no fish had come to their net, no traveler from Toltepec had sought to pass the crude barricade flung across the wagon road.

"Volgame!" announced Ortega. "God's Name, but this is slow work, eh, Chivo?"

The name meant "Goat" in Spanish, and the bearded vagabond who responded to it seemed well described.

"True, *Jefe.*" He nodded. "But one learns patience in your service. Also hunger. Hiding. Sand fleas. Body lice. How to use corn for money. How to live on water with no tequila in it. Many things, Excellence."

Ortega smiled and struck him full across the face with the heavy butt of his riding quirt. The blow opened the man's face, brought the bright blood spurting.

"Also manners," said the Colonel quietly.

Chivo spat into the dirt. *"Si,"* he said, "also manners."

Presently, the man on duty at the barricade called to his leader that someone was coming on the road.

"By what manner?" asked Ortega, not moving to arise.

"A burro cart."

"How many do you see?"

"Two. A man and a boy. Hauling firewood, I think."

"Pah! Let them go by."

"We do not search the cart, *Jefe*?"

"For what? Firewood?"

"No, *Jefe*, for *him*; these are *Indios* who come."

Instantly, Ortega was on his feet. He was at the barricade the next moment, Chivo and the others crowding behind. All watched in silence the approach of the small burro cart. Had they begun to pant or growl it would have seemed natural, so like a half-circle of wolves they appeared.

On the driver's seat of the cart, Diaz grew pale and spoke guardedly to his small son.

"Chamaco," he said, "these are evil men who await us. Something bad may happen. Slip away in the brush if there is any opportunity. These are the enemies of our leader."

"You know them, Papa? These enemies of our *Presidente*?"

"I know the one with the whip. He is Ortega."

"The Executioner?" The boy whispered the dread name, and Juliano Diaz, slowing the plodding team of burros, answered without moving his head or taking his eyes from the soldiers at the barricade. "*Si, hijo*. It is he, the Killer of Camargo. As you value your life, do not speak the name of El Indio except to curse it. These men seek his life."

El Indio was the name of love that the shirtless ones had given the revolutionary President who they had brought to power with their blood, but who now fought desperately for the life of his new Government, and for the freedoms that he sought to bring to the *descamisados* of all Mexico, be they Indians, such as himself and as Juliano and Chamaco Diaz, or of the Spanish blood, or of any blood whatever. To the small boy, Chamaco, El Indio was like Christ, only more real. He had never seen either one, but he knew he would die for his *Presidente* and was not so sure about the Savior.

He nodded now in response to his father's warning, brave as any ten-year-old boy might be in facing the Executioner of Camargo.

As for Ortega, perhaps the sinister appellation was only a product of ignorance and rebelliousness on the part of the incredibly poor *Indios* of the Motherland. He understood this for himself, it was certain. But being a soldier was hard work and the people never comprehended the necessity for the precautions of military control. This did not mean that one of the Spanish blood could not be gracious and kind within the limitations of his stern duty. The Colonel waved his whip pleasantly enough toward the burro cart.

"Good evening, citizen," he greeted Diaz. "You are surprised to see us here, no doubt. But the delay will be slight. Please to get down from the cart."

"*Que pasa*, Excellence, what is the matter?" In his fear, Diaz did not obey the request to step down, but sat numbly on the seat.

"Ah, you know me!" Ortega was pleased. "Well, it has been my work to get acquainted among the people of El Indio. Did you hear my order?"

"What?" said Diaz. "I forget. What did you say, *Coronel*?"

Ortega moved as a coiled snake might move. He struck out with his whip, its thong wrapping the thin neck of Juliano Diaz. With a violent heave, the guerrilla leader threw the small man from the cart onto the ground, the noose of the whip nearly cracking his vertebrae.

"I said to get down, *Indio*," He smiled. "You do not listen too well. What is the matter? Do you not trust your Mexican brothers?"

Diaz was small in body only. In heart he was a mountain.

"You are no brothers of mine," he said. "I am an Indian."

"Precisely," answered Ortega, helping him up from the dirt of the roadway. "And so is he whom we seek."

Diaz stood proudly, stepping back and away from the kind hands of Colonel Fulgencio Ortega. He made no reply now, but the boy on the seat of the burro cart leaped down and answered for him.

"What!" he exclaimed, unable to accept the fact anyone would truly seek to do ill to the beloved *Presidente*. "Is it true then that you would harm our dead—" Too late he re-

membered his father's warning, and cut off his words.
Ortega liked boys, however, and made allowances for their
innocence.

"Calm yourself, little rooster," he said kindly. "I said
nothing of harming El Indio. Indeed, I said nothing of your
great *Presidente* in any way. Now, how is it you would have
the idea that it is *he* we look for, eh?"

All of Mexico knew the answer to the question. For
weeks the outlands had thrilled to the whisper that El Indio
would make a journey to the United States to find gold and
the hand of friendship from the other great *Presidente*,
Abraham Lincoln. It was understood that such a journey
would be in secret to avoid the forces of the enemy en route.
But from Oaxaca to the Texas border the *descamesados*
were alerted to be on the watch for "The Little Indian" and
to stand at all times ready to forward the fortunes of his journey.

Chamaco Diaz hesitated, not knowing what to say.

His father, brave Juliano, broke into the growing stillness
to advise him in this direction.

"Say nothing, *hijo*," he said quietly, and stood a little
taller as he said it.

Chamaco nodded. He, too, straightened and stood tall beside his father.

They would talk no more and Ortega understood this.

"My children," he said, "you have failed to compre-
hend. We do not seek to harm the *Presidente*, only to detain
him."

If standing tall, Chamaco was still but a small boy. He
had not learned the art of dishonesty.

"Why do you stop *us*, then, *Coronel*?" he demanded.
"We are only poor wood-gatherers from Toltepec, going to
El Paso."

"Just exactly my problem," explained Ortega, with a
flourish of the whip. "You see, *pobrecito*, it is my order
that every Indian going across the border must be measured
against that line that you will see drawn on that dead oak

tree.'' He pointed to the sunblasted spar with the whip. ''Do you see the line on the tree?''

''Si, Coronel.''

''Well, it is drawn five feet from the ground, *chico*. That is just about the tallness of your great *Presidente*, not being too precise. Now the problem is that I, myself, am not familiar with this great man. I would not know him if I saw him. But we have his height reported to us and I have devised this method of, shall we say, ruling out the chance that El Indio shall get over the river into the United States and complete that journey.''

''Coronel,'' broke in Juliano Diaz, going pale despite his great courage, ''what is it you are saying?''

Ortega shrugged good-naturedly.

''Only that if you are an Indian not known to me, or to my men, and if your height is the same as that of El Indio, and if I detain you, then I have prevented a possible escape of your great *Presidente*, eh?''

''You mean that you think I, Juliano Diaz of Toltepec, am—'' He could not finish the thought, so absurd was it to his simple mind. Could this rebel colonel truly believe such a thing? That he, Diaz, was the leader, the great El Indio? Diaz gave his first hint of a relieved look. There was, after all, and even with the sore neck from the whip, something ironic about the idea. ''Please, Excellence,'' Diaz concluded, forcing a small smile for the sake of Chamaco's courage, ''take me to the tree and put me against the mark, so that my son and I may go on to El Paso. My good wife is sick and we need the pesos from this wood to buy medicine in Texas.''

''Chivo!'' snapped Ortega, no longer smiling. ''Measure this Indian.''

Chivo seized Diaz and dragged him to the tree. Pushing him against its scarred trunk, he peered at the line.

''He comes exactly to it, *Jefe*. Just the right size.''

''Very well. Detain him.''

The matter was finished for Colonel Ortega. He turned back to the fire. He did not look around at the pistol shot that blew out the brains of Juliano Diaz. To a scrofulous sergeant, even with the startled, sobbing cry of Chamaco Diaz rising behind him, he merely nodded irritably. "Coffee, Portales. *Jesus Maria!* but it is hot. Damn this river country."

What would have been the fate of Chamaco, the son, no man can say. Chivo was hauling him to the fire by the nape of his neck, pistol poised to finish him as well, with the Colonel's permission. Also, no man can say if Ortega would have granted the favor. For, in the instant of death's hovering, a thunder of hooves arose on the American side of the river and a rider, tall sombrero proclaiming his Mexican identity, dashed his lathered mount across the ford and to a sliding stop by the fire of the Executioner of Camargo.

"*Coronel!*" he cried. "I come from El Paso! Great news is there. El Indio is in the town. He has already been to see the American *Presidente* and is on his way back to *Mejico*!"

Ortega stepped back as though cut in the face with his own whip. The wolf pack of his men drew in upon him. Chivo, in his astonishment that El Indio had gotten out of Mexico and was ready to come back into it, dropped his rough hands from Chamaco Diaz. It was all the signal from above that the quick-witted Indian youth needed. In one scuttling dive, he had reached the crowding growth of river brush, and disappeared, faithful, belatedly, to his dead father's instruction.

Chivo, pistol still smoking, led the yelping rush of the guerrilla band after the boy. Ortega cursed on his men, raging about himself with the lashing whip.

"Kill him, you fools!" he screamed. "He must not get over the river. Shoot! Shoot! Stomp him out and shoot him. He must not warn the Americans that we know they have El Indio! After him, after him, you idiots!"

Deep in the brush, Chamaco wriggled and squirmed and raced for his life. The rifle bullets of the renegades cut the limbs about him. The cruel thorns of the mesquite and cat's-claw and black chaparral ripped his flesh. He could hear the soldiers panting and cursing within stone's toss of his heels.

He cried for his dead father as he ran, but he ran! If God would help him, he would reach the other side of the river, and El Indio.

As the desperate vow formed in his mind, he saw ahead a clearing in the tangled growth. Beyond it, the waters of the Rio Grande flowed silver-red in the sunset dusk.

Riding through the twilight toward El Paso, the thoughts of Charlie Shonto were scarcely designed to change the sun-burned leather mold of his features. Not, at least, for the happier.

A job was a job, he supposed, but it seemed to him that all the while the work got harder and the pay less.

Who was he, Charlie Shonto? And what was the Texas Express Company? And why should the two names cause him pain now, as he clucked to his weary buckskin and said softly aloud, "Slope along, little horse, there's good grass and water a-waitin'."

Well, there was an affinity betwixt the likes of Charlie Shonto and the Texas Express Company—even if it hurt. The latter outfit was a jerkwater stageline that had gotten it-self about as rump-sprung as a general freight and passenger operation might manage to do and still harness four sound horses, and Shonto was a "special agent" for said stage company. But Charlie Shonto did not let the fancy title fool him. There was a shorter term, and a bit more accurate, for the kind of work he did for Texas Express. If a man said it with the proper curl of lip, it came out something awfully close to "hired gun."

Shonto didn't care for the label. He didn't especially rel-ish, either, the risks involved in wearing it. But a "riding gun," be he on the driver's box with an L. C. Smith or Parker on his lap, or in the saddle with a Winchester booted under his knee, made good money for the better jobs. The better jobs, of course, were those in which the survival odds were backed down to something like, or less than, even money. So it was no surprise to Shonto to be sent for by

Texas Express for a "special assignment." The surprise
might lie in the assignment itself, but the suntanned rider
doubted it rather severely. It could be assumed that when
Texas Express sent for Charlie Shonto, the "opportunity for
advancement" was one already turned down by the Rangers
and the U.S. Army, not to mention Wells Fargo, Overland
Mail, or any of the big staging outfits.

Shonto clucked again to the *bayo coyote*, the line-backed
buckskin dun, that he rode.

"Just around the bend, Butterball." He grinned dustily.
"Billets for you and bullets for me."

Butterball, a gaunt panther of a horse that appeared
wicked and rank enough to eat rocks without spitting out the
seeds, rolled an evil eye back at his master, flagged the ragged pennant of his left ear. If he had intended further comment than this one look of tough disgust, the urge was
short-circuited.

Scarcely had the comment about "bullets" left Shonto's
lips, than a respectable, if well-spent, hail of them began to
fall around him in the thicket. Next instant, the sounds of the
rifle shots were following the leaden advance guard in scattered volleys.

Instinctively, he ticked Butterball with the spurs and the
bony gelding sprinted like a quarter-mile racer for the near
bend ahead. When he bore Shonto around that bend, the latter hauled him up sharply. Across the Rio Grande a tattered
company of Mexican irregulars were target-practicing at a
dark, bobbing object in midstream. Shonto's immediate reaction was one of relief that the riflemen had not been firing
at him. The next thought was a natural curiosity as to what
they had been firing at. It was then the third message
reached his tired mind, and his mouth went hard. *That was a
little kid swimming for the American side out there.*

The night was well down. In the Texas Express office in
El Paso, three men waited. The drawn shade, trimmed

lamp, the tense glances at the wall clock ticking beyond the waybill desk, all spoke louder than the silence.

"I wish Shonto would get here," complained express agent Deems Harter. "It ain't like him to be late. Maybe Ortega crossed over the river under dark and blind-sided him."

The second man, heavy-set, dressed in eastern clothing, calm and a little cold, shook his head.

"Shonto isn't the type to be blind-sided, Deems. You forget he's worked for me before. I didn't exactly pull his name out of a hat."

Deems Harter stiffened. "That don't mean Ortega didn't pull it out of a sombrero!"

Sheriff Nocero Casey, last of the trio, nodded.

"Deems is right, Mr. Halloran. I don't care for Charlie being late either. It *ain't* like him. If Ortega did hear we had sent for Charlie Shonto—" He broke off, scowling.

Halloran took him up quickly. "It's not Shonto being late that is really bothering you, is it? I counted on you, Sheriff. I didn't dare import a bunch of U.S. Marshals. I hope you're not getting cold feet."

"No, sir. It's common sense I'm suffering from. This job is way out of my bailiwick. The Government ought to send troops or something to see it through. It's too big."

Again Halloran shook his head. "The U.S. Government can't set one toe across that river, Sheriff. You know that. It's the law. That's why we've brought in your 'special agent.' Mr. Shonto is a man who understands the law. He appreciates its niceties, its challenges."

"Yeah, I've often wondered about that," said the sheriff. "But I won't argue it."

"Ah, good. You see, there is no law that says Texas Express cannot ship a consignment, such as our invaluable Item 13, into Toltepec. It will be done every day now that the new Mexican Central line has reached that city."

Agent Deems Harter interrupted this optimism with a groan.

"Good Lord, Mr. Halloran, what's the use of talking

about what we can ship when that cussed Mexican Central Railroad starts running regular between Toltepec and Mexico City? They ain't even run one work engine over that new line that I know of. Them damned ties into Toltepec are still oozing greenwood sap!''

Halloran's heavy jaw took a defiant set.

''Are your feet feeling the chill, also, Deems? I thought we had the plan agreed to. Where's the hitch?''

Agent Deems stared at his questioner as if the latter had taken leave of whatever few senses Government secret service operatives were granted in the beginning.

''Where's the hitch, you say? Oh, hardly anywhere at all, Mr. Halloran. You're only asking us to deliver this precious Item 13 of yours to railhead in Toltepec, Mexico, fifty miles across the river, tonight, with no one wise, whatever, right square through Colonel Fulgencio Ortega's northern half of the loyalist guerrilla army, guaranteeing to get our 'shipment' on the train at Toltepec safe and sound in wind and limb, and then to come back a-grinning and a-shrugging and a-saying, 'Why, shucks, it wasn't nothing. It's done every day.' Mister, you ain't just plain crazy, you're extra fancy nuts.''

''As bad as all that, eh?''

''Damn near,'' put in Sheriff Casey. ''We don't know if that Mexican train will be in Toltepec. We don't even know if those wild-eyed coffeebeans even got a train. All we know is that you Government men tell us they got the train, and that it'll be in Toltepec if we get this Item 13 there. Now that's some *if*.''

Halloran was careful. He knew that only these local people—Texans familiar with every coyote track and kit-fox trail leading into Chihuahua—could bring off the delivery of Item 13. Nothing must go wrong now.

''If we took Item 13 five thousand miles, Sheriff, surely Texas Express ought to be able to forward shipment the remaining fifty miles to Toltepec.''

''Huh!'' said Deems Harter. ''You got a lot more faith in Texas Express than we have. In fact, about forty-nine miles more. As agent, I'll guarantee to get your precious shipment exactly one mile. That's from here to the Rio Grande. Past that, I wouldn't give you a nickel for your chances of making that train in Toltepec. *If* there's a train in Toltepec.''

Halloran shook his head, unmoved.

''I'm not exactly thinking of my faith in terms of Texas Express, Harter. It's Charlie Shonto we're all gambling on.''

''Yeah,'' said Deems Harter acridly. ''And right now Charlie Shonto looks like a mighty poor gamble.''

''Well, anyways,'' broke in Sheriff Nocero Casey, who had drifted to the front window for another look up the street, ''a mighty wet one. Yonder comes our special delivery man, and it looks to me as though he's already been across the river. He's still dripping.''

Halloran and Harter joined him in peering from behind the drawn shade. It was the express agent who recovered first.

''Good Lord!'' he gasped. ''What's that he's toting behind him?''

Sheriff Nocero Casey squinted carefully.

''Well,'' he said, ''the bright lights of El Paso ain't precisely the best to make bets by, but if I had to take a scattergun guess at this distance and in the dark, I'd say it was a sopping wet and some undersized Chihuahua Indian boy.''

In the shaded office of the Texas Express Company, the silence had returned again. First greetings were over. Shonto and Halloran had briefly touched upon their past experiences during the War Between the States, and the time had very quickly run down to that place where everyone pauses, knowing that the next words are the ones that the money is being paid for. Sheriff Casey, Agent Harter, Shonto, even little Chamaco Diaz, all were watching P.J. Halloran.

''Now, Charlie,'' said the latter, at last, ''we haven't sent for you to review the squeaks you've been in before." He let the small grimace that may or may not have been a smile pass over his rough features. "But I did feel that some slight mention of our past associations might prepare you for the present proposal."

"What you're saying, Mr. Halloran, is that you figure your Irish blarney is going to soften up my good sense." Shonto's own grin was a bit difficult to classify. It was hard as flint and yet warmed too, somehow, by a good nature, or at least a wry appreciation of life as it actually worked out in the living. "But you're wasting your talents," he concluded. "I've had a couple of birthdays since I was crossing the Confederate lines for you, and now I don't sign up just for a pat on the back from my fellow countrymen. I've learned since the war that a man can't buy a bag of Bull Durham with a Government citation. Not that I regret my time in the 'silent service,' mind you. But a fellow just doesn't like to be a hog about the hero business. Especially, when he did his great deeds for the North, then went back to earning his keep in the South. You spend your time in Texas, Mr. Halloran, you don't strain yourself reminding the local folks that you took your war pay in Union greenbacks. *Comprende?*"

Halloran nodded quickly.

"Don't be a fool, Charlie," he said. "Harter, here, and Sheriff Casey were carefully sounded out before we ever mentioned your name. They are not still afire with the lost cause. We can forget your war work."

"I'm glad you told me, Mr. Halloran. Somehow, I still remember it every so often. Matter of fact, I still occasionally wake up in a cold sweat. Now I can put all that behind me. Isn't it wonderful?"

"Shonto"—Halloran's hard face had turned cold again— "come over here to the window. I want to show you something." He took a pair of binoculars from Harter's desk and Shonto followed him to the drawn shade. There, Halloran gave the glasses to him and said quietly, "Look yonder on the balcony of the Franklin House. Tell me what you see. Describe it exactly.''

From the other's tone, Shonto knew the talk had gotten to the money point. He took the glasses and focused them on the hotel's second-story *galeria*, the railed porch so common to the Southwestern architecture of the times. As the view came into sharp detail, he frowned uneasily.

"All right," he began, low-voiced. "I see a man. He's short. Maybe not much over five feet. He stands straight as a yardstick. Stocky build. Big in the chest. Dark as hell in the skin, near as I can see in the lamplight from the room windows behind him. He's dressed in a black eastern suit that don't fit him, and same goes for a white iron collar and necktie. Black hat, no creases, wore square like a sombrero. Long black hair, bobbed off like it was done with horse shears.'' He paused, squinting more narrowly through the binoculars. "Why, hell,'' he added softly. "That's a damned Indian dressed up in white man's clothes!"

"That," said P.J. Halloran, just as softly, "is exactly what it is." They turned from the window. "Up there on that balcony," Halloran continued, "is the most important man, next to Lincoln, in North America. I can't reveal his identity and you will have to know him as Item 13, until you have him safely on that waiting train at Toltepec."

"What train at Toltepec?" Shonto frowned. "Since when have they built the Mexican Central on into that two-burro burg?"

"Since today, we hope," said Halloran. "The idea was that, precisely as you, no one knew the railroad had been laid on into Toltepec. Those last few thousand yards of track were to be spiked down today. The gamble is that not even Ortega and the *rurales* would hear about it in time. Or, hearing of it, not realize a train was waiting to be run over it."

"That's what I'd call house odds, Mr. Halloran. This Item 13 must be one big table-stakes man."

"He is," answered the Government operative. "Anyway, Charlie, that train is supposed to be waiting at midnight in Toltepec. If we can get Item 13 there, the train can get on down past Camargo by daybreak, and out of Ortega's reach—if the train's waiting in Toltepec.''

"Longest two-letter word in the world," said Shonto. "Go ahead, drop the other boot."

"Well, we know that powerful enemies lie between El Paso and Toltepec. There's no point explaining to you the type of 'enemy' I mean. I believe you're familiar enough with Colonel Ortega and his 'loyal militia.' ''

"Yes, just about familiar enough. In case you're still wondering how Chamaco and I got ourselves doused in the Rio, it was meeting Ortega's loyal army, or as big a part of it as I came prepared to handle. I'd say there was twenty of them. They were pot-shooting at the kid swimming the river. He got away from them while they were murdering his father. Butterball got excited at the rifle fire and ran away with me. Bolted right into the damned river. Next thing I knew, I was in as bad a shape as the kid and, long as I figured two could ride as cheap as one, I scooped him up and we made it back to the American side by way of hanging onto Butterball's tail and holding long breaths under water on the way. I have got to get me another horse. In my business, you can't be fooling around with jumpy crowbaits like that."

"When you decide what you want for Butterball," put in Sheriff Nocero Casey, "let me know. I've been looking for just such a loco horse."

"Charlie," broke in Halloran, "are you interested or not? We've got to move soon."

Shonto nodded speculatively, a man not to be rushed.

"Depends. You haven't dropped that other boot yet."

"All right." Halloran spoke quickly now. "The small man in the black suit carries a letter of credit—a U.S. letter of credit—for an enormous amount of money. Some say as high as $50,000,000. That's $50,000,000 U.S., not Mexican. It's to bail out his revolution down there." Halloran gestured toward the Rio Grande, and Mexico. "I don't need to tell you, Charlie, what men like Ortega's will do to prevent that letter from getting to Mexico City. The money

means the rebels are through—loyalists, they call themselves—and that the revolution will succeed and will stay in
power. As you have already learned when your horse ran
away with you, Colonel Ortega has been assigned the job of
sealing off the border in Chihuahua State. Now, it becomes
your job to unseal that border.''

Charlie Shonto's grin was dry as dust.

"Shucks, nothing to that. Nothing that I couldn't do with
ten or twelve companies of Rangers, and a regiment of regular cavalry.''

"Don't joke, Charlie.'' Halloran pulled out an official
document, handed it to Shonto. "Here are my orders. You
don't need to read them. But check that final postscript at the
bottom of the page against the signature beneath the Great
Seal of this country you and I fought for, when *he* asked us
to."

Shonto glanced down the page, read slowly aloud:

. . . any man who may aid the bearer of these orders
in the business to hand will know that the gratitude of
his Government and my own personal indebtedness
shall be his and shall not be forgotten. Signed,
ABRAHAM LINCOLN

"My God!'' said Shonto, handing back the document, as
gingerly as though it were the original of the Declaration of
Independence. "Why didn't you say so, Mr. Halloran?''

"Like you,'' Halloran smiled, and this time there was no
doubt it was a smile, "I always save my best shot for the last
target. What do you say, Charlie?''

"I say, let's go. For *him* I'd wrestle a bear, blindfolded.
Who all's in it?''

"Just you, Charlie. I've brought our man this far. Sheriff
Casey and Agent Harter have handled him here in town. But
from here to Toltepec, he's your cargo. *If* you'll accept
him."

Shonto winced perceptibly.

"There's that word again. You got anything extra to go with it this time?"

Halloran picked up a rolled map from Harter's desk.

"Only this chart of the area between here and Toltepec supplied by the Mexican Government. You know this ground as well as any man on this side of the Rio Grande. Take a look at this layout of it and tell us if you spot any way, at all, of getting through Ortega's patrols, into Toltepec."

He spread the map on the desk. Harter turned up the wick. The four men bent over the wrinkled parchment. Behind them, the little Indian, Chamaco Diaz, had been forgotten. He stood silently in the shadows, wondering at the talk of these *Americanos*. Chamaco had been to school some small time in El Paso, and knew enough of English to follow the conversation in the rough. Lonely and sorrowful as he was, he knew who that other little Indian in the black suit was, and his heart swelled with love and pride for these *Americano* men, that they would talk of risking their lives that El Indio might live and might reach Ciudad Mejico with the United States money that would save the *Presidente*'s brave Government of the *descamisados* and *pobrecitos*, like his father, Juliano Diaz, who had given their lives to establish it. Now, Chamaco watched the four big *Americanos* bent over the map of Toltepec—his part of the beloved Motherland—and he waited with held breath for what the verdict of the one tall man with the dried leather face would be.

For his part, the latter was having considerable last doubts. The map wasn't showing him anything he didn't already know. Presently, he glanced up at Halloran.

"There's no help, here," he said. "I was hoping to see an old Apache route I've heard stories of. But this map shows nothing that wouldn't get me and the little man in the black suit stood up against the same tree that Chamaco's daddy was stood up against. Ortega knows all these trails."

"There's nothing, then? No way at all?"

"Yes, there's that Apache brushtrack. It was never found by the Rangers, but they know it exists. They've run the

Chihuahua Apaches right to the river, time and again, then seen them vanish like smoke into midnight air. If we knew where *that* trail went over the Rio, we might have a coyote's chance of sneaking past Ortega's assassins.'' Shonto shook his head. "But there isn't a white man alive who knows where that Apache track runs. . . ."

His words trailed off helplessly and the four men straightened with that weary stiffness that foretells defeat. But into their glum silence, a small voice, and forgotten, penetrated thinly.

"*Señores*, I am not a white man."

Shonto and his companions wheeled about. Chamaco moved out of the shadows, into the lamplight.

"I am an Indian, *Patrones*, and I know where the old trail runs."

The four men exchanged startled looks and, in their momentary inability to speak, Chamaco thought that he detected reproof for his temerity in coming forward in the company of such powerful friends of Mexico. He bowed with apologetic humility, and stepped back into the shadows.

"But of course," he said, small-voiced, "you would not trust to follow an Indian. Forgive me, *señores*."

Shonto moved to his side. He put his hand to the thin shoulder. Telling the boy to follow him, he led the way to the office window. He held back the drawn shade while Chamaco, obeying him, peered down the street at the balcony of the Franklin House.

"Boy," he said, "do you know who that small man is standing up there on the *galeria*?"

Chamaco's eyes glowed with the fire of his pride.

"*Si, Patrón!*" he cried excitedly. "It is *he*! Who else could stand and look so sad and grand across the river?"

Shonto nodded. "You think *he* would trust an Indian boy?"

Chamaco drew himself up to his full four feet and perhaps five inches. In his reply was all the dignity of the poor.

"*Patrón,*" he said, "he once *was* an Indian boy!"

Charlie Shonto nodded again. He tightened the arm about the boy's shoulders and turned to face the others.

"Don't know about you," he said to them, "but I've just hired me an Indian guide to Toltepec."

The men at the desk said nothing, and again Chamaco misinterpreted their hesitation.

"Patrón," he said to Charlie Shonto, "do *you* know who it is up there standing on the *galeria* looking so sad toward *Mejico*?"

"I could take an uneducated guess," answered Shonto, "but I won't. You see, Chamaco, I'm not supposed to know. He's just a job to me. It doesn't matter who he is."

The Indian boy was astounded. It passed his limited comprehension.

"And you would risk your life for a stranger to you?" he asked, unbelievingly. "For an Indian in a shabby black white man's suit? A small funny-looking man with a foreign hat and long hair and a dark skin the same as mine? You would do this, *Patrón*, and for nothing?"

Shonto grinned and patted him on the head.

"Well, hardly for nothing, boy."

"For what, then, *Patrón*?"

"Money, boy. *Pesos. Muchos pesos.*"

"And only for that, *Patrón*?"

At the persistence, Shonto's cynical grin faded. He made a small, deprecatory gesture. It was for Chamaco, alone. He had forgotten the others.

"Let's just say that I was watching your face when you looked up at the *galeria* a minute ago. All right, *amigo*?"

The dark eyes of Chamaco Diaz lit up like altar candles.

"Patrón," he said, "you should have been an Indian; you have eyes in your heart!"

Shonto grinned ruefully. "Something tells me, boy, that before we get our cargo past Ortega tonight we'll be wishing I had those eyes in the back of my head."

Chamaco reached up and took the gunman's big hand. He patted it reassuringly. *"Patrón,"* he smiled back, "do not be afraid. If we die, we die in a good and just cause. We lose only our two small lives. Him, up there on the *galeria*, he has in his hands the lives of all the poor people of *Mejico*. Is that not a very fair exchange, our lives for all of those others, and for his?''

Shonto glanced at the other men.

''Well, Chamaco,'' he said, ''that's one way of looking at it. Excuse us, gentlemen, we've got a train to catch in Toltepec.'' He took the boy's hand in his and they went out into the street. Halloran moved to follow them. At the door he halted a moment, shaking his head as he looked back at the express agent and the sheriff.

''Do you know what we've just done?'' he said. ''We've just bet $50,000,000 and the future of Mexico on a Chihuahua Indian kid not one of us ever laid eyes on prior to twenty minutes ago.''

The coach bounced and swayed through the night. Its sidelamps, almost never lit, were now sputtering and smoking. They seemed to declare that this particular old Concord wanted to be certain her passage toward the lower ford would be noted from the far side—and followed.

The idea was valid.

The lower crossing—the old Apache route—was the way in which a mind of no great deception might seek to elude examination by the *rurales* at the upper, or main, crossing. The driver of the old Texas Express vehicle, a canvas-topped Celerity model made for desert speed, held the unalterable belief that the Mexican mind was so devious as to be very nearly simple. It twisted around so many times in its *Latino* tracks, trying to be clever, that, in the end, it usually wound up coming right back where it started.

The driver was banking on this trait.

He was depending on Colonel Fulgencio Ortega to think that when the planted rumor from El Paso reached him by avenue of his kinsmen in that city, he would say, ''Ahah! This stupid *Americano* stageline company thinks that if they announce they will try to cross with El Indio at the lower ford, that I shall at once conclude they really mean to cross at the new upper ford, and that I shall then be waiting for them at the new upper ford and they can cross in safety at the lower place. What fools. I shall quite naturally watch both crossings, and this they realize full well. What they are trying to do is see that I, personally, am not at the lower ford. They think that if they can contest the crossing with my men—without me—it will be a far easier matter. Well, now! *Ai, Chihuahua!* Let them come . Let them come. Let them find out who will be waiting for their disreputable stagecoach and its mysterious passenger at the old lower ford! Hah! Why will they attempt to match wits with the Executioner of Camargo? *Idiotas!*''

Of course, if Colonel Ortega did not reason thus, the driver of the coach would have made a grievous error, for the entire plan depended on meeting the Executioner.

The driver, a weatherbeaten, leathery fellow, wrapped the lines of the four-horse hitch a bit tighter. He spoke to his leaders and his wheelers, tickled the ears of the former and the haunches of the latter with the tip of his fifteen-foot coaching whip.

"Coo-ee, boys!" he called to the horses. "Just so, just so." Leaning over the box, he spoke to the muffled, dark-faced passenger—the only passenger—in the rocking stage. "*Señor*, is it all well with you, in there?" He used the Spanish tongue, but no reply came in kind from the interior. Indeed, no reply came in any tongue.

A very brave fellow, thought the driver. His kind were not many in the land below the Rio—or any land.

"You are a very small boy," said the somber-looking little man. "How is it that you are so brave?"

"Please, *Presidente*. I beg of you not to say more, just now. We are very near to the place, and there is great danger." Chamaco spoke with awed diffidence.

"I am not afraid, boy." El Indio patted him on the shoulder. "Do I not have a good Indian guide?"

"*Presidente*, please, say no more. You don't know Colonel Ortega."

"I have dealt with his kind. I know him, all right. They are all alike. Cowards. Jackals. Don't be afraid, boy. What did you say your name was?"

Chamaco told him, and the small man nodded.

"A good Indian name. It means what it says. How much farther now, boy, before we cross the river?"

They were moving through a tunneled avenue in the river's brushy scrub of willow and rushes. It was the sort of thoroughfare frequented by the creatures of the night. None but very small men—or boys—might have used it, at all, and then only very small Indian men or boys. If the Rangers had wanted to know one reason, just one, why the Apaches raiding up from Chihuahua had been able to disappear before their eyes on the American side of the Rio, it would have been that they were seeking some "hole" in the brush that would accommodate an ordinary mortal—not a Chihuahua Indian. But Chamaco Diaz was not only a small Indian boy; he was a patriot.

"*Presidente,*" he now pleaded, "will you not be quiet? *Por favor*, Excellence! We are coming to it this moment."

The small man in the black suit smiled.

"You dare to address me in this abrupt manner!" he said. "You, an Indian boy? A shirtless waif of the border? A brush-rat of the river bottom? *Ali!*"

"*Presidente,*" said the boy, "I will ask it one more time. I know that you do not fear the Executioner. I know that I am only a *pobrecito*, a *reducido*, a nothing. But in my heart you live with the Lord Jesus. I will die for you, *Presidente*, as I would for Him, even sooner. But I have sworn to guide you across the river and to the rendezvous. I have sworn to get you to Toltepec by midnight this night. Therefore, why should we die, when you must live for the people of our suffering land? I am taking you to Toltepec, *Presidente*. And if you continue to speak along the way, I will die for nothing and *Mejico* will never get the money you bear and she will not be saved. But mostly, *Presidente*, you will be dead. I cannot bear that. You are the life of all of us.''

They had stopped moving. El Indio, in a streak of moonlight penetrating the arched limbs above them, could see the tears coursing down the dark cheeks of Chamaco Diaz. He reached quickly with his fingers and brushed away the tears.

''An Indian does not weep,'' he told the boy sternly. ''Go ahead, now. I shall be still.''

Chamaco swallowed hard. He dashed his own hand quickly at the offending eyes. His voice was vibrant with pride.

''It was the brush, *Presidente*. The small limbs snapping back and stinging me across the face. You know how it is.''

El Indio nodded once more.

''Of course, boy. I have been in the brush many times. Go ahead, lead the way. I have been an old woman talking too much. We are both Indians, eh? *Vámonos!*''

Straight as a rifle barrel, Chamaco Diaz stood before him a moment. Then, ducking down again, he scuttled on ahead. El Indio watched him go. Just before he bent to follow him, he glanced up at the patch of moonlight. The beams struck his own dark face. They glistened on something that seemed more moist and in movement than his coffee-colored features. But then, of course, in moonlight the illusions are many and the lunar eye is not to be trusted. Had he not just said, himself, that Indians did not weep?

The coach of the Texas Express Company splashed over the old Apache Crossing and came to a halt before the flaring bonfire and wooden barricade across the Toltepec road. *''Que pasa?''* the tall driver called down to the leering brigand who commanded the guard. ''What is the matter? Why do you stop me?''

''De nada, it is nothing.'' Lieutenant Chivo smiled. ''A small matter that will take but a moment. I hope you have a moment? *Si? Muy bien. Coronel!*'' he called to the squat of-

ficer drinking coffee by the fireside. "The stage for Toltepec has arrived on time."

The Colonel put down his tin cup and picked up a long quirt. Uncoiling the whip, he arose and came over to the barricade. He stood a moment looking up at the coachman. After a moment, he nodded pleasantly enough and spoke in a friendly manner.

"Please to get down," he said.

"Sorry, I can't do it," replied the driver. "Company rules, Colonel. You understand."

"Of course," said the guerrilla chief easily. "Without rules nothing is accomplished. I'm a great believer in discipline. Did I introduce myself? Colonel Fulgencio Ortega, of Camargo. Now do you care to get down?"

"*The* Colonel Ortega," said the American driver, impressed. "*Jefe*, this is a great honor. And these are your famed *rurales*?" He pointed with the handle of his own whip to the surly pack stalking up now, to stand behind the Colonel and his lieutenant. "My, but they are a fine-looking troop. Real fighters, one can see that. But then why not? On the side of justice all men fight well, eh, *Coronel*?"

Ortega ignored the compliments.

"Did you hear what I said?" he asked. "I wish you to get down. I do not believe I have met your passenger, and I think you should introduce me to him. My men will hold your horses."

His men were already holding the horses, the driver was keenly aware. Also, he did not miss the fact that the soldiers were holding something else for him. Their rifles. Pointed squarely at him. But he was the steady sort—or perhaps merely stupid.

"Passenger?" he said. "I carry no passenger, *Coronel*. Just some freight for Toltepec."

Ortega stepped back. He looked again into the coach.

"Freight, eh?" he mused. "Strange wrappings you have put around your cargo, *cochero*. A black suit. Black hat with round Indian crown worn squarely on the head. And see how your freight sits on the seat of the coach, just as if it were alive and had two arms and two legs and might speak if spoken to. That is, if fear has not sealed its cowardly Indian tongue!'' His voice was suddenly wicked with hatred, all the smile and the pretense of easiness gone out of it, and out of him. ''Chivo!'' he snapped. ''Please to open the door of this coach and help *El Presidente* to dismount!''

The stage driver straightened on the box.

''El Presidente?'' he said to Ortega. ''Whatever in the world are you talking about, *Jefe*?''

''We shall see in a moment.'' Ortega nodded, in control of himself once more. ''Hurry, Chivo. This *cochero* does not understand the importance of his passenger. Nor is it apparent to him that jokes about 'freight' that walks and talks like an Indian are not laughed at in Chihuahua just now. You fool! Get that coach door opened!''

Chivo, grinning stupidly, threw open the door of the Concord and seized the lone passenger by the arm. With an oath, he pulled the small figure from the coach and hurled it viciously to the ground.

His surprise was understandable.

It was not the usual thing for a victim's arm to come off at the shoulder and remain in the offending hand of its assaulter while the remainder of the torso went flying off through the night. Neither was it the usual thing for the poor devil's head to snap off and go rolling away like a melon when the body thudded to earth.

''Santissima!'' cried one of the brute soldiers of the guard. ''You have ruined him, you dumb fool.''

But Lieutenant Chivo did not hear the remark, and Colonel Ortega, if he heard it, did not agree with the sentiment, except perhaps as to Chivo's intelligence. For what the guerrilla lieutenant had pulled from the Texas Express Company's Toltepec stage was quite clearly a dressmaker's dummy clothed to resemble a very short and large-chested Mexican Indian man who always sat very straight on his seat and wore his black hat very squarely on his head.

Moreover, Colonel Fulgencio Ortega was given no real time in which to comment upon his soldier's awed remark, or his lieutenant's amazed reaction to the arm in his hand and the head rolling free upon the firelit banks of the Rio Grande. For in the small moment of stricken dumbness that had invaded all of the *rurales* when *El Presidente*'s body had come apart in midair, the American driver of the Toltepec stage had wrapped the lines of his four-horse hitch, stepped to the ground in one giant stride from the precarious box of the old Concord, and all in the same motion slid out a long-barreled Colt's revolver and buried its iron snout in the hairy belly of the Executioner of Camargo.

"Jefe," he announced quietly, "if you make the one false movement, your bowels will be blown out all over this river-bank," and this statement Colonel Fulgencio Ortega had no difficulty whatever in comprehending.

"Chivo!" he cried out. "Hold the men. Let no one touch trigger!"

"Yes, Chivo." The leather-faced American *"cochero"* nodded, spinning Ortega around so that the muzzle of the Colt was in his spine. "And so that you do not in greed seek to replace your beloved *Jefe* in command of the *rurales* of Camargo—that is to say, that you do not in this moment of seeming opportunity make some move deliberately to get me to shoot him—permit me to introduce myself."

"Ah?" queried Chivo, who truly had not yet thought of this obvious course of treachery to his leader. "And to what point would this be, *cochero*? Do you think that I am in fear of stagecoach drivers?"

The tall driver shrugged.

"Well, I think you ought to have the same break I give any other man I'm paid to get past."

There was something in the way that he spoke the one word "paid," that penetrated Chivo's wily mind. He hesitated, but two of the soldiers did not. Thinking that they stood well enough behind their companions to be safe, they moved a little aside from the pack to get a line of fire at the big *Americano*. The instant they were clear of their friends, however, flame burst from behind the back of Colonel Ortega—one lancing flash, then another—and the two soldiers were down and dying in the same blending roar of pistol shots.

"Shonto," said the stage driver to Chivo, the smoking muzzle of the Colt again in Ortega's spine. "Over there across the river, they call me Shonto."

"*Jesus Maria!*" breathed Chivo, dropping his rifle, unbidden, into the dirt of the wagon road. "Carlos Shonto? *Por Dios, pistolero*, why didn't you say so?"

"I just did." Charlie Shonto nodded. "Now you better say something. Quick."

Chivo shrugged in that all-meaning way of his kind.

"What remains to die for?" he inquired. "You do not have El Indio in the stage. You have fooled us with the dummy on the ground over there. Somewhere, *El Presidente* is no doubt riding through the night. But it is not upon the stage for Toltepec. Another of our guards will get him. For us, the work of the day is over. Command me."

Shonto then ordered all the soldiers to drop their rifles and cartridge bandoliers. All knives, pistols, axes, went into the common pile. This arsenal was then loaded into the stage, along with Colonel Fulgencio Ortega, bound hand-and-foot by his faithful followers. The work went forward under Chivo's expert direction, the spirit of the *rurales* now totally flagged. With their chances of snaring El Indio had gone their interest in being heroes. Like soldiers everywhere, they were of no great menace in themselves. Deprived of leadership, they were just so many surly dogs quarreling among themselves. Shonto had gambled on this. And gambled exceedingly well.

Yet, as in every risk, there is lurking one element of the unknown, one thing that cannot be depended upon except in the name of "luck."

Shonto's luck ran out with the command he now issued to the scar-faced Chivo.

"All right, Lieutenant," he said. "Up you go. You'll be the *cochero* now. I'll ride shotgun. *Sabe usted la escopeta?*" With the question, he reached for the double-barreled Parker laid across the driver's box, and Chivo nodded hastily. He "savvied" shotguns very well. One did not argue with them at close range—not ever. But Shonto had made his basic mistake some time ago. It was when he had put the thought of succeeding to Ortega's place of power in Camargo in the mind of the brutal lieutenant. Such towering aspirations had never flooded his dark brain. True, he would have seen Ortega killed in a moment, should that suit his purpose. This much was exactly what Shonto had guessed. What the wary gunman had not foreseen, however, was that, until he, Shonto, had mentioned the matter, Chivo had never really thought about the possibility of promoting himself over his Colonel.

Now the prospect inflamed his jackal's mind.

"Whatever you say, *Jefe*," he told Shonto, fanging a smirk that the latter hardly supposed was a grin of good nature. "You see, I climb to the seat gladly. I take the lines and am ready to drive for you. Come on. Let's go."

Shonto started to swing up after him. For one moment both hands were occupied. It was in that moment that the boot of Lieutenant Chivo drove into his face. Shonto fell backward, landing hard. The shotgun was still in his grasp but was useless from the angle. Above him, Chivo was shouting the horses into motion. The coach lurched forward. Shonto made it to his feet in time to leap for the trunk straps in the rear. He caught one of them, held on, dragged behind the moving stage for fifty feet. He still had the shotgun in his right hand.

The soldiers, sensing his helplessness, ran toward him. They seized up clubs and rocks on the run. Chivo, in response to their yells, slowed the stage, thinking to allow them to beat and stone the dragging *Americano*. Shonto held on to the trunk strap. When the snarling soldiers were near, he raised the shotgun and fired it with one hand into their faces. The first barrel and the second blasted as one. The soldiers screamed and fell away, three to stagger and fall mortally wounded, two others clutching at their shredded faces, screaming in agony.

Chivo, on the driver's box, turned in time to see Shonto

haul himself up over the rear of the Concord. He had no weapon, now, but neither did the lieutenant. Chivo knew the one way open to him, and took it. Over the side he went, rolling to the ground and free of the speeding wheels, the excited teams running wild the moment he flung away the lines. Shonto, weaving precariously, made it to the driver's box and threw himself down between the straining horses to recover the lines.

His luck now returned. He was able to gather up the harness and to return to the box, the coach under control and still upright on the wagon road to Toltepec. But now he knew the wolf pack behind him had a leader again. He could guess how long it would take Chivo to mount the survivors and take up the pursuit.

"Coo-ee, coo-ee," he called to the snorting teams. "Steady down. You've not begun your night's work yet."

Where he had said he would be waiting beside the wagon road to Toltepec with *El Presidente*, there Chamaco Diaz waited when, half an hour's loping run from the Rio, Shonto pulled up his panting horses and hailed the underbrush. The Indian boy had guided his charge without fail and on foot through the night and between the prowling soldiers of Colonel Ortega four miles south of the river. The ancient and secret Apache escape route from Texas, which the two had traveled to reach their rendezvous with Charlie Shonto and the stage for Toltepec, lay still unknown behind them. Shonto did not ask Chamaco where it ran, and the boy did not tell him. He was an Indian, even now, and Charlie Shonto was a white man.

Swiftly, then, the last part of the plan was put into operation. The four horses were unhooked from the coach. Four saddles and bridles were brought from the coach trunk and the mounts were readied. Colonel Ortega was removed from the stage and hung over the saddle of one mount in the manner of a sack of grain. Shonto tied his hands to his feet under the horse's belly, halfway hoping the ropes would not hold. Where the rutted track of the road bent to go past the rendezvous, an eighty-foot bluff rose above the Chihuahuan plain.

Over this drop, Shonto and his two Indian friends now tossed the Concord's load of firearms. There was no time for more effective disposal. Mounting up, the party set out, away from the road, Chamaco leading, Shonto bringing up the rear with the packhorse of the Executioner of Camargo. The goat path along which the small Indian boy took them disappeared into the desert *brasada* within the parabola of a pistol's shot from the wagon road. Shonto had no more idea where the trail led than did Ortega or *El Presidente*. No options remained in any event. Behind them, along the road from the river, they heard now the shouts of men of Mexican tongue, and the hammer of horses' hooves in considerable number. In a pause to listen, they all recognized the high yelping tones of Lieutenant Chivo discovering the abandoned stage and guessing, amid a goat's beard of rotten curses, the manner of flight of his enemies. And more. From Chivo's murderous bleats, they made out that he had with him another patrol of Ortega's, evidently encountered along the way. These new soldiers, whatever their number, would be armed and were, clearly, being commanded by the Colonel's good lieutenant. All might still have been well, yes, surely would have been so, considering the depth of the *brasada* and the blindness of its cover. But in the press of time and because he had not thought ahead to the complication of Chivo picking up more arms en route, Shonto had not taken the precaution he ordinarily would have of gagging the captive Colonel.

He thought of it, now, as Ortega's galling shout echoed down the slope they were climbing.

"*Aqui, aqui, muchachos!* I am here. I am here—"

His head was hanging on that side of the horse nearest Shonto. The shout for help was cut off by the toe of the gunman's boot knocking out four front teeth and knocking out, too, the owner of the teeth. But the price of poker had just gone up, regardless.

"Chamaco," he said, "we have one chance—to split up."

"Never, *Patrón*."

"Listen, kid," Shonto's voice went hard as glass, "you do what I tell you. I'm running this show."

"No, my *Americano* friend, you are not." The denial did not come from the boy, but from the small man in the black suit. "It is I who must say what will be. And I say we stay together. You are not with Spaniards, my friend. You are not with traitors who call themselves Mexicans. You are with Indians. Lead on, boy."

Shonto knew he was helpless. He knew, as well, that they were helpless. That it would be but a matter of minutes before the *rurales* would come up to them, blind brush or not. They were so close behind that they could follow by ear the sounds of their horses breaking through the *brasada*. The rifle-firing would commence any moment after that, and a bullet, unaimed except by the noise of their ponies crashing ahead, would soon enough find all and each of them. There was no other end within reason.

Yet Chamaco Diaz was no victim of such knowledge.

He had been supported by his *Presidente*, had heard him with his own ears say "we" are Indians. What was not possible in the service of such a man?

"Patrón!" he now called to Shonto, voice high and sharp with excitement. "There is a way. Follow me and don't worry about making noise. You know those Rangers from your *Tehas* side of the river did not always obey the law!"

Their horses were ploughing on up the slope now, and true to Shonto's fear, the guerrillas were beginning to fire blindly at the sounds of their progress. The bullets hissed and sang about them. But the boy's shout had intrigued Charlie Shonto.

"What's that?" he yelled back.

"The Rangers," answered the boy, laughing for the first time in Shonto's memory of him. "Many times they would run the Apaches right on across, *Patrón*. Then the Apaches had to have another way on this side to 'lose' them. I know the way, *Patrón*. Ride hard and jump your horse when I demand it."

Shonto wanted to know more about that "jump" busi-

ness, but the guerrillas were too close now. All he could do
was bend low in the saddle and hope the bullet with his name
on it went astray. It did. They came to Chamaco's "jumping
place" without a wound. The place, itself, was a declivity—
dug by hand, and centuries gone—in the trail where no rider,
not knowing that it waited beyond the steeply descending
hairpin turn that hid it from above, could ever lift his mount
over it in time. The animal's momentum, coming down the
roof-steep pitch of the decline, would have to carry it and its
rider into the "Ranger trap." And this is the way that it
worked with the eager soldiers of Chivo. All of the horses of
Chamaco's party, even the packhorse with Colonel Ortega's
unconscious form, cleared the break in the trail, leaping it
like deer because they were spurred to the effort by their
desperate riders. But the mounts of the guerrillas, scrambling around the hairpin, snorting and digging furiously
with the urgings of their savage masters, the scent of the kill
hot in the nostrils now, so close were they, had no chance to
see or to lift themselves and their riders over the yawning
pit. Into the waiting blackness of the man-made chasm the
first dozen horses and soldiers went screaming and kicking.
Another dozen soldiers and their mounts piled up in the trail
above and did not plunge into the abyss with the others. But
neither did they seem to retain their previous eagerness for
the blood of *El Presidente* and the elevation of Lieutenant
Chivo to the rank of Executioner of Camargo.

As for Chivo himself, Shonto never knew if he was
among the first group of riders, or the second. All that he did
know was that he did not hear again the harsh yelping voice
of the bearded lieutenant.

"My God, Chamaco," he said to the Indian boy, in the
first moment of stillness following the piteous cries from
above, "what is in that Apache trench up there?"

"Tigers' teeth," said the youth. "Their points burned to
hardness of iron, their butts set in the cracks of the mother
rock."

"Lord God," breathed Shonto. "A staked pit!"

"For a pack of animals, the death of a pack of animals."

The Oaxacan accents of *El Presidente* seemed sad. "Let us go on and catch that train at Toltepec. There is so much work to do in Mexico. The people cry out to me, and there is little time, so little time, for me to answer them."

Shonto did not answer, feeling the moment belonged to another. Chamaco understood the courtesy.

"Si, Presidente," he said softly. "Please to follow your humble servant."

At once the small man in the black suit spurred his pony up beside that of the Chihuahua Indian boy.

"You are no one's humble servant," he said sternly. "Remember that always. You are a citizen of Mexico. A free man, humble to no one. If you believe in a god, you can thank him for that. If you believe in a man, you can thank a man."

"Si, Presidente, I thank you, and God."

"In that order, eh, boy?" A trace of warm amusement crossed the dark Indian features. "But you are wrong about the man, *muchacho*. It is another *Presidente* whom I charge you to remember. See that you don't forget his name, citizen. Burn it in your mind, if you are a true Mexican. You owe it your life. *Abraham Lincoln . . ."*

It was all downhill from there. But minutes short of midnight, Shonto rode into Toltepec with his charges. By a quarter past the hour "Item 13" was aboard the waiting train. Steam being up and the dawn all too near, the parting was abrupt. Camargo must be run past in the dark. Also, for the benefit of good health, those who must remain behind when the train pulled out would do well to be drawing in American air come sunrise of that risky day. *El Presidente*, surrounded by his faithful guard aboard the train, was virtually "taken away" from Shonto and Chamaco. So, as well, was the one-time Executioner of Camargo. In a last-second view, *El Presidente* seemed to spy the tall American and the tiny Indian boy sitting their horses in the lamplight spilling from his car's window. Shonto and Chamaco thought they saw him wave to them, and they returned the wave, each with his own thoughts. If the Texas gunman saw the bright tears streaming down the dark cheeks of Chamaco Diaz, he said nothing of the matter, then or later. Each man is permitted his own manner of farewell. But when the train had pulled away from Toltepec, before, even, its smoke had trailed into the Chihuahua night behind it, Charlie Shonto knew all he ever cared to know of the ending of the story. His big hand reached through the dark to touch the knee of his companion.

"Come along, Chamaco," he said. "We had better make long tracks. It's forty-nine miles to the river."

The boy nodded obediently, saying nothing. They turned their horses and sent them into a weary lope.

As they rode, Shonto's rawhide features softened. He was watching the proud set of the thin figure riding by his side. He was aware, surely, that the small Indian man in the ill-fitting black suit had been Benito Juárez, the liberator of Mexico, his people's Abraham Lincoln. But that part of it did not impress the big gunman unduly. For Charlie Shonto, the biggest Indian that he saw that night was always a little Chihuahua boy who barely reached to his gunbelt. History would not record, Shonto suspected, the secret fact that Juárez had been spirited to the Capitol in Washington, D.C. History would never record, he knew certainly, the added fact of the strange manner in which the legendary "El Indio" had been returned safely to his native land. But Charlie Shonto and Texas Express would know the way that it was done—and so would the tallest Indian in all of Toltepec!

When he thought of that, somehow, even Charlie Shonto felt better. When the shadows of the Toltepec hills closed behind them, he was sitting as straight in the saddle as Chamaco Diaz.

But of course not as tall.

FAWCETT ROUNDS UP THE *Best of the West*